By the time the sun was stabbing into my eyes like pins into a suicidal pincushion, I'd gotten maybe four hours of sleep. Leave it to Lucy to put a voice to my fears. My best option was to tell Tabby outright, and while I knew she was used to unusual things, how could I be sure this wouldn't be so far out of left field she'd think I was insane? She probably already thought me nuts, but that was beside the point.

By Danielle DeVor

SORROW'S POINT
SORROW'S EDGE

TAIL OF THE DEVIL
THE DEVIL'S LIEGE

CONSTRUCTING MARCUS

DANCING WITH A DEAD HORSE

STRANGE DARKNESS

Short Stories
THE CASE
CRABS
REFLECTION
THE DARKEST DREAM
LOVE ME TO DEATH
EMMY'S PUPPY
DAWN
THE SHROUD
PAPAP'S TEETH
DUST

Anthologies
THE DARK DOZEN
LOVE POTION #9

BOOK TWO OF THE MARKER CHRONICLES

SORROW'S EDGE

DANIELLE DEVOR

CITY OWL
PRESS

SORROW'S EDGE
The Marker Chronicles: Book Two

CITY OWL PRESS
www.cityowlpress.com

Cover Design by Tina Moss. All stock photos licensed appropriately.

Edited by Tina Moss.

For information on subsidiary rights, please contact the publisher at info@cityowlpress.com.

Print Edition ISBN: 978-1-944728-05-2

Digital Edition ISBN: 978-1-533766-67-0

Printed in the United States of America

For my father, the Western King.

- Danielle

Chapter One

It's All Coming Back to Me Now

I GOT THE phone call at three. Just as Lucy said I would. I was really starting to hate the true "witching hour." I needed sleep, dammit.

I let the phone ring a few times, hoping that whoever was on the other end would just hang up. I wasn't that lucky. I dragged my tired-ass body up, grabbed my phone off the nightstand, and swiped the screen.

"Mr. Holiday?" the man asked when I grunted into the phone.

"You realize it's 3:00 AM, right?" My head hit the pillow. I did not want to be doing this right now.

The man sighed. "It couldn't be helped. We need you."

I twitched. Who the hell was this guy anyway? Kind of presumptuous to call somebody at random this late at night when you'd never met the person on the other end. Apparently, manners weren't his strong point.

I glanced around the room. The lamp in the corner was on. The light glowed just enough to keep my mind at ease. I'd gotten into the habit of sleeping with a light on ever since Sorrow's Point. Yeah, it was irrational, but hey, I was trying to keep the beasties at bay. From the dim light, I could see Lucy sitting on the floor in front of the TV. I, just barely, made out the program through her. Her hair was as pale as usual and so blond it seemed almost white. She wore the same white nightgown she always did.

"How did you get my number?" I had to know. I mean, I doubted Will would suggest me to someone else. Things hadn't exactly ended on a positive note.

"You came highly recommended."

That was news to me. A very small group of people even knew I did something besides graphic design. "By who?"

"That's not important right now. You're needed. That's what should matter."

I sat up. Not important to him, maybe, but it sure as shit was important to me. I squeezed the phone so hard my knuckles began to ache. If I broke it, this asshole was going to owe me another phone. "Listen. I'm not about to traipse around and do whatever the hell it is you want me to when you won't tell me who you are or who told you about me."

"O'Malley said you'd be difficult."

I froze. Father O'Malley had been the one who allowed me to see the church as a vocation when I was a kid. But there was one problem. He'd been dead since before I left the church. I didn't care where he got the information. That was a low blow. I clenched my teeth.

"I'm going to hang up now. I'd appreciate it if you didn't call here again—"

"No, wait!"

The desperation in his voice was the only thing that kept me from hanging up the phone. "All right. I'm listening."

"O'Malley told me about you in a dream. When I woke up, your phone number was scrawled on my hand."

Yeah, I knew that kind of weird. I had firsthand experience with it. Having a dead person talk to him in a dream wasn't that different from a disembodied soul speaking to me in a nightmare. Yeah, my life was *really* interesting. Though I'd never drawn on myself in my sleep. That was a new one. "Who is it who needs an exorcism?"

The guy hung up. I literally heard the phone hitting the cradle. Who used an old phone like that anymore? I almost threw my cell phone against the wall. I mean, what the hell? Wake me up in the middle of the night for what?

I scratched the sleep out of my eyes and glanced over at Lucy. "Don't you ever sleep?"

She stared at me and grinned. Her blue eyes almost sparkled. "I don't have to."

I shook my head. Of course a kid would think it great to not sleep. I, on the other hand needed my rest—strange phone calls or not. And if someone else called, I'd probably be facing a murder charge.

"Do you think Tabby will like me?" Lucy asked. She stayed dressed in this little white frilly nightgown. I wasn't sure if it was her favorite or if there was something else at work keeping her dressed that way. When I'd done her exorcism, she sure wasn't in frills.

Now that was the question, wasn't it? I'd been toying with the idea of not telling Tabby about my ghostly child, but it appeared that was no longer an option. And with my luck, Tabby would eventually see her, freak out, and the whole thing would be blown out of proportion.

"I'm sure she will…" I hoped that was true. "After she gets used to the idea."

Lucy stared at me for a bit. I could tell she wasn't buying it. Best I start remembering there was more to her than to a regular six-year-old.

"It will all work out," I told her. "Eventually." Part of that was me trying to convince myself. There was only so much oddness a normal person could take, and I figured I was probably getting close to the threshold.

"Uh-huh," Lucy said, back to watching the TV. How she could just sit in front of the TV for hours on end, I didn't know. It was almost like she became somehow hypnotized by it. I laid my head back on the pillow. Hopefully, I could go back to sleep. Hopefully, I could stop worrying about that odd phone call. Hopefully…who was I kidding? I was seriously screwed. Again.

#

By the time the sun was stabbing into my eyes like pins into a suicidal pincushion, I'd gotten maybe four hours of sleep. Leave it to Lucy to put a voice to my fears. My best option was to tell Tabby outright, and while I knew she was used to unusual things, how could I be sure this wouldn't be so far out of left field she'd think I was insane? She probably already thought me nuts, but that was beside the point.

I got out of bed and crawled into the shower. The heat and the steam felt good. I needed to relax more, but it wasn't like my life lent itself to a lot of relaxation. My shoulders were so tense they hurt every time I tried to move my head. I ran my hands over my hair, getting the last of the soap out.

I needed a hobby. Something calming, like fishing. Too bad it was too cold. And, then, I wasn't the most patient person in the world. Yeah, no fishing.

"Jimmy?" Lucy asked through the door.

I turned off the shower so I could hear her better. "What?"

"The phone's ringing."

I swiped a towel off the rack, wrapped it around my waist, and headed toward the door. Out of the corner of my eye, a brown disembodied head passed through the mirror. I left the bathroom and held the towel around my middle in a death grip. No sense in giving Lucy an eyeful. Yeah, she was a spirit, but she was alive too—long story. I wasn't about to take any more of her innocence away when the demon took most of it. Of course, I went through all of that and the phone had already stopped ringing. I picked it up—no notification of voicemail. Then I glanced at the missed calls. I was almost afraid Mr. Creepy had called again. But no, it was Tabby.

I called her number and waited, starting to hang up when she answered at last.

"What the hell are you doing?" she asked.

I was glad she couldn't see my eyeroll. If she could, I probably would have been socked in the arm. "Um. Getting a shower?"

She made a grunting noise like she was trying to move something heavy. I could imagine her pushing her long red hair out of the way while she tried to get a handle on the boxes. I loved her hair.

"Did anything strange happen last night?"

How did she know? Sometimes her insight was just creepy. "Yeah. There was a phone call."

"Another one?" A little hint of sarcasm in her voice. I wasn't sure if she was annoyed with me, the situation, or packing.

"Maybe. It's kind of complicated." Well, as complicated as *Attack of the Killer Tomatoes*, but whatever.

"Everything is always complicated with you, Jimmy. When I get there, I'll be expecting details. But is this something you want to do again?"

Good question. Heck, I wasn't even sure if the phone call had been a stupid prank. "I'm not sure if I have a choice."

"I thought God was all about free will, and all that?"

For normal people, he was. I gave some of that away when I became a priest, and some of the stuff I swore to I still kind of believed in. "To a point, yeah. But we could talk theology for hours."

"True."

"How much longer till you get here?" I asked. Having her here was going to be a change, but I viewed it as something good.

She sighed. "Who the hell knows? I've got so much stuff here."

If I hadn't needed to get my house moved around for her to put her stuff in here, I would have been up there to help. "Okay, okay. I'll stop pestering you."

She snickered. "If I didn't want to be pestered, I wouldn't have called you."

I grinned. She liked my bugging her. "I miss you."

"I miss you, too," she replied.

Too bad her witchiness wasn't strong enough for her to wave her hand and make her packing do it by itself. But then, real magic didn't work that way. "I'll let you go. Get back to packing."

"Okay. Be good."

I snorted. "Always." That was a lie. I played being good really well, but I was way too ornery to do what I was supposed to and leave it at that.

#

During the rest of the morning, I finished straightening up the house. No sense in letting Tabby freak out about the state of the place. I wasn't the type of guy to live in a pigsty, but I had some clutter too. The clutter had to go, for the time being at least. I mean, Tabby needed more than a path to move her things into the house. My books needed to be picked up from the floor. After rearranging things, I'd even managed to make room in the living room for her to add some bookcases. Between the both of us, we had a lot of books.

Lucy stayed in front of the TV, mostly to stay out of the way, I think. I didn't know if things passing through her hurt her; she'd never said. Of course, she'd been quiet all day. She hadn't spoken to me since I'd refused to let her watch a horror film.

"What are you doing?" I had asked.

She had turned around. "This is so fake."

Some scary thing was ripping out a guy's stomach on the TV. Spirit or not, she was six. I knew her dad wouldn't want her watching that stuff.

I snatched the remote off the coffee table and turned off the TV.

"Hey!" she said.

"Hey, nothing. I don't have permission from your dad for you to be watching something like this." I wasn't exactly sure, if I had a kid, if I'd want them watching something like that at her age either.

She glared at me. "I've seen worse anyway."

Damn. It was hard. She was this sweet kid. I couldn't deny that she'd seen and experienced worse. If I could, I'd take it all away. "I hope you can put that behind you one day."

Her gaze fixed on me. "I'd rather have him where I can see him."

I was unable to argue with that.

As I was walking into the kitchen later, I suddenly noticed all of the light in the house had grown dimmer, almost as if something was blocking out the sun. I went to the front door, opened it, and peered outward. The sky was clear yet darker somehow. Almost like something big, yet not totally opaque, obstructed part of the sun. I didn't want to think about omens, but if I'd paid attention to some signs with Lucy, maybe things would have turned out better.

The darkened sky with no clouds was a hell of a clue, but of what? Usually, it meant a storm was coming, but there weren't any storm clouds I could see. Definitely strange.

"Are you seeing this, Lucy?" I knew she could hear me. It didn't seem to matter how far away; she always heard me. I peered up at the sky, probably doing a damn good meerkat impression.

"You need to listen," she said from behind me.

To what? I was looking at stuff, not hearing anything. I turned around. "Lucy, the only thing you were talking about was some dumb horror movie."

She nodded. "And you didn't listen."

I closed the door and crouched down in front of her. Maybe I should start paying better attention. "What did that movie have to do with this?" I pointed at the sky.

She shrugged. "Doesn't matter now. He's coming." Then she disappeared.

"Who's coming?" I asked, hoping she wouldn't ignore me. She didn't answer. Not good.

The doorbell rang.

#

I'd like to say the doorbell ring connected to someone who could help with all of this, but no dice. It was the postman delivering a package. I probably should have thought about its arrival more intensely, but I was too worried about the dark sky and Lucy than the package.

I opened the door, staring for a minute. I'd begun to sweat. My palms were damp, and my heart was trying to tap dance. I don't know what I was expecting. Maybe some tall guy in black who could take over and save the day. But no, the guy shoved the box toward me. I took it. He left. There was nothing strange about it.

The box was square, about fourteen by fourteen and six inches tall. It wasn't real heavy, but I could tell there was something in it. I held the box up to my ear. No ticking. Not that I knew anyone who would send me a bomb, but hey, you couldn't be too careful. I lowered the box, closed the door, and wandered into the living room in a daze. I felt like I hadn't slept for about four days. Something had wiped me out.

"What's that?" Lucy asked. The sunlight from the window was passing slightly through her. It cast a shadow on the floor that was sort of a shadow and sort of not.

I glanced up. "I have no idea."

After walking into the kitchen to get some scissors, I leaned against the counter and studied the package— regular brown shipping box with clear packing tape and no name on the return address. Just an address in Tombstone, Arizona. I didn't know anyone in Arizona, and to be honest, it didn't give me a happy feeling getting something from a place called Tombstone. I'd had enough of this omen shit. I didn't need to be hit over the head with a cinder block, for God's sake. I wasn't that stupid.

I took a deep breath and sliced through the tape. Nothing happened. No explosion. That was promising.

"Is that a good idea?" Lucy stood in the doorway to the kitchen now. Kind of disconcerting to have a kid that you could never hear walk around the house. I was always thinking she was up to something just because she was quiet.

I shrugged. "We won't know unless I open it."

"That's what the girl thought when she opened that box in that movie."

I set the scissors on the counter. "What have you been watching when I go to sleep at night?" I vaguely remembered seeing a trailer for a movie like that. Something about a possession. She didn't need to watch that type of stuff. How in the hell did you get a therapist for a spirit?

"Stuff."

I rolled my eyes. Yeah. Stuff. Great. That left me feeling really relaxed about the whole thing. Right.

I opened the flaps on the box and took a deep breath. Something was wrapped and taped in bubble wrap. I picked up the scissors again and cut through the tape. Nestled amongst the plastic wrap lay a silver flask, the initials J.H.H. were etched into the side. I searched through the packing, but there was no note, no nothing. Okay, why did someone send me this?

"Is it okay?" Lucy asked.

"I guess so. No strange smells or anything." Just a silver flask. Nothing odd I could detect about it. Except that I was sent it, but that was beside the point.

She crept over to look at it. I held it down to her level. After a minute, she shrugged and sauntered out of the room.

"Okay. Guess it isn't dangerous," I said to no one.

The lack of danger had me nervous. Who had sent it, and more importantly, why? I had a sinking suspicion that phone call wasn't a prank after all.

Chapter Two

Time Is On My Side

THE CLOCK ON the microwave read a quarter to eleven, but I was hungry enough for lunch. Part of me wanted to offer Lucy a sandwich or something, but she couldn't eat. No kid should ever be deprived of chocolate. Or Easter. Or birthdays. Jesus, I was starting to depress myself.

I knew if Tabby didn't get her chocolate fix, she'd be a force to reckon with. Maybe it was a good thing Lucy didn't appear to get hungry. No sense in tempting fate, though. I was worried about Tabby's impending arrival, but it paled in comparison to the strange shit. I'd rather have Tabby around when all this crap happened. At least she could help me make sense of it. But I'd better make sure the house was stocked up.

I took out a pan, fried myself an egg, and made a sandwich. It would have been better with bacon, but I was out. Another reason to hit the grocery store. Bacon was a staple.

I went into the living room and plopped onto the sofa. It was an old brown thing I'd picked up ages ago. All of my furniture was old, but it was me. Lucy was watching some dog show on the Animal Channel. That, at least, I could approve of. Dogs were safe. Little kids liked them. I could relax.

"When can I go home?" she asked me suddenly.

I froze, my sandwich poised in mid-air. Crap. I had no idea

how to answer her. "I don't know. It's up to God, I guess."

Lucy nodded and turned back to the TV. I wished I could do more for her besides give her a place to hang out, but there wasn't anything else I could think of. It wasn't like I was all that smart or knew what I was doing. If I could make a magic carpet to carry her soul back to her body, I would. Hell, if I could somehow manage to make her body whole and nothing wrong with it, I would. Where were the medi-wizards when you needed them?

I picked up my phone and called Tabby. I needed to hear her voice. I needed some point of normalcy. After a bit, she picked up.

"What's up?" she asked.

What was left of my sandwich stared at me from the plate. I wasn't all that hungry anymore. "You leave yet?"

She snorted. "Uh. No. I thought I told you I'd call you when I left."

Dammit. I couldn't just come out and say that things were hard. I was at a loss. If I did that, I'd have to explain Lucy. "Yeah, but weird shit keeps happening."

I heard her rustling things in the background. "Just wait 'til I get there, okay? It's not like it's going to take me forever."

"Six hours." For now, that felt like a lifetime. I knew I was being ridiculous, but I needed her.

"It's not that long," she replied.

"I just didn't want you to drive at night." Bad things were out at night. Things I couldn't control.

She chuckled. "No, you're scared and you don't want to admit it."

Yeah, she had me. She was so damn smart. Hard to hide anything from her.

"So," she said. "Let me finish packing and maybe I'll actually get there tonight."

"Okay." It had to do. She was going to handle things her way, and nothing I said was going to make her change her mind. She laughed again and hung up. I was starting to wonder when I was going to get my balls back.

I'd run out of things to keep me occupied. The house was more spotless than it had ever been, the refrigerator and pantry were stocked with food—I'd made sure to include tons of chocolate—and I'd made room for Tabby's things in the bedroom. I was even prepared to haul some of my shit out to the garage if needed.

Sharing a bed with her again would be strange. I missed her smell and her heat next to me. But there was the small problem of Lucy. Most parents did their thing when their kid went to sleep. With Lucy never sleeping, I was going to be a celibate man for a while. I'd have a hard time explaining that to Tabby. I didn't even want to think about it. Stranger still that I was kind of sticking to the old priestly ways. Though, I had to admit, it was no longer by choice. The usual advantage of being with Tabby was gone, at least while Lucy was with us.

About eleven at night, my doorbell rang. I'd been getting ready to shut up the house for the evening and go upstairs to sleep. I glanced at Lucy. She shrugged.

Staring through the peephole, I flung the door open. Holy shit.

"I was starting to think you'd leave me out there all night," Tabby said.

I picked up the bag she had in her hand. I couldn't stop myself from grinning like an idiot. She was here. "I thought you said you weren't traveling at night."

I let her enter the house and then I shut and locked the door behind her. It was such a relief to have her here. Safe.

"You sounded so odd on the phone that I figured I'd better get it over with."

"Where's Isaac?" I asked. He was this goofy cat who would rub his eye teeth on your hands if he liked you. I missed his fang-bumps.

"At Mom's. I dropped him off on my way down."

That explained it. "Are you hungry?"

"I'm more tired than anything." She took off her jacket and threw it on the sofa. I'd pick it up in the morning.

I wanted to kiss her and hold her for a while, but we weren't quite that close yet. We'd been taking everything slow this time. Probably for the best, with how badly I had botched things up before. Maybe I'd been too young, or maybe I'd been too green just leaving the priesthood. Having a relationship with her wasn't sunbeams and rainbows. Somehow, I never connected marriage counseling and me having a relationship with the fact that bonds weren't something like at the end of a sappy movie. Real people had problems. I just hadn't expected one of them to be me.

"I'm going to bed," she said. Bed, yeah, I could do that. Eventually.

"Okay. I'll be up later."

I don't know why I didn't follow her upstairs. Being chickenshit probably. But I needed a moment to pull myself together. To get centered so I wouldn't do or say the wrong thing. I guessed the talk about Lucy would have to wait until tomorrow.

Lucy stood near the TV looking at me. I waited until Tabby went upstairs. "I'll tell her tomorrow."

Lucy glared, and then sat back down in front of the TV. I was messing it all up with her too.

"You're going to rot your brain," I chided her.

"I don't have a brain, remember?"

Shit.

I went upstairs after that. Me staying down there irritating her wasn't going to solve anything. I knew the conversation with Tabby about Lucy was going to be a disaster. Just like everything else lately.

I headed to my bedroom. The white walls seemed accusatory, my bed representing the judge's bench. Tabby was pulling up her hair into a ponytail.

"Who were you talking to?" she asked.

Oh, shit. I did not want to do this now. I wiped my eyes with my hand. "I'll tell you tomorrow."

Tabby turned around and put her hands on her hips. "Tell me what tomorrow?"

I took a deep breath. "Please." I could tell the big fight was coming and I was stepping right into the pile of shit in the middle of it. "You're tired."

She rolled her eyes. "No, now I'm pissed off."

I hunkered down on the bed. When was I going to learn? I wanted to protect her too much, maybe. "This was not how I wanted this to go."

"You think?"

It was like all the old hurt, pain, and fuckup we'd had before Lucy was crawling up out of the rock it had been hiding under. All of my righteousness, all of my opinions between right and wrong that Tabby had to beat out of me, resurfaced. I remembered some of the stupid crap I used to say. I was such an idiot. No sense in putting it off. Tabby needed to know. "Lucy's still here."

"What?"

I sighed. "Lucy never left." How else do you explain to someone that a spirit had been following you around for about four months? My only strong point was that she wasn't going to think I was crazy, at least I hoped not.

"What the fuck are you talking about?"

Yup. There it was. "Lucy's soul."

Tabby froze. "You can't be serious."

It was time I put it all out there. The time for hiding was over. I needed to start treating her like the strong person she was instead of the little girl I wanted to protect. "When I did the exorcism...she was separated somehow from her body. Then, Peter came—"

"Peter who? Who's Peter?"

I stared up at her. "The Pearly Gates?" Crap. Any moment now, she'd be grabbing her cell and calling the guys in the white coats to cart me off. Did they even wear white coats anymore?

"You're shitting me." Her hands dropped down to her sides.

"Nope."

"She's here?" A hint of interest. Maybe this wasn't going to be that bad after all.

"Downstairs, watching TV." At least she was when I had left her down there. She could be doing who knew what by now. I found it hard to believe she spent all her time watching TV when I wasn't around. But what could she be doing instead? That was kind of a scary thought.

"Can I see her?"

"I don't know." And I didn't. So far, no one had noticed her when I went to the grocery store, but that didn't mean that there would never be someone who could see her. Tabby would be a good candidate with her witchiness, but I really didn't know.

Before I could stop her, Tabby rushed past me and down the stairs. She was going so fast I was afraid she was going to fall. The stairs were a little narrow, and I'd fallen down them a couple of times myself. I tried to follow as close behind her as I could without taking a header. This was going to be either okay, or completely shitty.

I followed Tabby to the living room. The only thing left on

was the TV. Usually, Lucy went upstairs to bed with me, so I turned that TV on for her, but she'd stayed downstairs. Probably because of Tabby. I couldn't say whether Tabby would mind or not. That remained to be seen. Lucy looked at us like we were on Mars.

"Lucy?" Tabby asked. I watched her turn her head back and forth in front of the TV.

"Hi," Lucy said quietly.

Tabby slowly turned her head just slightly toward Lucy's voice. Then, she froze. "I can see you now."

I leaned against the wall. Okay, no freaking out. This was going better than I'd thought.

"Is it okay I'm here?" Lucy asked. Her eyes were on the verge of spilling tears. If she did cry, where would the water go? If there was water? I was so confused. The strangeness meter had upped its ante.

Tabby nodded. "Just let me know if you're around. I wouldn't want to trip over you."

Lucy smiled. Her tears stopped. "You should be okay. Jimmy hasn't killed me yet."

I snickered. I couldn't help it. My mind had just completely split in two. I was no longer losing my mind. I'd lost it.

"He is goofy, isn't he?" Tabby asked Lucy.

Lucy's whole demeanor seemed brighter. Happier, somehow.

"Uh-huh. Very goofy," Lucy replied.

That was it. I was officially outnumbered by two females. God help me.

#

Nothing else happened. I slept like the dead. No dreams. No strange noises. It was almost like I had my own little happy family. I knew better. Hell was on its way, and there was nothing I could do about it. The omens hadn't been about

Tabby coming; they had been about something else. Something
I didn't want to deal with, but would probably have no choice
about. Lucy stayed downstairs though. Maybe she felt we
needed some alone time.

The next morning, I woke to the smell of bacon sizzling. I
sniffed and opened my eyes, making sure I wasn't crazy. Nope,
I could hear someone rattling around in my kitchen. Looks like
I didn't have to feed myself this morning. I got up and
wandered downstairs. I found them at the tiny kitchen table.
Lucy was smiling—a nice thing to witness.

"I see you finally woke up," Tabby said.

Awake was kind of a misnomer. Moving around was
probably a better way to put it. I shrugged. "You make a man
bacon, and he'll come."

She rolled her eyes.

"Morning, Lucy," I said and glanced down at her. She
grinned smugly. Maybe having Tabby here and knowing about
Lucy would be good for the kid. Prior to Tabby, Lucy just
followed me around or watched TV. It could be the female
thing. The mother figure. What was I talking about? I knew
nothing about psychology.

"Is there anything I can help with?" I needed to make an
effort. I couldn't exactly stand around and do nothing.

Tabby shook her head. "Why don't you install yourself at
the dining room table? I'll be there in a minute."

I knew better than to ignore her. I was lucky enough she
was making me breakfast. It felt awkward being nudged out of
my own kitchen. I went into my "dining room." Really, it was
just extra space that was technically part of the living room. The
important part was that it fit the old table.

"Are you okay?" Lucy asked.

I was starting to think that, now that Tabby was here, Lucy
was more in tune with emotions. Weird. I gave her a smile.

"Yeah. Sure. I'm okay."

"You don't look okay," she said.

She seemed a little sad. I pulled out the chair next to me and patted the seat. She sat.

"I'm fine. Just getting used to having more people in the house." It was true. I'd been by myself for a while. And I was having to get used to Lucy taking part of Tabby's attention away from me. Yeah, it was juvenile, but with my family, you had to fight for any attention you got. It took Lucy being here for me to realize I was still carrying that around with me.

Lucy nodded. "You're gonna have to learn to deal with it."

I snorted. I couldn't help it. It sounded so funny coming from her. "Why do you say that?"

She stared up at me, her eyes wide. "You don't think I'm going to be the only one, do you?"

I froze. Oh, shit. I did not want to be the guy everyone thought was crazy because I spent all my time talking to dead people. Later, there would be these movies about my life that would actually be mostly false, but everyone would think was the gospel truth. Yay, me.

Suddenly, Tabby came in with a big platter of bacon and eggs. Food. Thank God.

"What are you guys talking about?" she asked.

I leaned back in the chair. "Stuff even I'm not ready to deal with."

Tabby snorted. "You might as well get with it. I don't think you have a choice."

I snatched a piece of bacon and bit into it. The salty goodness made things a little better. Not much, but some. "Probably not."

"You are going to have to deal with this sometime," Tabby said, after she wiped her mouth with a paper towel.

"Can we let my bacon settle, please?" I didn't want to be

having this conversation. I wanted to sit back and reminisce about my bacon time. Stupid, yes. But I wasn't exactly considered intelligent most of the time.

"Nope. Whether we talk about this now or not, your bacon is going to have to adjust. I have a full U-Haul sitting outside."

Oh yeah. Crap. I'd forgotten about that. The pack horse must do his duty. I downed the rest of my coffee. "When do you want to get started?"

"As soon as possible. If I don't turn that thing in before closing time, I'll have to pay for another day."

I saluted her. "Yes, ma'am."

"Smartass."

#

In all truthfulness, it wasn't that bad. Tabby had a lot of her furniture in storage. At some point, I supposed, we could figure out what of my crap we were keeping. But for now, my things would do. The hardest part wasn't the little bit of furniture or the books. Yeah, they were heavy as hell, but that wasn't what was unusual. When I began hauling in boxes that had Tabby's witch stuff, there was a sort of glow around them. I knew her magic had color, but I had thought it came from her. Either the magic came from the books, or these books had been used so often that Tabby's magic had imbued them.

"Aren't you done yet?" Tabby asked from the front door.

I'd been huffing and puffing boxes around for what seemed like hours. I was only one person. I needed a team of minions. "With what?"

"You've been standing there, holding that box, for about five minutes."

Oops. Okay. Having a complete blank-out wasn't good. Plus, my back was going to hate me for it. "Sorry." I hauled my ass into the house and set the box down beside the door. I stood up, popped my back, and stared at her.

"How much more is left in the truck?" Tabby asked.

"Just your bookcases."

After we got the truck dropped off at the U-Haul place, Tabby and I went home, got cleaned up, and I threw a frozen pizza into the oven. I knew I didn't feel like going out. My back ached and I wanted to just take it easy.

"Jimmy?" Lucy was standing in front of me.

"What's up?"

The kid seemed paler than usual, if that was possible. She was shaking.

"I'm scared," she said.

Oh, shit. Lucy saying she was scared was not a good sign. In fact, it scared the crap out of me. It was something like Tabby saying she didn't like chocolate. This was not cool. "Scared of what?"

"I have a bad feeling."

Okay. Bad feeling. Check. I wished I could hug the kid. Jesus. A bad feeling coming from her meant something was seriously wrong. But what? I couldn't imagine God giving her soul to the devil. I suspected it had something to do with that darn phone call.

"What's the feeling about?" I asked.

She wrapped her arms around herself. "I don't know yet."

Great. I figured I needed to put it out there. Maybe I was wrong, just maybe. "Are we going to Arizona?"

Lucy glanced up at me, her eyes wet. "You need to go."

Needing to go and wanting to go were two different things. Needing meant there would be consequences I couldn't deal with if I didn't go. It figured. If I had any luck at all, it was bad.

"Does it have anything to do with that flask?" I'm not even sure why I brought that up. Something was linking it all together in my brain.

She shrugged and left the room.

I blinked. Seriously? Sometimes I wished she could communicate better, but it wasn't her fault. She was only six, after all.

It was going to be interesting to break it to Tabby that we were going to have to haul ass to Arizona. I knew she was exhausted and it would be better to wait, but Lucy's bad feeling had me nervous. Did I want to go to Arizona? No. I wanted to stay home and get settled and try to find a job. Plus, I didn't want to be responsible if there was something big and bad that was able to take Lucy from me. Or do something bad to someone else. It wasn't like I was experienced at this. Doing one exorcism did not make me an expert, and I didn't know enough about the whole process. I had no idea how I could make heads or tails of any of this; there was too much that was unnatural. I'd tried searching online for "marker" and all I got were Sharpie advertisements. It wasn't like Lucy was walking around with a black check mark on her forehead.

"Is everything okay?" Tabby asked when she came into the kitchen.

"No," I said. The beeper on the oven went off. I got a pot holder out of the drawer and got the pizza out of the oven.

She sat down at the table. "Okay?"

"Lucy is scared." I waited for that to sink in. The last time Lucy had been scared was when the demon had her in his grip, and she still hadn't talked about it to me.

"Okay. So she's scared. She's six." Tabby leaned back in her chair.

I picked up the pizza cutter and attacked the darn thing. Sometimes Tabby made stuff hard. If she would just think for a minute, it would be clear. "This isn't what you think it is. Lucy spends a lot of time watching scary movies, for God's sake. If she's scared, it's bad."

"Did she say what she was afraid of?"

I gnashed my teeth together. I loved Tabby, I did, but sometimes she made me practice my patience. I shook my head. "She said she had a bad feeling about Arizona."

"And what's in Arizona?"

Now, that was a question I could answer. Sort of. I shrugged. "It's where the flask came from."

Tabby glared at me. "What flask?"

Ah ha! My turn to be irritating. "The one I got in the mail the other day."

"Someone sent you a flask in the mail?"

"Yeah, I guess." It sounded stupid. I knew that. But it wasn't. It was a sign of stuff to come.

"Who?"

I rolled my eyes. "I don't know. There wasn't a name on the return address." If I'd have known who sent me the damn thing, I would have Googled them and I wouldn't be freaking out like this.

"Jesus, Jimmy. The weirdest shit happens to you. Did you open it?"

"What? The package?" Why wouldn't I open a package addressed to me? I guessed if I were someone important like the president, I'd have a minion to open it for me. That way, if it had a bomb or something, they'd be blown to smithereens and not me.

"No, doofus. The flask."

I paused. I hadn't even thought about it. I'd been so relieved there was nothing scary in the box I took it at face value. "No…"

"Where is it?"

I pointed to the box on the floor next to the garbage can where I'd left it.

She grabbed it from its spot. After sifting through it, she glanced up at me. "Did you throw anything away?"

"No. There wasn't a note or anything." All there had been was that bubble wrap.

Tabby shook the flask. A faint sloshing sound came from it. "If this is blood, I'm going to shit myself."

"You won't be alone." I didn't want it to be anything gross or creepy. I had had enough of that with Lucy. Please, God, let it be something normal.

She unscrewed the cap and held it up to her nose. Then, she jerked back. "Jesus Christ!"

"What?" I had a moment of terror, afraid her nose was melting off her face or something.

She stared at me and rubbed her nose. "Worst rot-gut whiskey I've ever smelled."

I did my best not to laugh. "Who would send me bad whiskey?"

"You're asking the wrong questions. More like, who would send you a flask with these initials?"

Now, she had me confused. What did the initials have to do with anything? "Why?"

"I think this might have belonged to Doc Holliday." She turned the flask over in her hand studying the etching more closely.

"Nah."

She nodded. "Yeah. See, the silver has a faint bluish tint to it. Not like today's silver."

"Couldn't that be faked?" Not that I knew much about silver. Most of what I knew had come from Tabby, and that was all about the magical properties of the stuff, not antiques.

"No. The silvering process is different today. The engraving could be more recent, but I doubt it."

Heh, its being old didn't exactly instill confidence. "Why?"

"Because why would someone send you a fake flask to get you to come to Arizona? It doesn't make sense."

"Nothing makes sense." A hang-up phone call about a sort of exorcism and a box from Arizona that had an old flask in it had nothing to connect the two, as far as I could tell.

"That's the damn truth, but there's something here. Lucy's feeling notwithstanding."

Of course there was. "Fuck me."

"When are we going to Arizona?"

"When I can get a flight, I guess." I was so not looking forward to this trip. I could imagine running around and asking people on the street if they'd heard of Father O'Malley. I'd be in an institution before the day was out.

"What are you going to use to pay for it?" she asked.

Yeah. That had been the thing I'd been keeping in the back of my head for a long time, trying to ignore it. I wasn't all that far off from being broke. My steady job had gone bye-bye. After Lucy's body was put in the hospital, and all the loose ends were tied up, I didn't have a good enough excuse. I thought I'd probably be able to pick up another job, but the bottom had fallen out of the market for graphic design as badly as everything else. My unemployment was going to run out in a couple of months, and even then, it wasn't enough to pay for everything. My savings were shot.

I served us both up a piece of pizza. "Guess we aren't going to Arizona."

Tabby drummed her fingers on the table. "I do have a credit card."

I grabbed her hand. "No. We aren't going to do that. You don't have a job. I can't have you ruining your credit." I wasn't about to let her go into debt for me when it had to stand on something this flimsy. It wasn't worth the risk.

"What are we going to do?" she asked.

"I don't know."

#

If I said I slept, I'd be lying. I didn't want to do badly by Lucy, but I couldn't make myself financially destitute either. If I were a more religious man, I'd probably decide to take the "God provides" frame of mind. But even as a priest, I was more realistic than that. God gave me a brain. It was up to me to know how to use it.

If I had to go get a job at McDonald's, I would. I had Tabby to think of now. Sure, she'd probably get a job, but I wasn't about to put the whole monkey on her shoulders. I wasn't that type of guy.

If only my "profession" gave me a stipend or something. Yeah. Great wishful thinking there, Jimmy.

"Jimmy?"

I woke up, never remembering having fallen asleep. Tabby was standing over me. I glanced at the clock. A little after seven. "What?"

"Did you go somewhere last night?"

I searched the room; nothing was out of place. What was she talking about? "No...I came up to bed when you did, remember?"

"You have to see this."

She took me by the hand. I threw back the covers, got out of bed, and followed her downstairs. She was moving so fast that I missed a step and somehow didn't go down.

"Sorry," she mumbled.

I caught up to her in the dining room. She paused in front of the table.

"What?" I asked.

"Look." She pointed at the table. On it was an iPad. I didn't own one.

"What the fuck?"

"I don't know. It was sitting here this morning when I came down to make breakfast."

I knew there wasn't a magical iPad fairy. Something was up.

"Did you ask Lucy?"

"She's been strangely quiet this morning."

Hmm. Usually, that meant the kid was involved, but I knew it wasn't the case here. Lucy was a spirit. Yeah, she could go through doors, but there was no way she could make a tablet pass through a wall. This hadn't been the first time something had appeared at random. When I had to get the demon away from Lucy, the vestments I needed to do the exorcism had somehow appeared in my suitcase. I hadn't packed them, and Tabby hadn't been with me when I brought my suitcase to Sorrow's Point.

I picked it up and pressed the "on" button. Maybe I could find out who the damn thing belonged to. Burglars took stuff out of your house; they didn't leave it. When it powered up, a video suddenly began.

A guy was sitting at an ornate gold desk. The walls in the background were this odd color of yellow.

"Mr. Holiday," the man said.

The dude on the screen appeared to be this old priest, dressed in white robes. He was not unlike my old mentor with bright white hair, but this guy had an Italian accent.

Tabby stared over my shoulder.

"Welcome to the Order of Markers. Fate works in mysterious ways and all that."

My eyebrows rose. "Yeah, no kidding," I said aloud. More like I wanted to know who broke into my house. Why couldn't they have knocked on the door, said, "Hey dude, we want to help," and handed me the sweet iPad. But no, I had a random technological device sitting on my dining room table.

"Eventually, you will need to come to Rome for your official training, But for now, your services are needed. We apologize for not introducing ourselves earlier."

He pulled up the robe on his right arm and displayed the inside of his wrist. He had a mark too. It was hard to see, but I could swear it was exactly like mine.

"Sometimes it takes a while before we know another mark has made itself known. I'm sure you've been alerted to your next project, so I'll keep this brief. If you haven't noticed, there should be a credit card taped to the underside of the device you are holding. Think of it as your corporate account. Use it for anything to do with your work."

I glanced at Tabby. She stared back at me. Maybe wishes really did come true. But I was feeling uneasy about all of this.

"On the device, you will find forms to fill out so we know where to deposit your salary. Welcome to the church...again." He chuckled and the screen loaded up the normal home screen I'd seen on these devices at the mall. Like he said, there were a few files that seemed like the documentation I needed to fill out. I turned the thing upside down and sure enough, there was a credit card.

I pushed the *too good to the true* thoughts from my mind. This was something I'd needed. I wasn't going to mess it up. "Guess I don't have to look for a job after all."

"Fuck, Jimmy. This isn't right." Her eyes practically popped out of her skull.

Part of me wanted to chuckle. I'd never seen Tabby this freaked before—minus the demon, that was. It was kind of cute. Finally, she readjusted herself and glared at me.

"What are you?" she asked.

A rhinoceros? Yeah, it was a good thing she couldn't read my mind. I'd be so dead. "A marker, I guess."

"It's like you've just entered the mafia or something."

I couldn't argue about it. She was right. "I kind of have. Think about it. Secret organization who gets their funds via secretive means in order to accomplish various agendas and be a front for the big boss."

She blinked. "I think you just described the church."

I patted her on the head. "It will be okay."

"You sure about that?"

Chapter Three

Mr. Roboto

YEAH, I KNEW Tabby had a point. I should probably have been more concerned with the fact that someone had broken into my house to deliver an iPad. It wasn't like that was any sort of normal church behavior, but I knew there were other forces at work here too. And the Big Guy never did things subtly, not as far as the records went. I mean, who would notice if suddenly all the crumbs in the house were gone? God needed more blatant shows of his power.

The guy on the video had a mark, and he was also a priest. Part of me wanted to trust him because of that. But I knew better. Not all priests were good. And I'm sure my no longer being a priest had some in the Order grumbling. With that swanky desk and all, there was a lot of money involved, and money made people mean.

All of this didn't make me nearly as uncomfortable as Lucy and her bad feeling.

"Jimmy?" Tabby broke into my thoughts.

"What?"

"What are you doing?"

I glanced around. Nothing was out of the ordinary. "I'm thinking."

"Yes. Think away. You know about all of this strange crap

going on. What are we doing? Are we going to stay here and unpack, or are we going to go on your bizarre quest?"

Good question. But with this credit card, I was tempted to go for it. I'd never been to Arizona, and the worst thing that could happen if I found nothing was that Tabby and I would have a vacation. Even I chuckled over that. No way was it going to be that easy.

Her phone rang. "Yeah, Mom?"

That couldn't be good. Tabby didn't exactly get along with her mom. On the best of days, it was strained. The woman wasn't quite sane, which made things worse.

"He's never done that before," Tabby said. She tapped the table with her fingernails. "Okay. Okay. We'll come get him."

She hung up. "We have to go to Huntington to pick up Isaac."

"Why? What's wrong?"

"He bit Mom."

I snorted and she glared at me again. I stopped myself from telling her I didn't blame the cat, but I also knew better than to let that out of my mouth. It was better for me to stay neutral. "Is she okay?"

"Yeah. She just can't keep Isaac anymore."

"I'll go get the keys."

#

We were quiet in the car. Not much to say. We had to drop everything because Tabby's mother was a pain in my backside. There were times that I wished Tabby would wipe her hands of her mother, but that was the funny thing about love. Sometimes you loved people who treated you like crap.

Lucy "sat" in the back seat. I knew now not to ignore little things, and animals sometimes could see and sense things humans couldn't. But I'd be crazy if I didn't worry. Lucy, after all, had killed her own cat when the demon, Asmodeus, was taking control of her. While she hadn't been violent in her spirit form before, the possibility was there.

"Hey, Tab? Want to get some lunch before we go get Isaac?" I asked.

Tabby rolled her eyes at me. "Isaac needs to be away from Mom. Besides, I'm sure he'd want a hamburger too."

"Oh, yes, anything for the cat."

Lucy giggled.

Tabby's mother's house was an old ranch-style thing with fake brick on the outside and a big window near the front door. It was once red brick, but had faded to a more orange color. The windowsills needed painting and the front walk had weeds growing up through the cracks in the pavement. The weeds were trimmed though; I had to give her mother that.

"Will you look at this?" Tabby's mother said as soon as she opened the door. She was holding her arm at an odd angle.

Instead of inviting us inside, she stuck her hand in Tabby's face. I could faintly see a red mark. There was so much I wanted to say, but I bit my tongue.

"Yes, Mom. I see. That's why we're here." Tabby sighed.

When she finally let us into her home, it was normal. Actually, it was cleaner than my house. The front door opened into the living room with a blue couch, matching recliner, and a TV. One picture hung on the wall. It must have been taken when Tabby was in high school. She was pretty even then.

I found myself thinking of Poe—the whole tap, tap, tapping at my chamber door bit. Tabby's mother's voice was like that. It crept in like a woodpecker hammering at a piece of wood while you were trying to catch the last zzz's of the morning.

"Jimmy?" Tabby asked. "You remember my mom, Kathy."

"Of course." I reached out my hand and all I got for my trouble was a glare that made me feel like I was the dog shit on the bottom of her shoe. Nice lady. I chose to be silent about it for Tabby's sake. "Where's Isaac?"

Just hearing me speak his name, Isaac barreled from where he'd been hiding under the sofa and jumped into Tabby's arms. He was this huge darker-colored Siamese with bluish eyes. He did not look happy.

"All righty, then," I said. Poor thing. I wouldn't want to stay with that woman either. It was hard to tell what she'd done to him to make him bite her.

Tabby snorted. "Okay, Mom. I know you want him out of here, so we'll be going." With that, she turned toward the door.

Her mom grunted. I glared back at her. She did not want to get me pissed off enough that I let it all out, did she?

I held the door open for Tabby and we left. I made myself calm down before I reached the car. Her mother and the way she acted wasn't a good reason to get into an accident.

In the car, Isaac stared wide-eyed at Lucy for a minute, and then settled down into the seat beside her.

His initial uneasiness didn't do a lot to quell my fears. I hoped Lucy was benign. But beyond God coming out and saying all the badness had left with the demon, all I could do was watch. I silently hoped her obsession with horror films was just one of those things and not an instruction manual.

"Hamburgers?" Tabby asked when we were a bit down the road.

"Where do you want to stop?" I searched along the highway, but there wasn't anything yet.

"Oh, anywhere. A drive-through would be best."

"Yeah, I can't see a restaurant enjoying having 'his royal highness' come visit."

Lucy giggled from the backseat. I glanced at her in the rear view mirror. Isaac was fine. Thank God. I was being paranoid. I had enough on my plate without adding to the stress. And I needed to stop thinking about those horror films. Plenty of people watched horror films, even as kids, and came out completely normal. Right?

"Lucy, what do you think of Isaac?" I asked her.

"I don't think he likes Tabby's mommy very much."

Her insightfulness was something else. As far as I knew, she'd stayed in the car when we collected Isaac. Or maybe, she had more power than I thought.

"Why particularly?" Tabby asked.

Lucy paused. "He doesn't like how she treats you."

Tabby and I stared at each other. There was no way Lucy could have known anything about Tabby's past. And Isaac—he was a cat. I didn't want to think I was getting any crazier than I already was. Too bad it was possible.

"Does he talk to you?" I asked her.

"Kind of. It's like I look at him and these pictures appear. Like a movie or something."

I calmed down. She was a soul. It made sense that she could see other souls. Interesting that Isaac had one, though. The church taught me that animals didn't have them, and thus, couldn't be granted Heaven. One more thing the church was wrong about. I should have started keeping a list.

#

When we got back to the house, Lucy went straight into the living room and plopped down in front of the TV. I turned it on for her.

Isaac barreled through the house, his way of making the place home, but still funny having a cat run like a maniac around the place. It was kind of nice to have the house not be so quiet.

"What are we going to do now?" Tabby asked.

"What do you mean?"

"I somehow don't see Isaac participating in an exorcism."

I chuckled. "Hey, you never know. Besides, he's your

familiar, right?" Of course, I knew he wasn't doing spells for
her and things like that, but any animal that belonged to a witch
could be considered a familiar. At least, that's what I thought.
"Well, sort of."

"Then he goes. We can get him a seat on the plane."

Tabby shook her head. "I'm not even remotely going to
pretend that this isn't a dumb idea."

I shrugged. "Animals can sometimes sense stuff before we
can. He might be able to help." I could see a demon screaming
at Isaac's noxious fumes. They were *that* bad.

"It's your funeral," she said.

I ignored her and booted up the tablet. No sense in waiting
any longer. Familiar or no familiar, we needed to get to Arizona.

#

I wasn't dumb enough to get first-class tickets. Even I
couldn't have been able to justify that in my head. Isaac or not,
coach it was going to be. If my legs had to stick up my butt, so
be it. I wasn't going to let this company credit card thing get out
of hand.

We were supposed to get into Tucson, Arizona, about 8:00
PM. I'd found a hotel that accepted animals, but I wasn't sure
how long we'd be in that room. I was starting to feel like the
Scooby Doo gang. I had a mystery to solve, but I didn't know
what it was. I had too many pieces to put together—the strange
phone call and the flask to start. Logic told me the flask was
sent by the same person that made the phone call, but why?
And if Tabby was right and the initials belonged to my ancestor,
then that was another level to the madness.

The number hadn't shown up on my cell's call list, which
was odd enough, but the call itself was the strange part. No way
the guy could have known about O'Malley by getting in a
database for my phone number, so that left me to believe he
was telling the truth…at least about that part. Whether he

needed an exorcism or not was the problem. Kind of. The possessed wasn't usually the one asking for help from the church; the family was. So that meant he was lying about who needed an exorcism.

Again, why? It made no sense to me.

One thing: I didn't like being lied to. It didn't matter if the possessed person was a real bastard or something, I'd still help. It wasn't like Lucy was nice in her possessed form. So how would this be any different?

Sometimes, I found myself wanting to dive back into doctrine and look for things, but honestly, I knew it wouldn't help. I'd had better luck with the exorcism when using the words Tabby and I had made up. Maybe there was something to that. Could it be as simple as being defrocked meaning that the church's ritual wasn't available to me, or was it all in my head?

And if doing an exorcism like a witch's ritual worked, who was I to argue?

Chapter Four

Piece of My Heart

"WHAT TIME DOES the flight leave?" Tabby asked. It was Thursday. We were flying out tomorrow. I wasn't really looking forward to it, but it was better than staying around here and wondering what might have been.

"Seven forty-five." It meant getting up at the butt-crack of dawn, but nowhere near as bad as getting there at like 2:00 AM.

"Ugh." Tabby popped her neck and lowered herself into one of the dining room chairs.

I shrugged. "At least it puts us in Arizona at a decent time."

She raised her eyebrow. "Decent for who?"

I didn't want to be mean to her, but if I could have somehow pulled a perfect flight out of my butt, I would have. It was either early going or getting in late. "What? We'll get there at eight."

"Uh. Huh. Did you get us a rental car?"

I stared at her. Shit. Of course, she'd zero in on the thing I forgot. "I'll be right back."

She snorted. I took off to the computer and added a rental car to our reservation. It wasn't like I was trying to be stupid, it just came out that way. Or, maybe, stuff in the world like to see me fail. Yeah, that sounded good.

I had to believe it would all work out; otherwise, I'd just

screwed up the first assignment I had since getting marked. Great way to start a new job—mess up your first assignment. Good going, Jimmy.

After booking the rental, I plopped on the sofa and watched Tabby rush around the house. She'd gotten some stuff moved in, but it wasn't anywhere near done. If we didn't have to leave this soon, it would have been a lot easier for her. I probably could have helped with some of it, but I was comfortable on my couch.

Lucy rested on the other end of the couch, alternating between sort-of petting Isaac and watching Tabby.

"What's it going to be like?" Lucy asked.

I glanced at her. "What's what going to be like?"

"Arizona."

I thought for a bit. I had to find a way for this kid to have fun on the trip. It wouldn't be fair otherwise. "Hot, mostly. Do you feel temperature?"

She shrugged. "I don't get cold anymore."

I guess that made sense. She didn't have a body. Not one she was attached to, anyway. But a kid should be able to do stuff like play in water when it's warm. Lucy being in this state wasn't doing her any good. I just didn't know what I could do about it.

"Is Isaac going?" she asked.

I chuckled. "Yes, Isaac is going."

She beamed.

Okay, cat made her happy. Check.

#

I'd shuffled my crap together as best I could. I did manage to get a case for the iPad. Traveling with the thing exposed would be stupid, and I didn't know if I should leave it at home. It was probably better if I had it with me in case they needed to contact me or something. It was getting way too complicated.

I guessed it was connected to some cell phone or something. Yeah, they broke into the basic lock on my house without a security system. I had trouble believing they would hack my network. I didn't know enough about the thing to check to see how it was connected, though it seemed like a hell of a lot of work for something I could have done myself. I wondered if they meant for me to travel with it.

"What are you doing?" Tabby asked.

"Trying to figure out how it's linked." I searched around the house and stared out the window, but I didn't see anything unusual.

Tabby stared at me. "I've never had one, so I don't know how to check the settings. You could look it up."

Yeah, technically she was right, but I wasn't feeling like messing with the internet. Going on a jaunt was more fun anyway. "I'll just go outside."

Tabby raised an eyebrow. "Why?"

"If I walk down the street, out of range, the net connection will quit." If it was connected to my house, at least.

She shook her head and walked away.

I went outside, heading down the street. My neighborhood was one of those old housing subdivisions from the fifties. Tons of neat little houses in rows, almost as far as you could see. At one time, there had been a little supermarket settled within the grid of all the houses that had its own butcher. Way before my time.

I continued along the sidewalk. At the corner, I stopped and loaded up the tablet. It came to life just like it had in the house. I checked on the internet app and it brought up the Apple homepage.

Yeah. Okay. I was covered. Maybe. Hell, I didn't know. It would be kind of cool if the Order had its own huge server or something. More likely, the server was connected to a cell tower format, so I could just surf the net wherever there was service.

I probably should have looked up how to check the settings like Tabby said, but since the thing didn't belong to me, what business did I have messing with it?

I went back to the house. I needed to know more than I did—like usual. But even I had to admit I was probably better off not knowing.

#

Needless to say, getting on an airplane with a disembodied spirit and a cat presented quite the interesting scenario. The Isaac part wasn't too bad. I hoped there was no one on board who was allergic to cats. I wouldn't want to give someone an asthma attack or anything.

Lucy, however, stressed me out. Because she didn't have a seat, she wandered around the plane. Sometimes getting really close to people. Too close. I kept expecting for someone to sense her, but I was lucky. No one did.

I wanted to set her down and tell her to chill, but I couldn't exactly be seen as a total nutcase on a plane. Isaac even stared at me like I was mad several times. Be great if I got myself on a no-fly list.

Finally, when we landed, my heart stopped hammering in my chest. If I couldn't calm down, I was going to need anxiety medication or something. I almost welcomed the annoying assembly line getting off the airplane.

"Are you better now?" Tabby asked as we headed toward baggage claim.

"Yeah, kinda." Maybe being enclosed with a lot of people in a septic tank had my hackles up.

"I haven't seen you that uncomfortable in a long time."

"Did you see what Lucy was doing?" My brain bounced back to Lucy staring at people, dodging the drink cart, dancing in front of the bathroom door. Yeah. The flight was not a fun time.

"Yeah?" She seemed so unconcerned. I don't know how she managed it.

"What if someone noticed?"

Tabby giggled. "I think Lucy has control over who can see her. Even I didn't see her at first."

"True." I said it, but I didn't necessarily believe it. There was always going to be someone stronger, faster, more amazing. And it was just a matter of time before we ran into one.

#

After we got into our hotel room, I allowed Isaac to take a dump in his travel litter box, and got my shoes off. That's when Lucy reappeared. Why she'd run around invisible in the airport was beyond me. I wasn't the one she had to worry about seeing her.

"Did you have fun?" I asked her.

She perched on the bed beside me. "You were funny."

The bed had one of those odd undulating wave patterns on the bedspread. At least it was blue. In pink, it would look like vomit. "You about gave me a heart attack."

"It wasn't that bad," Tabby said, coming in from the bathroom.

It amazed me. All she had to do was brush her hair and wash her face, and she'd be back to normal. Me, I'd look like shit until I got a good night's sleep.

"So you say," I replied.

Lucy stared at me. "Why were you scared?"

"What if there was someone who could see you?" I needed to put it out there. She needed to think a little more. I knew she was young, but she had different needs than a normal kid.

She stopped for a minute and then bowed her head. "I didn't think about that."

I would have liked to put my hand on her shoulder, but her

not being corporeal really made that impossible. "It's okay. Just try to keep calm when we're around a lot of people."

She nodded.

"Can we let this go and get something to eat?" Tabby asked, a hint of annoyance in her voice.

"Wanna see if there's a pizza place that will deliver? I'm tired." All I wanted to do was get a shower and some sleep. I was leaning away from food. Though I'd probably wake up in the middle of the night starving to death.

Tabby went for the phone on the stand between the two beds. "Sometimes you do have good ideas." She hit the button for the front desk.

"Only sometimes?" I asked.

"Don't make me hurt you."

It was past midnight by the time Tabby fell asleep. Isaac snoozed at the foot of the bed by her feet. I had the TV volume turned down low. Lucy didn't complain. She lounged on the other bed and watched me flip channels.

In the dark, Lucy seemed sad. Her eyes lost that sparkle they usually had and there were shadows on her face I hadn't seen before. I had no way of knowing if she could tell anything about what was happening to her body or not. Who knew what God's plan was for her? Part of me wondered if it would be more humane for her to go on to Heaven instead of having to live with the pain and disfigurement her own body now had. It was probably a good thing that it wasn't my call.

#

"How do you want to handle this?" Tabby asked me after I finished getting dressed the next morning.

"To be honest, I don't know. With Lucy, I knew where I was going because Will took me. This…this is something new." Somehow, I had a feeling it wasn't going to be as easy as typing the address into the GPS.

"True, but we came here because of the package," she said.

"Yeah. Let's try that." I mean, it wasn't like I had any other plan.

First off, we had to get to our new hotel in Tombstone. I was glad I had the foresight to have us crash for a night in Tucson. Somehow, I don't think I could have driven all the way there last night.

Tabby plugged the address of the hotel into her phone's GPS, and after checking out, we were on our way. Isaac seemed a bit more nervous. I don't know if it was the recovery from the plane trip or not, but he couldn't settle down. Every time I glanced back at Lucy, she was doing nothing. If she'd been hurting Isaac, he would have made some sort of noise. All I had were sort of snorts from him. Not exactly worry-worthy.

The closer we got to Tombstone, the more my heart raced. The animal side of me was sensing something that the logical side wasn't. Logic told me I had nothing to worry about because we were simply going to look up an address. But logic wasn't exactly my best friend.

"Jesus Christ!" Tabby grabbed onto my arm.

I slammed on the brakes. The biggest badger I had ever seen stood in front of the car. He was staring like he wanted to eat our tires. The dumb thing must have weighed forty pounds.

I revved the engine. It growled and prowled the car like a lion.

"Jesus, Jimmy. Did you have to do that?" Tabby asked.

"How was I supposed to know?"

"It's getting closer." Lucy pointed from the backseat.

I rolled down the window. I had to do something. Yeah, the thing probably wasn't going to get into the car, but I'm pretty sure the rental place would have an issue with their car being totaled by a badger attack.

"Hey," I shouted.

The beast stopped and growled.

"I'm sorry I disturbed you." I motioned with my hand for the thing to continue its way across the highway. "Go ahead."

It glared at me for another minute, and then it started crossing the road.

Just as I was about to relax, it turned his head around. Almost like he was saying, "You sure you don't want a piece of this?"

I didn't move. Finally, after the creature disappeared into the sagebrush, I drove off.

"That was interesting," Tabby said.

"Is that what you want to call it? Badger attack wasn't part of the itinerary."

"Just get us to the hotel. I don't want to fight." Tabby flicked her wrist.

Who was fighting? But I said nothing. It was better to keep the peace than to wreck us because Tabby and I had a knock-down-drag-out in the car.

#

After we deposited Isaac and our stuff into our hotel room, I punched in the address of the package into the GPS on Tabby's phone. Whatever it was, it was on a street called Toughnut. That alone should have been enough to make me laugh my ass off, but the general feeling of it all wasn't funny. Dread tightened my gut. It wasn't like when I finally entered Sorrow's Point or anything, but it was there. Nineteen-seventy-three Toughnut Street turned out to be a vacant lot. Now I knew someone was fucking with me. When we pulled up to the destination, I thought the GPS had puked.

"This can't be right," Tabby said, staring at the empty space.

A few houses rested on either side of us, but nothing seemed out of the ordinary. I knew it wasn't going to be this easy. I just knew it.

Lucy stayed strangely silent.

"I guess we'll check it out."

We got out of the car. Tabby shielded her eyes from the bright sunlight. I wandered over to the house nearest the car. The number on the outside read nineteen-seventy.

I motioned to Tabby. "I think someone is playing us."

Tabby raised her eyebrow at me. "Maybe we should ask Lucy?"

I nodded and stuck my head in the car window. Lucy glanced up at me.

"Any ideas, Lucy?"

She sighed. "Someone needs your help here."

I leaned my head against the roof of the car. My patience was wearing thin. The heat from the roof soothed my forehead. "Any idea who?"

She shrugged. "Guess he'll find you when he wants you."

Not an answer I wanted. I'd rather know what I was up against so I could take care of it, leave, and go home. "What do we do until then?"

She shrugged again. "Whatever."

I don't know what I'd been expecting, but it seemed pointless to travel all the way out here for nothing. I could have found Southwestern food somewhere back home. And Lucy wasn't a lot of help.

I waved Tabby over.

"What now?" she asked.

"We find something to amuse ourselves with." Or I could find who brought me here for a fool's errand and beat the shit out of him. Either one worked for me.

"What about the address?"

"A red herring, I guess. Lucy says the guy who wants our help will find us, but I can't help to think we're going to be psychically mugged."

Tabby chuckled. "I don't think Lucy would let that happen."

"I sure as hell hope not."

#

We left Toughnut Street and found a decent place to park. Then we went down Allen Street on foot. Allen Street served as the main street in Tombstone, and part of it was where the shootout with Wyatt Earp happened. Glad I wasn't around back then. My temper combined with my general smartass behavior would have left me dead before I was twenty. I couldn't see myself bowing down to some random outlaw just because he thought he was a big shot. Yeah, I probably shouldn't hang out in Vegas either.

The old-timey look of the place was quaint. All the signs were printed with the type of font you saw on Western movies. A few people milled about in period clothes. The rest seemed like tourists. The scenery was nice, but the heat left something to be desired. Being from the east coast, I couldn't stand the intense daytime. Like walking around in an oven. Not fun at all. If this was what Hell felt like, all the more reason for me to never go there.

"Let's go in here." Tabby pointed.

It was a saloon. The place even had those old-style swinging doors. She was probably right; a cold drink would ease our suffering. Plus, it was kind of dark inside…and cooler.

Tabby grabbed a pamphlet from a rack beside the door. "Jimmy?"

"Yeah?"

"Who told you that you were related to Doc Holliday?"

I blinked. Not something I expected to be asked today. "My mom. Why?"

"His name has two ells."

I shrugged. "I don't think that makes too much of a

difference. Families alter the spelling of names all the time."

Tabby raised her eyebrow at me.

"No, really. This guy I knew in seminary had at least four different family members that changed the spelling of their last name."

"Ah ha. Do you believe you're related?"

"Probably not. It was just one of those things Mom always said." I think my mother wanted to be famous in some way. Too bad; her life was daytime movie material all right; the Lifetime movie about what happens when you're an alcoholic and your kids have to learn to cope. Not that I was bitter or anything.

She nodded. "That flask is strange."

I couldn't argue with her there. It likely would be something highly prized by a collector somewhere. Hell, I would have been fascinated had I seen it at an antiques show, but having received it at random through the mail? That was creepy. "Yeah. A lot of things are odd."

"Don't you think it's interesting that the flask has Holliday's initials on it?"

I began to chuckle. First, how would I have known Holliday's initials? And second, what did that have to do with anything? "Do I even need to mention how many name configurations could have those same initials?"

"Fuddy-duddy."

I pulled her into a hug. This trip had been hard enough for both of us. "Hey, we have enough mysteries without you creating more for us."

She pulled away and glared at me. I'd screwed up now. Yeah, I should have handled this better, but I was already annoyed enough with the false lead.

"I'm sorry," I said.

Tabby grunted and headed toward the bar. I followed

behind. I guess I deserved the silent treatment, but damn she was being harsh. I'd done a lot worse than this.

"You know, you could have just checked Google Earth," she snapped. She stopped in the middle of the aisle and stared at me.

"Google Earth wouldn't have told me who sent the flask, now would it?" Yeah, I definitely shouldn't have snapped at her, but I was tired of being treated like her own personal punching bag.

"All right. Jesus, Jimmy. You're driving me crazy. I concede. Yes, there is a reason we're here. What is it?"

As I was about to answer her, a deep voice answered for me.

"That's a question we've all been asking, little lady." He was dressed in this out-of-time way with a vest and a suit coat. He had a black hat, but he was holding it in his hand. His hair, unlike his hat, was ash blond. He also sported a matching mustache.

Tabby looked like she'd swallowed a bug. Her hands shaking and she was on the verge of losing the pamphlet. What was her problem?

On a whim, I asked, "Sir, do you know anything about Toughnut Street?"

The man laughed in an awkward way. Like my question was the funniest thing he'd had in a while, but then he stopped abruptly. "Strange things on Toughnut. But nowhere near as weird as me."

I didn't doubt that. He wasn't exactly a normal guy, not with the way he was acting. But I didn't really have room to talk. I wasn't normal either.

"What is your name?" Tabby asked.

He smiled. "You can call me Doc."

Then he disappeared.

"Fuck." Tabby and I stared at each other. That was the first time I'd spoken to what was probably a real ghost. Lucy didn't count. She was a soul separated from her body. A technicality, but still.

Tabby sucked in a breath. "Maybe it isn't a man that needs an exorcism but the town."

I had this vision in my head about a circle of exorcists chanting in the town square like a scene in a movie. "Then we're going to need a lot more exorcists."

#

Seeing Doc didn't stop us. I left Tabby standing in the aisle and sauntered up to the bar. I knocked on it to get the bartender's attention. He was dressed in a white shirt with a ribbon tie around his neck. His hair was black and parted down the middle. I guessed he was told to look the part. He stopped washing glasses and came over to me.

"Whatcha need?" he asked.

"Did you see that?" I pointed toward the area Doc had been sitting.

He shrugged. "Doc is known to show himself here from time to time. He won't hurt ya."

I blinked. I wasn't used to a place where ghosts were that commonplace. "Oh, I'm not worried about that." I paused. I had more to worry about than talking to ghosts. I took a deep breath and stilled myself. It was time to get back to my real problem, figuring out who had sent that flask and why I'd been called here. "Have you heard of anyone looking for a Jimmy Holiday?"

Tabby came up behind me and put her hand on my elbow. The bartender raised his head and glanced over at her. "They got ya, did they?"

"Who? What?"

He leaned in close. "There's a lot of odd shit in this town.

And we get people coming here looking for something all the time. Most, we never see again."

It was starting to sound like a bad horror movie. What was next? Being warned about the black dog that appeared only at the full moon? "Look. Someone sent me a silver flask from an address on Toughnut. No name. Empty parking lot."

"No, there wouldn't be." He leaned forward so that his nose was only inches from mine. "House there burned down a few years ago. The family wasn't real careful with their gas. Lady left a pot on the stove, flame went out, and when the furnace kicked on downstairs—boom!"

"Was everyone okay?" Tabby asked.

He nodded. "She'd gone to the store when she left the pot on the stove. Lost the whole house, though, and there was damage to the other houses around it. Took about a year to get everything set to rights."

"If the house was gone, then who sent me the flask?"

He shrugged. "Wasn't the lady that lived in that house. She left and moved to Philadelphia. No, stick around a while, and he'll find ya, but don't say I didn't warn ya."

I didn't like the idea that this bartender knew who he was talking about, but he didn't bother to tell me. It was my life that being fucked with, not his. As I was about to say something about it, the bartender put down the last glass and went into the back of the saloon.

Tabby grabbed me by the arm. "We are so screwed."

"Tell me about it."

Chapter Five

You Spin Me

SO I GUESS we did the stupid thing. I stopped getting myself worked up and Tabby calmed down. When the bartender came back, I ordered up a couple of beers and some chicken strips and fries. I knew I wouldn't be able to live with myself if I didn't at least wait for a while. The dude was supposed to show. I started wondering if this had happened before. Tabby hadn't said much at all.

I almost wished I hadn't left Lucy in the car. Who knows what could have happened if she and old Doc had gotten together? But that's something I didn't do, so no sense in worrying about it now. But it might have been something cool to see.

"Jimmy?" Tabby asked.

I glanced up from my food. "Yeah?"

"I'm sorry I was so hard on you earlier."

Holy shit. Tabby was apologizing to me. It was one of those things that like almost never happened. Ever. Maybe spotting a ghost changed her perspective on a few things.

"It's okay. I know I can be a pain in the ass sometimes. Besides, we're in this together, right?" It was the least I could do. I'd been just as much of a prick. I needed to own up to it.

She wiped her mouth with a napkin. "Right."

"I wonder when Mr. Creepy is going to show up."

"Which Mr. Creepy?"

I snorted. It was kind of sad she had to ask. We'd been through so much bizarre shit that it was an honest question. "Whatever it is we're supposed to be waiting for. Part of me hopes he looks like he's from *The Hills Have Eyes* or something. The other part of me hopes he's a normal guy, an antique collector or something."

"In your case, either one would be bad." She took a sip of her soda.

"How so?"

"Because you're an exorcist. Any of the people you encounter will likely be possessed."

Shit. She was right. Though, not everyone I encountered was possessed. I mean, her mother wasn't demonfied; she was just a bitch. "Or a pissotsky."

"What the hell is a pissotsky?"

I laughed. "It's a guy possessed by a certain type of demon. When he gets horny, he gets *horny*."

She rolled her eyes. "And what movie did you get that from?"

I grinned. "The fruit burger classic, *My Demon Lover*."

She held her head in her hands. "I sure as hell hope that the higher power knows what he's doing making you into this thing."

"Maybe it's my charm." I knew she liked me. Otherwise, she wouldn't put up with my goofy ass.

She swatted me on the arm. "You done?"

"Yeah. I give up. Let's get back to Lucy." I pushed my food away. We'd waited here long enough. I hadn't seen anyone come in to the place. It was time to cut my losses, do a little sightseeing, and go home.

I went up to the bar to pay the bill while Tabby waited for

me by the door. The bartender didn't say a word to me as he settled my tab and ran my credit card. In fact, he seemed a little odd. Stiff almost. I shrugged it off as a guy being tired, but I felt that strange feeling again.

It wasn't until I got the receipt that I knew all hell was breaking loose. Instead of my total on the receipt, there was a hotel name and a room number printed. The only problem? It was my hotel, the Marian Motel, and my room number, fourteen-oh-eight. After a minute, the text changed back to what it should have been, a normal restaurant receipt.

I grasped Tabby by the arm. "We have to go."

"What the hell, Jimmy?" she asked as I dragged her over to the car. I knew I was likely hurting her arm, but she was too stubborn to just come when I needed.

"We have to get back to the room, now." Maybe it was the panic in my voice that did it. I let go of her arm and she followed me down the street.

She didn't argue anymore. We both jumped into the car and I got us to the hotel as fast as I could. It probably wasn't fast enough. I just hoped that Lucy was there and I wasn't about to find Isaac spread about the room in pieces.

We ran from the car after I parked it and dashed up to our room. I could hear Isaac yowling from within. This wasn't good. I slid the key card into the lock and the light went green. God help me if the bastard hurt the cat. I opened the door.

We headed in, Tabby bringing up the rear. Isaac was on the bed with his back hunched and his lips pulled into a snarl. He was glaring toward the window. I glanced over at the little table in front of the window. A man was there sitting in the chair, staring at us.

He was tall with these long skinny legs I could see defined by his white suit. His hair stood out as white as the suit and billowed down to his shoulders. He wore black-plastic-framed glasses.

"Close the door, if you will," he said to Tabby and motioned with his hand. The nails on his fingers were long and perfectly manicured.

Tabby complied, her eyes wide. Only, I think, because we didn't want to let the whole hotel know our dirty laundry. Though, if having a random guy break into your hotel room wasn't cause enough to create a disturbance, I don't know what was.

"Who the fuck are you?" I opened without the bullshit.

He wrung his hands together and sighed. "I had hoped things would be more civil."

Where I was from, you didn't chitchat with someone that broke into your house. You shot them. Good thing I didn't own a gun.

"Look, buddy. You broke into our room, sent Jimmy a flask from who the hell knows where, and you want us to be civil?" Tabby's eyes began to glow red. The idiot hadn't seemed to realize that she was the violent one.

I would never have come right out with the stuff about the flask. She was so flipping cool.

"I'm guessing you're the one who called me?" I asked him. I needed to get the spotlight off Tabby. She was having a hard enough time keeping her cool. At least this way, if he fucked up, she could catch him broadside.

He uncrossed his legs, stood up, and gave a strange little bow. "Allow me to introduce myself. I am Nicholas Vespa, a spiritualist."

I nodded. He sounded more like a motor scooter salesman than a person who dabbled with the occult. I wasn't completely ignorant when it came to spiritualists. Yeah, I'd read about one with the whole Sorrow's Point mess, and I suspected she was more of a witch than a spiritualist, but whatever. If this guy was what he said he was, then I was confused as to why he was in my hotel room, and, apparently, why he sent the flask. "You said on the phone that you needed an exorcism."

He smiled like that female vampire from the old *Fright Night* movie with his mouth pulled up just a little too wide at the sides. "Not exactly. I'm not sure if an exorcism is called for, in fact. It is more of an agreed-upon possession."

Things had stopped making sense, and when stuff didn't make sense, it wasn't true. "Why did you lie?" It was a lie, after all. He'd said on the phone that he'd seen O'Malley and he'd needed an exorcism. I did not like being lied to, especially when the person lying to you thought you were stupid enough to take them at face value.

"So you're aware, lies are one of my pet peeves." I was blocking the doorway with my body. "And how the hell did you get into my room?"

Tabby moved and lay on the bed next to Isaac. The cat cuddled up to her and stayed there. It didn't escape my notice that the cat was claiming his spot. I was second place.

"Does it make a difference? I am here now. That is what matters."

This was not going to happen. I had better things to do than listen to some old dude lording it over me. "Look. There's this thing called free will, and if you piss me off, I do have the choice not to help you."

Vespa coughed. "Truly? I should think your superiors would have something to say about that."

Now what would a "possessed" guy know about the Order? "Why do I suddenly feel like I am fighting with a demon instead of a man?"

Vespa grinned. His eyes turned yellow and the pupils turned to slits. Ooh, big scary.

"Jimmy?" Lucy asked from behind me. Her voice shook a

little. Not good.

"Yes?"

"He wants to take me."

I stared down at her and her body was more transparent than usual.

Fuck this shit. I was not going to let anyone mess with me a second time. I stilled myself to ready for a fight. "Foul being. Dark bearer. Hear me. You have not been invited." I put strength into my voice. "Being invited is critical. And I take great offense to those who hurt my friends."

The demon blinked. "What is it you think you can do?"

Okay, play time. The power bubbled up inside of me. I knew how to put it out there. All I had to do was speak a certain way and blammo. "You are not invited. Lucy's soul is not yours. It bears my mark. Be gone."

With every word, I could see ripples of power move through the air around me. He'd done it. Maybe it would teach him a lesson not to piss off a marker.

Suddenly, I heard a loud bang. Vespa collapsed onto the floor.

"Oh, shit." Tabby jumped off the bed. "Should we check on him?"

I eyeballed his chest. He was breathing. Good enough. "I'm not touching him. It could be a trick."

Tabby nodded. After a few minutes, Vespa woke.

"Where am I?" he asked.

"Marian Motel. My room." I leaned against the wall in front of the door. I wasn't going to let the dude run away. I had some questions.

"What am I doing here?" he asked me.

Crap. This wasn't normal.

"You don't remember?" Tabby asked.

He got up from the floor. "I get these spells where I

remember nothing. Sometimes I miss entire days."

Yup. If I hadn't already seen the demon, I would have suspected he was either possessed or had some psychological disorder. But with those eyes, I was thinking possession.

"Who are you?" he asked me.

"Jimmy Holiday." Or marker extraordinaire, cool guy without a robe. I was getting ahead of myself.

"Oh, thank God. I had to be sneaky, you know?"

I blinked and felt a tension headache coming on. "Sneaky how?"

"It wouldn't let me contact you again. So I had to wait until I had the power, when he was asleep. Then I was able to send you the package."

And back to the flask we were. I ignored the fact that my brain was now thinking like the little green dude from *Star Wars*.

"What does the flask signify?" Tabby asked.

I glanced at her, then back at Vespa. Something was going on there, and Tabby being a hell of a lot more astute than I was, apparently picked up on it.

"It…belongs to a famous spirit. I knew you'd come here if I sent it." He brushed off his suit.

"What famous spirit?" I asked.

"Why, your ancestor, Doc Holliday, of course."

Fuck me.

#

Vespa left the room soon after. He did give me his cell number so that we could reach him. I'd told him I needed to think things over. The truth was, I was so pissed off about the invasion of my privacy, I wasn't sure if I wanted to help him. Demon or not, you don't saunter into someone's hotel room unannounced. It wasn't cool.

Lucy kept staring at the door, almost as if she expected him to come crashing in. I couldn't blame her. The fucker had tried to take her away. I still didn't quite understand what the marker power did, but it was able to make the bastards go somewhere else. Lucy seemed okay now, just nervous. Isaac was curled up against where Lucy's leg sort of was, asleep.

"What are you going to do?" Tabby had plopped on the bed again.

"I don't know." It was true. I wasn't even sure if I was going to bother to help the guy after all that. It would probably be best to haul our asses back to Virginia and take our chances.

Tabby rose and hugged me. "I'm not crazy about this either."

Her arms felt good, both soft and strong at the same time. I took a deep breath. "With Lucy, I cared because she was this little girl, ya know?"

Tabby stepped back. "When you were a priest, would you have done the same for all of your parishioners?"

"Not all, but most." But none of my parishioners had tried to steal the soul of a little girl, either. It did make a difference.

Tabby came over and tapped the top of the little table. "What is it about this guy that bothers you most?"

"Honestly?"

"Yes, honestly."

"That he freely invited the demon in. I don't have a problem when someone is attacked, but to make deals with these things, that's evil too." Not to mention what he'd just done. I wasn't a hundred percent sure that he wasn't aware of what the demon was doing. Lucy certainly was. She'd indicated that in the dreams I had about her at Sorrow's Point. I knew enough now not to ignore things most people would discount.

"If it really bothers you, why don't you call them?"

"Call who?"

"Your employers or whatever they are. Surely, they could send someone else."

I hunkered down on the bed. Lucy watched me. Calling the Order would be a hard thing. Telling them that I wasn't able to do this job...that would be failure almost. Maybe Tabby and Lucy should head back home and I'd stay here? No, Lucy couldn't be that far from me. Shit. That wouldn't work either.

"What do you think?" I asked her.

"You said you'd protect me."

Leave it to a kid to blatantly put it out there. "Yes, I did, and I will." That was the end of it. I had a job to do—protect Lucy. Whatever went along with it, I'd just have to deal with it.

She petted Isaac, or sort of at least. Her hand passed through his coat. Isaac opened one eye, feigned interest, and then fell back asleep. "You saw what it was doing to me. You have to send it away."

I was starting to think that Lucy was the best thing to ever happen to me. She kept my conscience straight. That was it, then. I had to deal with Vespa. "Thanks, Lucy."

She beamed.

"How are you going to do this?" Tabby asked.

Good question. I knew nothing about this type of possession. The church assumed that no one would ever want to be possessed willingly. "I guess I'd better get to know what a spiritualist actually does. After that, I'll call Vespa."

"What can I do to help?" Tabby reached for her purse.

"Find out everything you can about Doc. I want to know what the connection is. Why would a possessed man send an artifact that belonged to my ancestor to me? There has to be something there."

Tabby nodded. "I'll see what I can find."

She left the hotel room. I didn't want to do this exorcism. Of course, I hadn't wanted to do Lucy's either, but that was beside the point. The one thing I did know was that if I didn't get rid of this thing, it was going to take Lucy. That was not an option.

#

I loaded up the iPad. Immediately, I got a pop-up informing me that my forms had been received and I should get my first check in about two weeks. Yee fucking haw. I guessed that meant that I'd be getting a paycheck sometime this century. Online bill pay was going to be my friend for a while.

I pulled up the browser and searched for spiritualist information. Most of what I got was people proclaiming to do spells for money, et cetera. Definitely not what I needed. Finally, I found a site that had a lot of old photographs with ectoplasm and séances. The historical stuff. Many of the photos were debunked, but there was one that gave me chills. The guy could have been a double for Vespa: the shoulder-length white hair, the long mustache, it was all there. I saved the photo to the desktop. If Vespa was that old, that might explain the power the demon had. But with a man being possessed that long, how could there even be any of his soul left? Besides, I'd never read anywhere that a demon could prolong human life for hundreds of years. Yet again, more questions than answers.

Logic said this guy was likely a descendant, an uncanny one, but a descendant nonetheless. So that left me with one question. Who in their right mind would willingly let a demon inhabit their body? Even a normal person knew that demons weren't exactly easy to get rid of. I didn't buy the fame and fortune crap. Pride maybe. Power certainly. But money? It would be easier to rob a bank. Plus, if you got caught, you'd serve a light sentence if it was your first time doing something that bad. If you told them a demon made you do it, the judge would laugh you out of the courtroom.

Of course, the only person who could answer that for me was Vespa himself, and I wasn't in the mood to talk to him so soon. I wanted to get all of this over and done, but I wasn't about to risk anyone's well-being again. The only reason I wasn't beating myself up over Lucy is that we were all broadsided with Vespa. Now I was on the alert, and I was going to make sure nothing like that had a chance to happen. The church would probably feel it was my duty to help him. I didn't agree. I was only helping him so nothing else bad would happen. He could shove the rest of it up his ass as far as I was concerned. It was enough that I was actually going to do this. It didn't mean I had to like it.

#

Tabby came back a few hours later with a crapload of pamphlets and a book. Her hair had escaped its bun and wafted out around her face, almost like a halo.

"Damn," I said when she dropped it all on the bed.

"Your ancestor is kind of popular, if you haven't noticed." She kicked off her shoes and walked across the room.

I chuckled. "Something tells me he wasn't like the way he's portrayed in movies."

"No one is like how they are shown in movies." Tabby sat in a chair at the table, opened the pop bottle she had in her hand, and took a swig.

I flipped through the pamphlets. "Can you imagine living back then?"

"Nope."

"Why not?"

"Because it was fucking hard. We're too used to air conditioning and buying our food at the grocery store. Hell, just to have a sandwich you had to bake the bread, butcher a pig, and then cook the ham, make the mayo if you wanted it. No, I couldn't do it."

I grinned. "Yes, you could. You can do anything."

She took another drink of her soda. "You wouldn't be much better. I can't see you riding a horse to go to the next town."

She had me. Way back when, before we'd broken up the first time, she'd tried to get me on a horse. The poor thing stood there. I couldn't get into the saddle. So I fed it carrots instead.

"Yeah...my ancestor. What do you think he was like?"

She paused for a minute. "None of these guys were sweet, Jimmy. They were total assholes. They had to be. It was survival of the fittest."

"How about Wyatt Earp?"

She chuckled. "He only took the role of marshal so he could kill the killer of his brother. Doc Holliday was a gambler. These weren't petting puppies kind of guys."

"I would love to know what my ancestor has to do with a possessed spiritualist." The link was out of my reach.

"Then maybe, just maybe, it's time for you to calm down and we'll ask him. We could meet him for dinner somewhere." Tabby raised a brow.

I stared at Lucy, but she was ignoring me and watching TV. I didn't really have any other choice. I'd exhausted all the avenues I knew of to get information. And I seriously doubted if a biography of my ancestor would have an occult section. Hell, this was the first time I'd heard of it.

"I guess that would be okay," I said.

Tabby tossed me Vespa's card. "Get on with it, then."

I dialed his number...and got voicemail. I couldn't win. Why couldn't things work out the way I needed them?

"Yeah. Mr. Vespa? This is Jimmy Holiday." I gripped the phone harder. "We'd like to meet with you for dinner. Call me back when you get the chance."

I hung up. Some days, it would be better to dig yourself into a hole in the ground.

"At least, you did all you could do," Tabby said.

"Yeah. I guess."

Part of me was upset for dragging my feet earlier. Yeah, true, I had a reason to be pissed, but once I decided to do something, I followed through. I should have told him we'd meet him later so I'd have a chance to calm down and get some of these questions out of the way. I was more concerned with keeping myself from beating his ass. Now, I hoped it wasn't too late.

"Isaac's hungry," Lucy said.

"How do you know that?" Tabby stared at my little charge.

She shrugged. "He told me."

Lucy's ability to communicate with Isaac was getting really odd. I wondered if she was putting words in his mouth or if he actually was telling her these things.

"Isaac has food." Tabby turned her attention back to a pamphlet.

"He wants fish," Lucy said.

This was getting stranger by the minute. Just what I needed, a spirit living in my house that could talk to animals. What was next, a cockroach conga line?

"There is fish in his food." Tabby glared at the cat, "Besides, he knows better."

Said cat let out a rowr in response.

"That's it. I'm losing my mind," I said. It was time I wore one of those spit hoods and drooled constantly.

Tabby chuckled. "Nope. You lost it a long time ago."

"So you say." I watched Lucy. She was back to staring at the TV and Isaac was trying to sleep.

Then my phone rang.

#

Vespa wanted to meet us at a Southwestern restaurant outside of town. I didn't care, but the farther he was from where we were staying, the more comfortable I felt. I didn't want him getting close to Lucy any more than I could help it. It was too dangerous.

"Any way you can ward our hotel room?" I asked Tabby. It wasn't a bad idea. If there was a safe place for Lucy to stay, maybe I could convince her to stay there instead of sticking to me like glue. As far as I knew, it wasn't like there was a thread connecting us. It was more like I was her marker, so thus her caretaker.

"I don't know. It's not a usual dwelling, but I can try."

"It would be a good idea, though, right? I mean, we don't need anyone or anything coming in without an invite."

Tabby sighed. "Yes, Jimmy. I know."

It was time for me to shut up. I was pushing her too far. Sometimes I rambled on and on, not letting her speak, but I wasn't sure I was being all that bad. Though her getting annoyed was probably proof enough. Maybe I needed to not be such a smartass, but it wasn't like I was trying to offend her.

"Are we there yet?" Lucy asked from the back seat.

I glanced at her through the rearview mirror. She was smiling. "Smartass."

She giggled.

Tabby spun around in the seat. "Lucy, why don't you stay in the car? I don't think it will be a good idea for you to be around the demon."

Thank God for Tabby. I had been more wrapped up in the warding of the room than what to do about things immediately. I swear, if I had a brain...

"Thanks."

She smiled. "Any time."

"I hope you get him gone soon," Lucy said.

I could hear the fear in her voice. Poor kid. She'd been through enough. I needed to step up my game. No sense in putting her through more crap than I had to. "I do too, Lucy."

By the time Tabby and I got inside, Vespa was sitting at a table toward the front of the place. The restaurant was your usual Mexican thing: dark with wooden tables and chairs. The walls were painted in murals all over the walls. On each table rested a clay pot with a lit candle in it. I guess it was supposed to give some atmosphere, but I was thinking more about what could happen with a klutz and an open flame.

"Thank you for meeting me," Vespa said when we approached the table. He stood up, nodded his head at us, and sat back down.

I pulled out a chair and draped a leg around it. Tabby followed suit.

"It isn't for you we are doing this, just so you know."

It wasn't that I was trying to be a dick or anything, but I wanted to be honest. I didn't trust Vespa, and at this point, I wasn't sure if I trusted the Order since they seemed to want this to happen. I had a hard time believing that they would knowingly put Lucy in danger. So it must be that they knew that Vespa was possessed, and that was about it.

If this exorcism didn't go right, I wasn't sure if I could handle Vespa's spirit bugging me for who knows how long. Plus, he was kind of creepy.

"I welcome the help nonetheless." Vespa seemed to curl into himself. It would take a lot for someone to accept hostile help. Interesting.

Tabby leaned forward. "How did you get yourself into this mess?"

Vespa took a sip of water and stared into the flame. "I wanted the power that my great-grandfather had. Stupid, I know."

I glared at him for a minute. "Why was the power so important to you?"

"You would have to understand my family. Spiritualism is

their religion. Since my birth, I was made to study, to make contact with the dead. Unfortunately, I wasn't very good at it. To my family, that was a blight on their good name."

He reached up and began picking at his face. I had flashbacks of that scene from *Nightbreed* where the guy peels his face off. But this wasn't real. It was fake. The latex pulled off in patches. When he finally took off the white wig, I found myself facing a kid that couldn't even have been twenty years old.

I closed my eyes and counted to ten. Blowing up in a restaurant would be a bad move. "Now would be the time to come completely clean. I hate lies. And I swear, one more lie out of you, and I'll walk away."

The kid's eyes welled up. It was strange seeing a young kid with close-cropped dark hair staring back at me where an elderly man had been. They did share the same facial features, but without the wig and the latex, he was just a boy. "I thought…I thought you'd ignore me if you knew how old I was."

"Is your name at least Nicholas Vespa?" At this point, I wouldn't be surprised if his name wasn't Tom Smith or something. Jesus Christ.

He nodded. "I was named after my great-grandfather."

"All right. Let's start this again." At least I did have his name. Shit. What a mess.

The waitress came over. She stared at Vespa for a minute, noticed the wig on the table, and slightly shook her head. "What can I get you folks?"

I had to admire her professionalism. "I'll take a Coke."

Tabby asked for one too. Nicholas stuck with water. After the waitress stepped away, he stared at me.

"Get on with it." I wanted to know the story and get the hell out of there. I had better things to do than listen to lies and that seemed to be the one thing Vespa was good at.

"I was supposed to be the one." His eyes took on a faraway look.

Tabby blinked. "The one what?"

"The one who could channel great-grandpa's powers. He was the one with the real gift. The others had to resort to tricks to get similar effects, but my great-grandfather was the real thing."

Of course there wasn't anything to prove that. Too much was left for me to simply believe, and I wasn't crazy about that. Not to mention the fact that he told me he had a demon possess him so he could hopefully pull off the parlor tricks his great-grandfather did. Was this kid really that stupid? Yes, he was. "You collared a demon to take up residence so you could have 'powers'?"

"Yeah. I know it sounds bad, but my family…we're broke."

Plenty of people went and got jobs to deal with their debt. This was the first time I had ever heard of anyone asking a demon to possess him to get rid of bills. It was probably a good thing he didn't have a giant student loan hanging over his head. He'd have invoked the devil then. I guessed you would either call this kid lazy or obsessed. I wasn't sure which yet. Either way, what he'd done was far from normal, incredibly stupid, and ridiculous. Evidently, the kid never learned to grow a set and tell his family to fuck off. If that was the issue here at all. I didn't believe a word that came out of his mouth.

"Why did they think you'd be the one?" Tabby asked.

"Because I looked like him," Vespa said. "They have all these old photos of Great-grandpa from the time he was about twelve until he died."

"Genetics decided to make you look like him, so they decided you needed to have his 'gifts'?" This part kind of rang true, I had to admit. I'd seen families this fucked up before.

The waitress came back with our drinks. The poor girl was

dressed in some sort of serape thing. With it being over eighty outside, I could imagine how miserable it was to work there dressed like that. I would have had heat stroke within half an hour.

"Have you decided?" she asked.

I ordered something with lots of chorizo. Needed to have my spice fix. Tabby got tacos, and the kid ordered some chicken platter. The waitress seemed to be trying to cheer us all up with her friendly demeanor, but crap was too frustrating for it to work. She picked up the menus a little sadly.

"Thanks," I said to her. I got a smile in return and she left. I kind of felt for her. She was here, working her ass off, and we weren't even playing along and trying to make this dining experience fun. Not much I could do about that. Present company put a damper on things.

"You channeled a demon? Invoked a demon? What?" Tabby asked Vespa.

"I found a spell on the internet that was supposed to bring me a demon guide."

I couldn't stop my eyes from rolling and I snorted. I couldn't help it. Vespa stared down the table and I could feel Tabby's gaze boring into me. She couldn't expect me not to laugh at that. Shit. You gotta be kidding me. "And it worked?"

"No. I ended up using a Ouija board."

Now that made sense. I knew Tabby didn't mess with them. And given her own experience with it, I didn't blame her. Bad things happened with those things.

"What did it promise you?" I asked.

"Power beyond my wildest dreams, stuff like that. I allowed it in. Now I can't get rid of it."

I exhaled. I wanted to give him a set of crayons and some paper and make him write lines like a child. Nobody did this. And with him agreeing to specific abilities, this meant there was a verbal contract of sorts. Damn. I knew nothing about this side of it. I'd never dealt with a demon contract before. It wasn't like I knew a warrior who could help me fight for people's souls or anything. Though, if they did exist, it would be damn cool.

"Can you get it out?" he asked.

Good question. It depended on what the contract actually said. "Maybe. You, doing an agreement with this thing or whatever it was, I just don't know."

"Could you mark him?" Tabby asked.

That was a very good question. I had marked Lucy's soul and that's what kept her around. But Nicholas wasn't dead and this demon seemed to be getting nothing out of living in the body. Not to mention, I didn't want to mark him if I could keep from it. I did not want him hanging around my house. Sorry.

"I don't know." I truly didn't. Of course, I wasn't exactly going out of my way to find out either.

"What? Mark what?" Nicholas asked.

"Don't worry about it." I waved it off. "One more question though. What's with all the connections to my ancestor?"

He stared straight into my eyes. "Grandfather used to channel him all the time."

I blinked. At least I sort of had an answer now. This whole thing was getting worse and worse. So we'd seen Holliday's ghost in the saloon. If Vespa's grandfather had somehow trapped my ancestor's soul here, I needed to take care of that too. Not like I didn't have a crapload on my plate or anything. "All I can tell you is that I'm going to have to research it. I don't know enough about demon contracts to know if we can even exorcise you."

He exhaled slowly. "O'Malley said you could help."

Yeah, twist my guts, why don't you? I missed my mentor. At least he died normally. A heart attack took him right after he performed his final baptism. He went out doing what he loved.

But I missed him. "I'm going to try."

#

After we all got back to the hotel, Tabby took Lucy around the complex. I guess there was this gift shop. Poor kid needed something to do. TV wasn't exactly going to keep her entertained forever, and it wouldn't be a bad idea to try to educate her either. I mean, hell, the kid, if she did get reunited with her body, was going to be so behind in school that it would be ridiculous. If she were my kid, I'd homeschool her anyway. The last thing she needed was for someone to ask her about her scars or something, and then all the mess would begin.

I relaxed on the bed with Isaac lying against my leg. Having a cat that liked me enough to use me as a pillow felt kind of nice. Every so often, I'd give him a scratch behind the ears. I had the "Holy iPad" in my hands. It wasn't like they expected me to know anything. They'd said something about training, after all, but I felt bad for contacting them. I shouldn't, I suppose, but it was like I wasn't capable of doing the job. But better to look like an idiot and ask instead of majorly fucking something up.

I jotted off an email letting them know about the contract and the possible trapped soul, and questioned what I should do about either one. Then I set the machine down and spoke to Isaac. "You should be helping me."

Isaac snorted, stepped over to the pile of brochures Tabby had brought back that afternoon, and dug at them until he uncovered the one he wanted. Heh. Who knew? Maybe I should ask him for help more often. I was going to have to tell Tabby about it.

I picked up the pamphlet. It was one about a ghost tour of Tombstone. Interesting.

"You saying I should go on this?"

Isaac let out a rowr at me and laid his head down to go to sleep.

I sucked my teeth. Who knew what would be in that ghost tour, but it was at least it was a lead of some sort, and until I heard from the organization, it was the only lead I had. Plus, I couldn't exactly ignore a suggestion from a witch's familiar. That was what he was no matter what type of spin Tabby tried to put on it. I didn't know of any normal cat who could have done what he had.

Chapter Six

Creep

"WE'RE GOING ON what?" Tabby asked when I tried to tell her about Isaac. Whether the cat told me either didn't register or she didn't care. She seemed stressed out, but I had no idea why.

"There's a ghost tour of Tombstone," I reiterated. It was a hell of a lead. Maybe I could learn something about my ancestor at the very least.

Lucy kept staring at Isaac like she was talking to him with her mind. I knew I sounded crazy, but if it got me the information I needed, so be it.

Tabby placed a bag from the gift shop on the table. Her shoulders slumped as if all the wind had gone out of her sails. I didn't know what I was doing wrong.

"When does this thing start?"

Okay, maybe she was just tired. I could deal with that. I picked up the pamphlet. "Says here that tours start after dark."

Tabby closed her eyes. I could swear she was counting. "All right. Let me get my coat. It gets chilly at night in the desert."

"Better stay here, Lucy." I winked, "Don't want to accidentally scare people."

Tabby turned around. "He got in here once before, and you want to leave her here alone? I haven't tried to ward the room yet."

Eek. I'd gotten way ahead of myself. Hell, she'd been with me the whole time. What the hell was I thinking? "Crap. I forgot. Why haven't you done it yet?"

That did it. She put her hands on her hips, her eyes flashing. I swear, she was about to catch me on fire with flames from her pupils. "All day it's been, 'Tabby, go get this; Tabby, do that.' What about 'Tabby is fucking tired, it's almost ten, and you want to go to a goddamn ghost tour'?"

I'd done it. Big time. Sometimes I was so stupid. "I'm sorry. You're right. Let's do it tomorrow."

"Let's." She stomped into the bathroom.

I was so totally screwed. The last time I'd seen her this pissed was the day she left me. Not good. I waved the pamphlet at Isaac. "Too bad you aren't a dog, I could borrow your house then."

He glared at me and then closed his eyes. Great. I'd pissed him off too.

"What about you, Lucy?" I asked.

"You aren't very smart." She plopped in front of the TV.

That was putting it mildly. The best thing I could do was keep my damn mouth shut until I knew Tabby had calmed down. "I know, Lucy. I know."

The next morning, Tabby wasn't talking to me, so I went out to get pastries for breakfast. The less she had to do at this point, the better. And I was hoping that chocolate might improve her mood. It was worth a shot. I knew I wasn't going to get out of this easily, but maybe if I made an effort, she'd forgive me a little more quickly.

I headed for the front desk of the hotel. The lobby was this all-white thing with a big concert-style piano in front of a large curved window. Kind of fancy-looking. After a moment, the guy at the desk turned his attention to me.

"Can I help you?"

I swallowed the spit that collected in my throat. I hated being nervous. Too bad my nervousness had to do with Tabby, and this dude at the desk was probably thinking I was strange. "Is there a bakery or something nearby?"

"There's a Walmart outside of town a ways."

I nodded, thanked him, and left the building and ambled toward the car. Walmart was better than nothing. I'd been hoping for a gourmet bakery, something that would impress Tabby, but I had to take what I could get.

Lucy had stayed in the room with Tabby. Part of me was thankful for the break, but the other part was kind of jealous. I'd gotten used to my funky sidekick. It was good to know for sure that she could be places where I wasn't.

I'd just unlocked the car when my phone rang. If it was Vespa, I would chuck the damn thing down the street. I snatched it from my pocket and glanced at the screen. It was Tabby.

"What's up?" I asked.

"You need to get back to the room."

This did not sound good. There was a strange desperation in her voice. "Okay. I'll be there in a minute."

"Hurry," she said, then hung up.

I clicked the clock on the car again and ran back inside. I tapped my foot at the slow elevator, but I didn't exactly know where the steps were, so elevator it had to be. Once I got up to the room, I could hear Isaac hissing through the door. I used my hotel room key card.

I didn't know what I expected to find. Maybe blood, maybe something worse, but that wasn't what I got.

I stepped inside. "What's going...," I stopped. A huge black cloud had amassed in the corner of the room. Lucy was hiding behind Tabby, standing near the bathroom. Isaac hissed at the thing from the bed. I wanted to call to Isaac to come closer to me, but I also didn't want to antagonize the black cloud any more than necessary.

I closed the door behind me. There wasn't a foul smell like you'd have with a demon, just this freaky-looking black cloud. It could have been anything. From my limited knowledge, it meant some sort of spirit. That was all I knew. I didn't even know if it was malevolent. Black didn't have the same connotation around the world that it did in the West.

"Isaac, get away from there," I said. Antagonizing be damned. I couldn't let Tabby's cat get killed right in front of her.

Isaac turned, ogled me, and then darted off the bed in my direction. Before I had a chance to do anything else, he leapt into my arms. I held him. Poor guy was shivering. I had to keep myself from smiling that Isaac went to me when he was in danger.

"Who are you, and what do you want?" I asked the cloud thing.

Slowly, it began changing form, undulating and shifting until finally settling on the shape of a man in an old-style Western suit. I recognized him immediately. It was my ancestor.

"You could use some help, pilgrim," he said.

I blinked. Shock grabbed me, but I'd take help wherever I could get it. "Yeah, I probably could."

He sat at the table and cocked a grin at Tabby. "I always liked redheads."

She twitched and blushed a little.

Then, my ancestor turned to me. "Tell your pretty lady friend I don't bite." He winked. "Much."

Tabby stepped away from the bathroom and stood near me. "What are you here for, Mr. Holliday?"

He stroked his mustache a minute. "Guess you could say I have better things to do with my time than let my relative get screwed."

I stepped forward, put Isaac down, and plopped on the bed opposite of Doc. "You knew his great-grandfather, didn't you?"

Doc let out a belly laugh, and then got stonefaced. "Now, that would be one way to put it. He promised me immortality in exchange for gold. Preyed on a man in a weakened condition."

I knew Doc had died of tuberculosis, drowning to death because of the fluid in his lungs. Not a pretty way to go. For someone to capitalize on that was despicable. And it was further proof that a Vespa was not a person to be trusted.

"You're what, a ghost?" Tabby asked.

"If that's what you want to call it. I could have done this myself. It still burns me up that I wasted all that gold." He adjusted himself so that he had one leg crossed and his ankle resting on the knee of his other leg.

"How come you're here? You didn't die in Tombstone," I said. It was a good point. Nothing held him here, as far as I could see.

He grinned. "I go anywhere I like. Sometimes I pay the swindler's family a visit."

Ah ha, now that made sense. See, people made it so hard to get simple honest answers.

"And you're here now because of the young Vespa?" Tabby asked. She was coming forward, a little at a time.

"Nah. I'm here because your boyfriend asked for help."

Now that caught me off guard. I'd sent off a message, not verbally asked someone for help. Tabby stared at me.

"I sent an email to the organization last night, but I didn't expect this." I motioned to Doc. "Not that I'm not grateful."

Isaac hissed at him. I had to keep myself from losing it. Though I probably should have been worried that Isaac so far didn't like him. Of course, appearing first as a big black cloud didn't help matters.

"Damn things never did like me. Wyatt always said it was my sunny disposition."

I chuckled. Then, I glanced over to the bathroom. Lucy was standing there. She seemed almost frozen in place.

"She isn't right, ya know," Doc said.

"What do you mean?" My head whipped around to him.

"She ain't all there. She's not like me."

I nodded. I should have figured he would know. "She's unique all right."

Lucy came forward. She was staring at Doc like he'd just insulted her in the worst way possible. "Ever been possessed by a demon, Mr. Holliday?"

He paused for a second. I thought that was something he never expected to come out of a little girl's mouth. "No, little lady. Can't say I have."

"It changes things," Lucy replied and plopped next to me on the bed.

"Come to think of it, you ain't right either." Doc waved a hand at me.

I coughed. He was pretty damn astute. "I don't think exorcists are supposed to be normal."

"Jimmy, you weren't normal before all of this," Tabby said.

"You're going to stick around for a while?" I asked Doc. If he was, he needed to get along with Lucy. And Isaac would tell me if Doc was really bad, I thought. At least I hoped so.

"As long as you'll have me."

Later, Tabby turned on the TV for Lucy, and Lucy explained modern things to Doc. It was kind of interesting watching her accept him. He must have been okay on some level for her to do that. I tuned them out after a while.

Was I happy for the help? Yes. But I didn't know if I could

trust him. Lucy accepting him said a lot, but I didn't know him. Vespa being involved didn't help matters. Tabby's earlier warning about how ruthless even the heroes of the Old West were ran through my mind. Doc wasn't *Casper the Friendly Ghost*. He was the ghost of a killer. For now, he seemed to like us, but what would happen if we pissed him off?

Letting my thoughts drift off, I finally got around to turning on the iPad. That way, I could see if I got an official reply. Doc showing up was either as a result of them, or one hell of an odd coincidence. Doc was behaving like a very strange grandpa. Lucy seemed to be happier, wearing a smile a little more often. At least, she wasn't disappearing or anything, but I was uneasy.

After the device booted up, I clicked on my email icon. I had mail all right. Too bad it was spam. I guessed I was in for a long wait. That or they wanted to see how much I could handle. I was annoyed at that thought. I mean, my test, my real test, was Lucy, wasn't it? She was still here. Kind of. If they wanted to see if I could mark someone again, they should have had me tag along with another exorcist. What did they hope I'd accomplish with this one? It almost felt like a red herring. Something felt wrong about the entire trip. The little things that kept getting added were almost like distractions to the issues at hand. Fuck.

I shut down the tablet and tossed it aside on the bed.

"Are you okay?" Tabby asked.

"Peachy."

#

Doc disappeared before lunch. I was getting testy, of course. Part of it might have been that I hadn't had my morning caffeine. And I was used to eating breakfast. I hadn't had my daily bacon fix. Believe me, bacon makes a difference.

"Where did Doc go?" Tabby asked Lucy.

Lucy turned her head away from the TV. "He said he was going to keep an eye on Mr. Vespa."

That I could live with. If he turned out to be trustworthy, it might not hurt to have a spy. And maybe the old bird figured we needed some time to get used to him hanging around. If so, he wasn't wrong.

"Want to get out of here for a while?" Tabby asked.

I glanced up. "And do what?"

"I don't know. Get out of this room; get something to eat." I was starving. "Food sounds great. How about you, Lucy? Want to get out of here for a bit?"

Lucy raised her hand toward the TV. It shut off. I clicked my tongue against my teeth.

Okay, that was new. She was getting stronger. I took her action as affirmative.

"Maybe I can find somewhere to buy a sage bundle." Tabby tapped her finger against her chin.

"For what?" I drew a total blank. What did she need that for?

Tabby glared at me. "To ward the room?"

"Oh, yeah, right." Now I felt like a doofus. I'd made such a huge stink about it yesterday, and today, I'd screwed up again. Hopefully, Tabby was just going to take my faults for what they were. I wasn't exactly doing a very good job at changing.

After that, I kept my mouth shut. My job was to take Tabby places, be her pack horse, and make sure she got something to eat. Nothing else. The last thing I wanted to do was to stick my foot in it again. It didn't last long, though. We had just settled into a booth in the diner. Lucy had come as well. She was sitting beside me nearest to the wall. It was better that I could see her and protect her than to leave her in an unprotected room.

"Why are you so quiet?" Tabby asked after the waitress brought our drinks.

"Because I'm starting to realize which one of us is the brains in this outfit." At one time, I'd thought I was smart. Heh.

Lucy giggled.

Tabby raised an eyebrow.

"No, really." I paused and took a sip of my coffee, "I'm okay at learning stuff from a book, but apparently, I don't have common sense for shit." It was true. I really wondered how I had managed not to totally screw everything up at Sorrow's Point before Tabby got there. Then, I remembered. I had been following the Roman Ritual. No wonder that part had worked okay. I'd had a guidebook. This here, I was flying solo, sort of.

Tabby rolled her eyes. "No, you're feeling sorry for yourself. Stop it."

I lowered my head. "Yes, ma'am."

"How do you do that thing?" Lucy asked. She was staring at Tabby instead of the TV in the corner of the restaurant. In fact, the picture on the TV seemed a little fuzzy. The news channel showed some sort of unrest in the Middle East. Perfectly normal, except for the fuzziness.

"What thing?" Tabby and I asked in unison.

"What you're going to do to the room."

Tabby paused, and then inclined her chin at me for help. I shrugged. I didn't understand it much myself.

"Um. Okay." Tabby put her head in her hands. "Let's see. You've been to church, right?"

Lucy nodded.

"You know how the minister prays for people?"

"Uh-huh."

I was so glad Tabby was the one explaining this. I couldn't imagine what it was going to be like when Lucy was a teenager. I just hoped she'd be back with her parents before I had to worry about the "sex talk."

"What I'll be doing is kind of the same," Tabby said. "I'll be praying for our room to be blessed so it will be a safe place for us."

"And so Mr. Vespa can't come in again?" Lucy eyes had turned a little watery.

"Yup."

"What about Doc?" Lucy asked.

Shit. That was a good question. Doc was supposed to be helpful to us, but could Tabby direct her wards to let him in? Or could they be like they were at Sorrow's Point? In a way, if they did get set to flat-out keep away things that meant us harm, that would be proof if Doc really was on our side.

"What type of ward are you going to do?" I asked.

Tabby waited when the waitress stopped by our table. We both ordered lots of bacon on our hamburgers. Bacon was becoming a staple with us, like milk and eggs.

After the waitress left, Tabby strummed her fingers against the table. I could tell a lot of this was making her nervous, more fidgety than usual. "I'm not sure."

"Can you do something like you did in the library at Blackmoor?" I figured I should make a suggestion. She needed some of the brunt taken off her shoulders.

"Maybe. I don't know. Hotel rooms are different than being in someone's permanent residence. I don't know if it falls under the same rules."

I never knew all of this could get so complicated. "How will you know?"

"I guess when I find out if it works."

I didn't like it, but it wasn't like I could blame Tabby for it either. We both were stumbling around in the dark with a lot of this. "At least we'll know one thing if it does."

"What's that?" Tabby asked.

"We'll know if Doc is really on our side." I kind of hoped he was. I mean, Lucy had perked up so much with him being here that I'd hate to lose that. It was almost like Lucy was relieved to find someone sort of like her.

"That would be a good thing to know," Tabby said.
I took a drink. "Yeah."

#

After we finished eating, and the waitress showed up with
the bill, I had a bright idea.

"Hey," I asked our waitress. Unlike the one at the Tex Mex
restaurant, she seemed happy. She wore jeans and a T-shirt with
the café's name on it.

"Yes, sir?" she asked me.

"Anywhere around here that sells fresh herbs and spices?
We were thinking of bring a bit of Arizona back home." I
figured, why not ask the locals? That way, we wouldn't be
stumbling around for hours trying to find something Tabby
could use.

The lady grinned. "Tombstone isn't really the place for that.
Mostly, just tourist stuff here. But if I were you, I'd ask at the
general store. Monti might know of a place somewhere nearby."

"Thanks." It wasn't what we were looking for, but maybe
we'd get something out of it.

"Don't ya find it odd that a guy manning a general store in
Tombstone has a name like Monti?" Tabby asked.

I snorted. "It's better than Slim."

"Not much."

Later and not surprisingly, the general store turned out to be
a bust. Yeah, it had that great Western look about it with flour
sacks stacked in the corner, jars of penny candy, that sort of
thing, but nothing really that we needed. Tabby did manage to
buy a cheap container of ground sage. It would have to do. I
didn't think the sage being ground up would make too much of
a difference. Now, how she was going to burn it, I left that up
to her. She was the witchy expert, after all.

After getting the sage, we headed back to the hotel. Our
room was just as we left it. I supposed it was going to take a

while before we would stop looking for Vespa—at least until this whole business was over. Isaac seemed to take it all in stride. He popped open one eye when we came in, and as soon as he saw it was us, he went back to sleep.

Tabby dug around in her suitcase until she pulled out this ceramic thing and a bag with small pieces of charcoal in it. Who carried charcoal with them on a trip? But I'd be lying if I wasn't happy she did. "You should have been a Girl Scout," I told her. She chuckled and put a piece of charcoal into the ceramic thing. Then, using a cigarette lighter, she lit the charcoal. After she got it burning decently, she sprinkled the ground sage on top.

It stunk. Not a pleasing stink either. Hopefully, the smell would dissipate before we got charged a clean-up fee by the hotel. I could see my superiors wondering what the bad smell in my room was related to and then me having to explain to them that, no, we weren't doing drugs. That had the makings of a fun conversation.

Tabby wandered around the room, chanting and drawing symbols in the air. Like the last time I'd seen her do this, the symbols glowed green. At this point, I chalked it up to me being weird. In a way, it was kind of cool that I could see Tabby's magic. But part of me missed being normal. Though Tabby would probably say that I'd never been normal.

When Tabby finished the circuit in the bathroom, she let the charcoal burn out and then flushed it.

"When will we know it worked?" I asked.

"Same as Blackmoor. When something tries to get in that we don't want in."

I wished she had this amazing ability to have a warning beacon, like a superhero, to help me know when the bad stuff was going to happen. But she didn't. "Or has plans to harm us."

"Yeah. That too."

"I'm scared," Lucy said. Maybe Lucy was my beacon. In fact, the last two times she'd said she was scared, something happened. It was something to think about. Her senses were more finely tuned than mine, and honestly, when she got scared, my asshole got tight. Why? Because I didn't remember one time while Lucy was possessed that her spirit said that she was scared to me. All she'd done was ask for help. Not a good sign.

Out of a whim, I picked up the iPad and turned it on. Minus Vespa, the email was the only thing I was waiting to implode. I loaded the email. Something labeled urgent caught my eye. Just as I opened the email, Doc popped in.

"Trouble's coming," he said.

I heard something that sounded like the ceiling crack. "Ah, hell."

This was so many levels of not cool that I couldn't even count them.

"Here we go again," Tabby said.

Chapter Seven

Fade to Black

WIND RIPPED THROUGH the room with a roar, crashing and moaning as fierce as any cyclone. Yet, as suddenly as it began, everything stopped. The pictures on the wall swayed as the storm died. Then, someone—or something—knock at the door.

Of course, it would all be left up to me. Tabby stared at me. Lucy and Doc alternated between looking at each other and the door. I shrugged, went to the door, and spied through the peephole. I stopped myself from punching the wall. It was Vespa, all right. And his eyes had the demonic snakelike pupil thing going on again. Despite my better judgment, I opened the door...but kept the chain on.

"What do you need, Nicholas?" If he asked for my firstborn son, I was going to take him out.

"To talk."

He said that now, but as soon as I took off the chain, all hell could break loose. Tabby's ward worked enough that it kept Vespa out...so far. The wind had made it in. Not sure if I should have been worried about that or not. Should I invite him in or tell him we'd meet somewhere? It wasn't like he was all alone. He had his demon friend with him.

I glanced over at Tabby. "What should we do?"

"Tell him that we'll meet him over at the diner in twenty minutes," she whispered.

I nodded. A public place worked for me. I turned back to my visitor. "Nicholas, go to the diner near the general store. We'll meet you there in twenty minutes."

"This best not be a ruse," he said, his mouth twitching at the corners.

I couldn't tell if he was trying to control a smirk or what. Oh, yeah. The demon was speaking. The question was, did Vespa know everything the demon did when the demon was in power? I had to pay attention to see if that was the case. Asking him wouldn't work. He'd already shown himself capable of lies. "We'll be there."

He turned on a dime and sprinted down the hall toward the elevator.

I could almost feel the mood of the room lighten as he left. I closed the door and relocked it. I left the chain on as extra protection. It might not keep someone from breaking in, but the extra noise would at least get my attention.

"At least we know the ward worked," I said.

They were all staring at me. It was odd. They were acting like a giant bug was about to crawl onto my head. I glanced up. Nope, no bug. "What?"

"What are we going to do now?" Tabby asked. Isaac let out a rowr in agreement.

Seriously? Since when did I become the leader? I was the guy who could sort of save souls, not a saint. I didn't know anything about wards and magic, and basically that stuff that was Tabby's expertise.

I sighed. "We go see what he wants, I guess. I doubt this demon will do much in a public place. After all, he's not like the one that had Lucy."

Tabby nodded.

It was true. I didn't like making blanket statements, but so far, Vespa hadn't pulled out monsters to throw me across the room or anything. Plus, this demon couldn't control Nicholas at all times. The kid could be himself. Lucy's demon, Asmodeus, was a big, nasty bastard. This one had to be further down the food chain.

"The next step is the exorcism." Tabby made it a statement, not a question.

She was right. There was no doubt that Vespa was possessed and we weren't waiting around for approval from the church. But there were a few problems. One: I didn't know if there were special rules regarding doing an exorcism on a willing possessee. Two: we couldn't do an exorcism in a hotel room. And three: where would we get the stuff I needed? Yeah, I could probably look like an idiot and jump in with a super soaker filled with holy water, but I wasn't about to pull a *Lost Boys* move either. I needed to do what I knew.

All we really needed was holy water, but I didn't even know if we could get roses this time of year in Tombstone. The rum was the easy part. I was starting to think about how good my bed at home felt. But no, I couldn't give up. If I did, I would be without a paycheck again, I couldn't take that risk.

"Looks like after we meet Vespa, we'd better go shopping."

Doc snorted. "You all act like you're coming back here."

Tabby and I exchanged a look. Did Doc know something he wasn't telling us?

"What do you mean?" I asked Doc.

"Somehow, I don't think this thing is going to be as easy as you think it is." He leaned forward a little, almost as if he was emphasizing the point. I didn't need that. I knew what was at stake—at the very least, Lucy's soul, but possibly all of us.

I closed my eyes for a minute to steady myself. "It's never easy. We plan as best we can."

Doc stared at me for a minute, nodded, and then disappeared.

"Stay here, Lucy. I don't want to risk losing you." Here she had wards to protect her. Out there, she had my sheer dumb luck. Wards were better.

Her big eyes widened. "Be careful."

I could only do my best. I hoped it was good enough.

#

We got to the diner with a minute to spare. Last thing I needed was for Vespa to be more pissed off. If Tabby didn't have time to make her holy water, I could always do my old priest blessings. I knew I'd feel off doing them, but if I had no choice... Besides, I was marked by God for this after all. Somehow, I didn't think he'd mind me using his blessing.

Nothing about the diner seemed off when we entered. There were no dimmed lights, no creepy feelings on the back of the neck. I was thankful. Vespa was at a table near the back. I couldn't tell if he was still pissed or not. Tabby and I steeled ourselves and headed for him.

"Nicholas," I said. He wore a pair of sunglasses, a dark turtleneck, and a black sport coat. How he wasn't dying in the heat, I had no idea.

"Please sit," he said.

I guessed he hid his eyes for the locals. Yet I was sure that people would assume he was wearing freaking contacts for a joke. Goth kids did that stuff all the time. Kind of funny, in a way. I'd seen it a few times in crappy eighties horror comedies. It didn't even work in the movies, so why did he think it would in real life? I was starting to think that Vespa was more naive than he put on.

"What did you want to talk about?" I figured I needed to get it over with. I didn't exactly want to share a meal with him if he was going to come up with some insane idea about trading one of us in exchange for his soul or some nonsense.

"I don't appreciate you sending spies to watch me," he said. At least he'd said it calmly, I could deal with that. I leaned back in the chair. "First, you asked for my help. It's not my fault you never checked into how I handle things. Two, if you think I have the ability to control our mutual friend, you are sadly mistaken."

The corners of Tabby's mouth jerked. At least, I hadn't lost my charm.

"I do not like being spied on," he said again. I'm not sure what he expected me to do. It had been Doc's idea, after all.

I shrugged. "Nothing I can do about it. Now, if you no longer want my help, we can head home and go our separate ways." It was best to be truthful about it. I hadn't wanted to take his case from the beginning. If I could get out of the whole thing because he wasn't happy about the way I worked, then so be it.

He took off his glasses. "I can't lose your help. My eyes won't go back now." He leaned forward, so we could see his peepers more clearly.

He had darker green eyes. I doubted if someone would notice unless they were close to him. "If you want me to help, you'll have to deal."

"*He's* not happy about it."

I did want to ask. I had to tread very carefully until I was going to do the ritual. If I didn't, the exorcism would fail for sure, and I'd be in deep doo doo. "*He's* going to be a lot worse once we begin getting him out of here."

Tabby tapped her fingers against the table. I hadn't seen her do it before this trip, but it was becoming a habit. Either she'd established a new twitch, or my job was too stressful for her. I guessed I'd have to wait and see which.

"When are we going to begin?" Vespa asked.

"I need to do more research first." I wasn't lying. I did not want to start an exorcism if there was some odd provision in the contract he'd agreed to. I wasn't going to accidentally forfeit anyone's soul, even someone as stupid as Vespa.

"Where will we do it?" Tabby cocked her head to the side.

I inclined my chin at Vespa. It was his call. He was the one who knew the area. Our hotel room wasn't going to cut it. For one, it wasn't soundproof. That, in and of itself, was important with the noises that demons tended to make.

"My house," he said. "I have my own place."

That worked. I would want to check out his house for hidden issues, but it was a place to start. "All right, then. I'll be in touch once I'm done with research."

"And it will be over?"

Sorry, buddy; it wasn't that easy. Hell, I wished it was.

Tabby spoke up next. "You should know that it might take a while."

Vespa smiled. It was unsettling with those snake eyes now that I really concentrated on them. "What, a few hours?"

I chuckled. I had a feeling he'd been watching some choice horror films. "Apparently, you've never actually read about exorcism."

His snake eyes narrowed. "No, I haven't."

That figured. Why was I not surprised? "It has been documented that some exorcisms have taken years."

He froze. "I could be like this for that long?"

Yes, idiot. You should have thought of that before making a deal with the devil. "Maybe longer. That's why people don't make pacts with demons."

Yeah, I knew I sounded like an ass, but I didn't care. He had to hear the truth sometime. I wasn't about to hold his hand and tell him it was going to be okay.

"But you'll try to get it out?"

What did he think I was here for? A vacation? I stopped myself from rolling my eyes. "Yes, I'll do what I can. I can't promise a good outcome though."

Vespa sighed. "Okay. Let me know when you know more."

"Will do." That was where I had to leave it. I couldn't comment for sure on anything until I knew what I was dealing with.

He got up and left. The waitress approached the table and asked what we'd like. I waved her off. She glared at me, but didn't say anything. I watched her walk away.

"Do something," Tabby said.

I paused for a minute, trying to see what she was getting at. She pointed at the table.

Oh. Yeah. I dug out my wallet and put a couple of bucks on the table. We'd wasted her time. Not cool. It wasn't her fault we didn't need anything there. Not then.

Tabby and I left the restaurant. What I needed was an email.

#

I was relieved we didn't have to try to exorcise a demon in the middle of a diner. One, trying to keep people safe would be a nightmare. Two, we likely would be arrested. That would be a first, for me anyway, not for an exorcist. Sadly, there had been a few cases where exorcists had been party to the deaths of their charges. I hoped I would never ever be in that type of situation. It had been close enough with Lucy.

Speaking of Lucy, she seemed happy when we walked in. She was humming, just slightly.

"The beast didn't kill ya?" Doc asked.

"Not yet, anyway." I wandered over to the bed, picked up the iPad, and turned it on. There had been something before Vespa threw his hissy fit. I hoped it was the response I'd been waiting for.

After it finished loading, I clicked on my email. Thank God

the letter was still there. It would have been my luck if the damn thing had disappeared. I forced myself not to let anything on to the others and clicked on the email. I needed it to be good news. I stared down at the screen.

Mr. Holiday,

Your request for help has been noted. We consider this a simple case, so unless there is a huge mistake, your request for help has been denied.

Fr. Johnson

"Fuck me." I couldn't stop it from coming out of my mouth. It felt like I'd been punched in the gut, sucker punched. Did they even care what happened?

"What?" Tabby asked and crossed over to me.

I turned the iPad so she could see. "I don't care that they don't want to help, but they should have answered my question. Dammit."

"Shit, Jimmy. What now?"

Back to stumbling around in the dark. I guessed the advantage of being part of the Order was the credit card and the paycheck. Woe be it that I actually need some help. "I have to find a new age store, something that might be able to give me pointers. I don't want to end up with Vespa bugging Lucy all the time."

Doc nodded. "He isn't a good one."

That was an understatement.

"Give me that thing," Tabby motioned for the iPad, "I'll see what I can find. Why don't you go get a shower? Release some tension."

It was as good an idea as any. No way did I want to leave the room again so soon. Who knew what the thing inside Vespa had in mind? I already recognized it wasn't going to go easily, and if it had the chance, it would kill me to keep its body. Not hard to figure that out.

I climbed into the shower and got the water steaming. It

helped to release the tension in my muscles. Other than that, it didn't do anything. My problems remained, staring me in the face. I needed an expert.

Too bad witch schools didn't exist like the ones in books, or I'd just go and track down the dark magic teacher, but no such luck. I was hoping I wouldn't have to contact a Satanist— I'd heard that there were perfectly normal people who were Satanists, but my upbringing and my former vocation made that idea hard to stomach. How could someone who worshiped a known evil being be a good person?

Somehow, being a witch was different. Being a witch did not automatically mean evil. All you had to do was watch old movies to know that. Tabby hadn't touched dark magic in her life. And it would be kind of hypocritical for me to not accept her weird when mine was so much more strange than hers. I mean, it's not like prior to Lucy that she regularly spoke to spirits or anything. That was all me.

Man, I was pissed at the Order. I could understand them not sending someone to do the job I was meant for, fine. But to ignore my question when I, in their own words, hadn't been trained yet? Bullshit. I should have listened to Tabby more before I signed up for this, though, if I hadn't we wouldn't have made it out here. The good old boy in me was pissed Vespa was so stupid, but I couldn't not help him. Losing Lucy to this demon was not an option. Besides, God never said that dealing with this stuff was going to be fun. And he tended to protect those who couldn't help themselves.

I got out of the shower, toweled off, and dressed. I needed to do the stuff I could do here. The best thing was to stop dwelling on the Order and take care of what I was able. It was time to get the ingredients for Tabby to make me some holy water. It had worked before. No sense in messing with the system now. Apparently I was supposed to fly by the seat of my pants again. But this time, I had to do it right, or I'd be saddled with this stupid fuck. I wasn't going to let that happen. Marking be damned.

#

When I came out, Lucy was playing with Isaac, Tabby was sitting on the bed, and Doc was gone.

"Where'd he go?" I wasn't completely sold on him. He wasn't doing anything to hurt us, true, but that didn't mean that he wouldn't accidentally leave us open to something.

"Said something about going to look for information." She shrugged.

Interesting. Maybe Doc wanted to help after all. "What time is it?"

"A little after three."

I lounged beside her on the bed. The weight of everything was getting to me. I needed to stop thinking so much. I sighed. "I should have known."

She didn't need for me to say more. She put her hand on my shoulder. "It's okay. You just expected more from them than you were able to get. That's all."

"It's just...why are people such assholes?"

"I'd say that would be something to ask your boss about, but it seems kind of disrespectful."

I snorted. I knew there was a reason I loved this woman. "I wonder how happy he is with the way the Order is being run?"

"Hard to say," Tabby said. "I imagine that if they at least get the job done, he can deal with it."

I could imagine God shaking his head.

Tabby got up and stretched her back.

"Why make me a marker?" I asked. "I didn't like the church before…"

"Maybe he wants you to change things."

I thought about that for a minute. I wasn't exactly the sanest guy around. I usually chalked it up to being a product of my environment, but maybe there was more to it.

Tabby went over to the TV and turned it off. I guessed she was tired of the background noise. Lucy glanced at her, shrugged, and then lowered herself in the chair by the table that Doc had vacated.

It was kind of funny that I, a defrocked priest, was suddenly chosen to help God claim souls. Maybe it had more to do with having a good heart than status. I didn't know. And now, it seemed like there were politics in play that I didn't know understand. I swore, if I lost Lucy because of some bigwig's political move, they wouldn't like me very much. The whole thing left a sour taste in my mouth.

"Stop dwelling," Tabby admonished.

I chuckled. She knew me too well. "What should I do instead?"

She shook her head at me. "Don't look at me like that."

"Like what?" I had something in mind that we could do if Doc took Lucy somewhere for a while. I wiggled my brows at her.

"Focus, you idiot." She threw me a wicked grin.

"Yes, ma'am." It was time for me to behave. Heh.

"First, we'll see what Doc finds," she said. "Then, we'll head out and see if any of the stores I found in Tucson will be able to help us."

"We're not staying here tonight?"

Tabby stared at me. "It's three, Jimmy. We're staying here. Tucson is tomorrow."

"Oh, right." I did need to focus, but sometimes she made me feel like an idiot. Of course, it would probably help if I thought things through. My brain didn't work like that, though. I was more of a doer. "What now?"

"We relax. Eventually get dinner and hope Doc finds

something that will help us." She said it so matter-of-factly.

I didn't understand how all of this could be so easy for her to put together, and here I was, freaking the fuck out over every little change. "Looks like we'll be starting an exorcism soon, huh?"

She nodded. "It isn't like there's much else we can do."

I slouched over onto my knees. I had made the mistake of thinking I was never going to have to do this again. I knew what had happened last time, how Tabby had gotten hurt. If I had anything to do with it, there would not be a repeat performance. "I don't like doing this."

Lucy wandered over and put her head in my lap. I felt nothing, but it was sweet nonetheless. She turned her eyes up at me and gave me the ol' puppy dog look. "We need you."

I reached to pat her head, but my hand went right through her. Was it really too much to ask to be able to comfort the kid? Jesus. "I know. It's just hard."

Lucy raised her head. "He knows."

#

After dinner, Tabby and I lounged around waiting for Doc to show. I wished he was able to figure something out. Lucy read over the pamphlets Tabby had found about Doc. Isaac snored.

"This is going to be a long night," Tabby said.

"I'm glad I'm not the only one that's bored." It wasn't exactly easy waiting for the thing you wanted most. "There's only so much you can do in a hotel after a while."

"It doesn't help that this is a small town that doesn't have much of a nightlife," Tabby replied.

"Except for ghost tours." As soon as it came out of my mouth, I regretted it. I closed my eyes.

"What are those? You talked about them before," Lucy said.

Actually, we had a hell of a donnybrook about one, but that

was beside the point. It was so easy to forget Lucy was only six. She seemed much older at times. The sad part was I didn't even know when her birthday was. I had no way of knowing when she would get older. I guess I could have asked, but I didn't want to remind her of her family more than I had to.

"Places that are supposed to be haunted by ghosts. Some people decided to make money off it," Tabby said. "They take people on a tour of the haunted places."

Lucy squinted her eyes just slightly. "How do they do that?"

"They walk you through a place and tell you about the people that died there, hoping that a ghost will appear," Tabby explained.

"Some of them even do fake stuff to make a place look haunted when it actually isn't," I said.

"That's not nice." Lucy crossed her arms over her chest.

"No, it isn't." I couldn't argue with her. Especially now that we knew a ghost, and Lucy wasn't all that far removed from one. If God hadn't figured out what would happen to her before I died, who knew where her soul would go then? Maybe being a soul or being a ghost were more closely related than I thought.

So a ghost tour was out. Lucy spent a good bit of time ranting about how people shouldn't be mean to Doc. I'd thought the start of the conversation had been calm, but I hadn't expected Lucy's temper. After a while, I couldn't even understand her anymore. What worried me the most was that, in her eyes, Doc had seemingly replaced her family. Being this attached to him wasn't necessarily a good thing. It wasn't that I didn't like Doc, but he didn't belong in Virginia.

Tabby finally distracted Lucy by showing her some witchy stuff. For some reason, Lucy was fascinated with Tabby's bag of rune stones. They were made of chunks of amethyst, and I thought it was the purple color that had her fascinated, but then

I paid better attention. Lucy kept stroking the painted gold letters on the stones. She understood so much, and yet she never spoke about it. I had to believe she had experienced a sort of hell while the demon possessed her.

What would happen when Lucy got her body back? Could she put all of this behind her and be a normal girl? More and more I was realizing that probably wasn't going to happen. She needed therapy now, and I had no way to find a therapist for a ghost. I guessed I'd better be cracking the psychology books. At least I had done some marriage counseling, but I knew with all my heart I wasn't good enough. The best I could do was keep her alive...and that knowledge hurt.

Suddenly I had a horrid thought as an old dusty book appeared on the ground near the table. "What the hell?"

A pop sounded and Doc was there in the chair. "Howdy."

I jumped. "You are going to be the death of me."

He chuckled. "Nah. Sources say you're gonna live a mighty long time."

I wasn't sure if that was a good thing or not. Besides, "long" could mean a lot of things to a spirit as old as Doc.

"What's with the book?" I asked.

"Might be of some help. I got it from Vespa's grave."

I blinked. It took me a minute, and then I realized he was talking about the original Vespa—the one who'd stuck him on this plane. I got that creepy feeling dancing along my spine.

"Is it a grimoire?" Tabby asked.

I swallowed, but the spit stuck in my throat. My brain stayed in first gear and I couldn't stop looking at the damn thing on the floor.

Doc stared at her. "A grim-what?"

"Never mind." I shook myself out of the daze. "Do you know what this book is?"

Doc's eyes turned red. "You calling me stupid, boy?"

Oh shit, now I'd done it. I jerked back. "No, sir."

His eyes returned to normal. "That's better. What kind of foolhardy question is that? Of course I know what the book is. I never would have brought some random book to you."

He had a point. But then, I wasn't exactly known for my astute grasp of knowledge either. Sue me for asking a dumb question. I glanced at Tabby. It was probably a good thing Doc couldn't read my mind.

"What is it?" Tabby asked.

"A demon manual, near as I can tell." Doc shrugged. "Might not tell ya everything, but it sure can't hurt."

"Thanks," I said to him. And I meant it. The Order might not be willing to help, but I had Doc. At least, he was doing something. I might be creeped out by the book, but it was something tangible. He was proving to be a hell of a lot of help.

Tabby walked around the bed and picked up the book. "It's heavy." She flipped through the pages. "And it's in Latin."

I grinned. I had been a priest. Latin was part of my education. This was doable. "It's been a while, but I can't be that rusty."

Doc chuckled. "If ya talk nicely to me, I might help you."

I grinned.

"You can read Latin?" Tabby asked.

"I was a doctor, ma'am."

I glanced back and forth between them.

Tabby, somehow, wasn't getting it. "How do you know Latin?"

Doc cocked a brow.

Time for me to clear things up. With Mom's obsession with everything Doc Holliday, I knew the answer for once. "In Doc's time, you had to be fluent in Latin to read most of the medical textbooks."

Doc grunted. "Don't doctors learn it now?"

I shook my head. "The only people who learn Latin now are those studying religion and other scholars."

Doc tsked. "Seems like they made medicine worse, not better."

"In some ways, I'd agree with you," Tabby said, flipping through the pages.

I held out my hand and she passed the book to me. It would have helped if I had a Latin dictionary, but I wasn't about to ask Doc to fetch one for me from somewhere. He wasn't my servant.

I opened to the first chapter. It was time to see what the elder Vespa knew. Hopefully, there would be something that would help us with the exorcism. But I had a sinking suspicion that this wasn't going to be as easy as the Order thought.

Chapter Eight

Die With Me

ONE THING, READING Latin wasn't exactly easy, especially when you hadn't read it in a long time. I was a hell of a lot rustier than I thought I'd be. In fact, the last time I'd done anything with Latin was when the demon spoke through Lucy during her exorcism. Speaking wasn't even using the same skill set as reading. The last time I'd read Latin? Back in seminary.

I had enough knowledge that I was able to make out a few things. Too bad it wasn't enough to know exactly what the book said. And with my limited knowledge, it was going to take me a while to work through it.

"Do you know what chapter we need?" I asked Doc. He was more of an expert on the language than me, and he had to have read part of it to know what book he'd been looking for in the first place.

"Depending on what you're wanting," he replied.

I swallowed my pride. It would be quicker to get honest help than to try to stumble through it. "Rules regarding exorcism, contracts with willing parties, stuff like that."

Doc motioned for me to put the book on the table. I complied. The pages shifted on their own, almost as if someone was flipping through them. If I hadn't been used to all the weirdness by now, I'd be seriously freaked. But it wasn't any different from Lucy doing the things she could. And in comparison to what I'd seen demons do, seeing pages in a book turn themselves was nothing extraordinary.

Tabby scratched something down on a piece of paper.

"What are you doing?" I asked.

"Trying to figure what types of herbs I'm going to need for the duration of this."

I nodded. "Might not hurt to recharge my ring."

She stared at my hand and almost seemed surprised that I still wore the ring she'd bought me. I wasn't that stupid. For me, the ring meant a couple of things. One: I was special enough to her that she was willing to do a spell to help me out—not a light thing. And two: it was a ring. Rings were about promises in our culture. She could have chosen anything, but she chose a ring. No way was I going to mess that up. I'd done enough the first time.

She scribbled some more on the paper.

"While we're up there, go ahead and get the vodka and stuff for the holy water."

"Right." She scribbled that down too. "Thank God you have that credit card. This is getting expensive."

I hoped the Order wasn't going to look at every single purchase. I mean, I could explain them all, but I didn't like being a bug under a microscope either. "At least, we don't have to worry about video cameras this time."

"Do you really think that's wise? What do you think got you off the hook with Lucy?"

She had a good point. If the exorcism hadn't been recorded, I probably would have been charged with attempted murder at the very least. Lucy's injury not being fake had something to do with it too. But I hadn't had any backing before, either. I'm sure the Order had lawyers. Besides, there was always the possibility that this exorcism would go off without a hitch. If it didn't, I could chalk it up to being my own stupid fault.

"Okay, I'll think about the video camera. Part of the reason we had it was Lucy's age." I didn't want to be accused of molesting her. I was a defrocked priest, after all. I knew what people assumed that meant.

"Yeah. And if anyone dies, there is going to be an investigation."

"That's what the Order is for." Yeah, I was probably being an idiot, but whatever. When you examined it closely, it was all out of my hands. I stared at Doc. "Find anything?"

"How do you ever get anything done?" he asked Tabby.

Tabby snorted. "What can I say? I'm used to him."

Doc grunted. "Give me some paper and a pen. I'll try to jot this down so he can stop being so impatient."

Tabby set her notepad and pen on the table.

"I'm not that bad, am I?" I asked her.

She raised her eyebrow at me.

#

I must have fallen asleep. I didn't remember anything after Doc agreeing to translate passages. If I were a more suspicious guy, I'd swear they'd figured out a way to knock me out, but since I didn't feel weird, I knew that wasn't possible. I searched the room with my gaze. Isaac and Tabby were curled up together under the covers. Doc was gone. On the table lay a stack of paper. Lucy was in front of the TV.

"Is everything okay?" I asked her as quietly as I could. I didn't want to wake Tabby.

Lucy stared back at me. "I think so."

"Okay, just checking."

She went back to watching whatever TV show her eyes were glued to. Who knew a kid would still get fascinated by a talking horse, even though the horse was in black and white. It was better than the horror films she usually watched. I could handle normal old TV.

I got out of bed, went and used the bathroom, and when I came back, I was sitting at the table. There was just enough light from the TV that I could read Doc's spidery handwriting. It was legible, but some of the letters definitely did not look like how they taught them today.

From what he translated, I had my hands full. Without knowing the full contract, I was kind of sunk. But it seemed like, for what Vespa wanted, he had likely sold his soul in some fashion. The book, near as I could tell, had nothing about "markers" in it. I didn't know if it would be as simple as my marking Vespa's forehead and rendering the contract void. Something told me it was going to be more complicated than that. But from Doc's translation, I got a better idea as to how binding the contract was. Yet I had to know the contract's specifics. Too bad there wasn't a demon-net or something I could log into to find out. If Hell was anything like Earth, the contract would be public record. I snorted. The idea of imps running around in starched white shirts sitting in cubicles was killing me.

I put down the papers and stared at the wall for a minute. I was starting to scare myself. My brain wasn't usually this colorful.

#

The next morning, Tabby and I headed for Tucson. It wasn't that big of a trip, but I didn't know how long it would take to find what we needed. She wanted to get there and look before anything else bad could happen. I guessed our goals were kind of the same, but I thought I was being a bit more chipper about it.

We took Isaac out for a walk before we left. That was an experience. He was okay with the leash, but he kept stopping and starting, and then looking back at the thing. Once we finished, we locked him in the hotel room, got Lucy in the car, and went toward our destination.

It took us about two hours to arrive. It didn't help that a cow had gotten loose from a farm somewhere and stood in the middle of the road for a bit. But when we finally made it at last, the first shop turned out to belong to this woman obsessed with angels. And when I mean obsessed, I mean really obsessed. She tried to sell Tabby a holy pillow. I could just imagine her running around after scantily clad men with white feathered angel wings, using a hoover to suck up the shed feathers.

The next store was manned by a kid who was young enough that she should have been in in school. Sixteen at the oldest. When Tabby asked to see the manager, the girl ignored her and continued texting her friends on her cell phone. The youth of America. No hope there.

When we made it to the last store, a thin Goth girl stood at the till. She too was young, but at least this one was probably eighteen.

Tabby stepped up to the counter. "I have a question?"

The girl glanced up from her book. It was one of those romance things with vampires that all the young kids liked. I didn't understand the appeal. I mean, sleeping with a vampire was technically necrophilia. Yuck.

"What can I help you with?" she asked.

Tabby took a deep breath. "A man we know was an idiot and made a pact with a demon."

The girl slammed her book shut. "I don't mess with the dark."

"You don't understand." Tabby sucked her teeth. "He wants out of the pact now. We're trying to help him."

The girl came out from behind the counter. "Sure he doesn't need an exorcist?"

I spoke up. "That's the thing. If the possessee signed up for the demon to use him freely, does that mean the exorcism will work the same way?"

The girl leaned against the counter. "That's messed up."

"Yeah. Tell me about it." I couldn't expect an eighteen-year-old to know more about this shit than I did, but hell, I'd expected to at least find someone who had some idea of what to do.

"We don't have anything like that in the shop. And I really don't know how to help," she said. She kept grasping and unclasping her hands. I couldn't tell if the subject made her nervous or if it was just us.

"Any idea how we could find out what the demon contract was?" I asked.

She paused. Then, she scratched her head with her left hand. After a minute, her eyes lit up. "It's kind of dangerous, but it might work."

I was willing to try anything, including tying a severed chicken foot around my neck.

"What's that?" Tabby asked.

"You could try a Ouija board."

Tabby said nothing until after we left the shop. She was walking so fast I could barely keep up with her.

"Look, I know you had bad experiences—"

She turned around and stuck her finger in my face. Shit.

"No, you look," she said, pointing her nail closer with each word. "I almost got possessed that night. I don't want a repeat performance."

I didn't want to piss her off more than I already had, but I didn't have a choice. There wasn't anything else for me to do. "How else are we going to find out?"

"We'll just ask Vespa again." Tabby opened the car door.

I grabbed her by the arm. "He said he doesn't remember.

Don't you think if he knew he'd try?"

Her shoulders slumped. "It almost sounds like the demon obscured his memory."

More like she didn't want to go near a board, but I wasn't going to put it like that. I knew she had a reason to be scared. Yet this was something that had to be done. "It's a go with the Ouija board or we try to hypnotize a demon. Which do you prefer?"

"Damn it," she sucked her teeth, and then nodded.

#

I was surprised at how hard it was to find a Ouija board. Back in the day, all you had to do was go to the local toy store and grab one off the shelf. Now, not one toy store had one. I began to wonder if it was a conspiracy. But it turns out they don't carry them anymore. Who knew?

If it hadn't been for Tabby's desire to run into the bookstore, we'd have been sunk. I don't know if she sensed we could get one there, or if she had a raging desire for a book. But when she came out of the store, she was carrying a big bag. No books.

"What's that?" I'd asked.

"It's what you think it is."

I took the bag from her and riffled through the contents. She'd found one. It wasn't your usual Ouija board. It was this weird circle thing, but who cared? It was supposed to do what we needed it to do. That's all that mattered.

"Thanks."

She rolled her eyes at me. "Okay. Now that we have this fucking thing, what else do we need?"

"Just the mix for the holy water. The roses and stuff." I didn't want to be any more of a pain than I had to be. Even touching the board was putting Tabby in a worse mood. No sense in my doing something stupid and really getting into a fight.

Tabby grunted and got into the car. I waited until she had her seat belt buckled before I started the engine. Then, I put the board in the back seat.

"Be careful," Lucy said from the back.

"About what?" I asked her.

"With that thing in the bag."

"See," Tabby said. "I knew this was a bad idea."

Having two women joining forces against me wasn't what I'd bargained for. Damn. Beat the guy with a stick why don't you? "If you have any better ideas, please let me know."

Tabby grunted again. I programmed the GPS to lead us to a liquor store.

#

Tabby was silent the entire trip back to Tombstone. My stomach growled. We hadn't even stopped to eat. I probably should have tried harder to come up with another way for us to uncover the contract, but using the Ouija board was the first promising idea. Did I want to do it? No. And I sure as hell didn't even know if it was possible. I kept quiet. I was kind of pissed now, but me blowing my ass wasn't going to help the situation any. The best thing I could do was let Tabby let off some steam before I brought up the board again. I knew Tabby didn't want to do it, much more than I didn't.

I'm sure fighting a demon when you're a kid does something to you. Shit, I knew Lucy was permanently scarred and not just physically. I felt for her. But I could understand Tabby's reluctance too. It wasn't like I wanted to do this. We'd just been backed into a wall. Too bad it meant Tabby doing something she swore she'd never do again.

"Stop somewhere." Tabby threw up her hands. "I'm hungry."

The lady was hungry, finally. Her wish was my command.

"Okay. Anywhere specific you want to go?"

"No."

Okay, it was going to be that way. Fine. If she got mad because she couldn't read my mind, I was going to find the nearest wall and punch it. I loved Tabby. I did. But I wished she could see it from my side too. If I didn't follow this through, Lucy was right. The demon would find a way to get her soul. The only thing standing between her and the devil's minions was me and my mark. I didn't even know if my mark would matter if I died.

Scary thought there.

We ended up back at the diner in Tombstone. By the time Tabby had decided she wanted to eat, there had been no place to stop on the way. I could tell it didn't help improve her mood. But she didn't say anything and didn't take it out on me. Thank God for small miracles.

"What can I get you folks?" the waitress asked. This one had red hair in an old lady bouffant hairdo.

We gave our drink orders and the waitress left.

"I'm getting dessert," Tabby said.

"Okay." I'm not sure why she felt she had to announce it to me. It wasn't like I had ever refused her sweets or anything.

She stared at me. "I'm ordering the biggest thing on this goddamn menu."

I didn't know what type of reaction she was looking for from me, but as far as I was concerned, she could eat a whole pie if that's what she wanted. It was a side of Tabby I'd never seen.

"Whatever you want," I said.

She brought the menu up to her face and pored over it. I set mine down on the tabletop. Finally, she lowered her menu. "Aren't you going to say anything?"

I blinked. "What do you want me to say?"

"You don't care if I eat like a pig?"

I closed my eyes for a minute, and then slowly opened them. "One, you aren't a pig. Two, if you are stressed out, I'm not going to bitch at you if you want to eat something that might make you feel better."

"Really?"

"Really."

"You don't care if I get to be over three hundred pounds?"

Okay, I could see where this was going. "I would worry about your health, but I'd love you. Weight wouldn't change that."

She slumped in her chair. Her spunk seemed to have calmed down a bit. "I'm still getting dessert."

"Whatever you want." I shrugged. What did I care if she wanted to eat a piece of pie? If she let me kiss her, her mouth would taste sweet. Yeah, better stop thinking like that now. Lucy was in the car and she didn't need to remotely see what happened when I…yeah, not going there.

I didn't bother to try to understand all of that. I knew she was stressed and pissed off, but where the weight talk came from, I was at a loss to understand. I'd never said a word about her weight to anyone. To me, she was great the way she was. Maybe she'd eventually talk to me about it. I could only hope that would be how it turned out. It seemed like something she needed to get off her chest. And if some guy had made her feel that way, I might just go and kick his ass.

After we got back to the hotel, I made it a point to grab the board. The least she had to touch it, the better. She didn't say a word, just grabbed up the rest of the bags. Lucy's eyes were rimmed with something that resembled water. I could tell already that this was going to be a fun evening.

Once we got into the hotel and up to our floor, Tabby

opened the door to our room. Nothing was amiss. And no Doc.
We set the bags on the floor near the wall. No sense in messing
with them now. It wasn't like we were going to do this tonight.
Isaac meowed at us. Tabby stopped to scratch him behind the
ears.

I wanted to grab her and hold her, but she was being too
stoic for that. I knew she liked to be the strong one, but
strength had nothing to do with needing support once in a
while. That made her normal.

"Want to do something fun later?" I asked.

"Like what?" She eyed me suspiciously.

"I don't know. Watch the reenactors or something?" Every
day in Tombstone, reenactors performed the shoot-out at the
OK Corral. While the Old West wasn't exactly my favorite
thing, it was something we could do that really had nothing to
do with exorcism.

"Maybe," she said.

It was better than nothing. I was at the table. Tabby lay on
the bed.

"Get over here," she said.

Far be it from me to refuse her. I rose from the table and
crawled into bed beside her. She curled up to me and put her
head on my chest. It felt nice. Maybe she was going to let me be
her comfort after all.

At some point, we both fell asleep. By the time I woke up, it
was after four. Tabby was snoring softly. It felt good to know
that even though she wasn't happy with me, she still wanted to
curl up to me. Demon contract or not, the rest of the day was
going to be about Tabby.

As far as I knew, as long as Lucy stayed in the warded
room, the demon in Vespa couldn't hurt her.

Without warning, Lucy shook me from my thoughts. "I
miss Mommy and Daddy."

I gently disengaged from Tabby and crawled on the floor where Lucy was. Damn. This wasn't fair. Had she been this depressed the whole time? "I know, honey. If I could, I'd fix it."

"I know." Unshed tears swam in her eyes.

I wanted to hug her and tell her everything would be okay. I silently prayed to God that he'd figure out a way to fix this. I couldn't take much longer of not being able to actually help her and being a mere holding place for her.

"Maybe it won't be much longer," I said.

Lucy nodded. "I hope not."

What I could do was find a way to distract her. Get her thinking about something else. My choices were Isaac or Tabby. I chose the latter. "I want to do something special for Tabby. Any ideas?"

Lucy paused. "What does she like?"

"Scary movies, good food, stuff girls like." How do you answer that question for a six-year-old?

Lucy laughed. "You're silly."

"I know. Tabby tells me that all the time." I thought of myself as more of a dork, but it wasn't like there was much of a difference.

Isaac hopped off the bed and trotted over to Lucy. She began petting him, actually petting him. It was different than before. How in the hell could she pet a cat? I mean, she rubbed his ears, they moved, the whole nine yards. Her form no longer passed through him. Maybe God had answered my prayer after all.

"How do you do that?"

"Do what?" She raised a brow.

"Pet Isaac." I motioned at her hand. I wasn't sure how much deeper I should go into the situation.

She shrugged. "I don't know."

"Something is different. When you touch me or Tabby, we

just feel a little coldness, but it's not like how you're petting Isaac now."

She shrugged again. "Maybe cats are different."

"Maybe." It was about the only explanation, minus the prayer, and it wasn't like I had time to explore it further right now. Besides, while I had been a man of God, I wasn't a huge believer in miracles. Sometimes things went how we wanted them to...and sometimes they didn't.

"What's going on?" Tabby asked from the bed.

Shit, we'd woken her up. "Nothing. I just noticed Lucy can pet Isaac. I mean really pet him."

"That's...," Tabby sat up and rubbed her eyes, "...interesting."

"Yeah. How are you feeling?"

"A little better." She popped her neck. "I'm hungry."

Food must be her medicine for the day. I wasn't going to say a thing, especially not with how the conversation went before. "Want to do an early dinner?"

She nodded. "Let me go get cleaned up."

I got the feeling there was something she wanted to talk about, but I wasn't about to ask. Not yet. Better to let her tell me on her own. Especially when I got the feeling it was something important. Maybe food wasn't her biggest focus. Maybe she just wanted to be away from Lucy for a while.

I got off the floor and changed my clothes.

Tabby came out of the bathroom. "Where do you want to go?"

"You pick." I pulled out the advertising stuff from the dresser drawer and handed it to her.

She took the booklet from me and flipped through it. "It's a little bit of a drive, but how does Italian sound?"

I shrugged. I'm not sure if there was anyone on Earth that would pass up lasagna. "Works for me. It's only four-thirty."

She beamed. I grabbed the keys. "Lucy, take care of Isaac. You're in charge."

"Can Doc come and play?" she asked.

Did she know how to call him? That might be a good thing to know. "Doc kind of comes and goes as he pleases. But if he comes, I don't see a problem with you making him entertain you." I winked at her.

She giggled.

Tabby and I left, making sure the door locked behind us.

"She's a good kid," Tabby said as we were heading toward the elevator.

"Yeah, she is." She deserved better than I could give her. They both did.

#

The restaurant had dim lighting and candles on every table. A series of murals of Italy encompassed the walls. I'd seen it before. Some restaurants, especially ethnic ones, liked to make you feel like you were in the country. Too bad I didn't know a lot of these scenes. The only painting I recognized was the one with the Leaning Tower of Pisa. The restaurant looked expensive with all of the decor and the crisp tablecloths. I felt seriously underdressed, but no one said anything to us. They were probably used to tourists.

"What are you going to get?" I asked after a bit.

Tabby shrugged. "Probably lasagna or something. That wasn't why I wanted to come here."

I kind of figured that, but I didn't have a clue what she wanted to talk about. "Okay…"

"We needed more garlic in our systems, and I wanted to explain a few things without Lucy being around." She arranged the napkin on her lap.

"All right." That made sense. I knew garlic had a lot of antioxidant properties and since Tabby was the witch stuff expert, I wasn't going to be upset about eating a little of it.

"I know I was being a bitch earlier." She sighed. "But it's hard."

I nodded. No sense in interrupting her. I was glad she apologized to me, but by now, it was unnecessary. Her thing at lunch proved to me there was more going on than just surface stuff. I was there for her, better and worse.

"You know the story of me with the Ouija board. I've told it to you a few times."

"Yeah, you have." She'd last spoke of it in Blackmoor. Sometimes, it felt like all of that had been a long time ago, but it was just this past November.

"What I've never told you is how it felt. It hurt, Jimmy. It was bad."

The waitress interrupted us. We gave our drink orders. Tabby continued after she left.

"Imagine feeling like something is trying to snatch what makes you the person that you are right out of your body. Then, imagine your brain being pulled out of your head through a small hole the size of pencil lead."

"Jesus Christ." That was worse than how I'd heard childbirth described—squeezing something the size of a watermelon out of a hole as small as a lemon.

"That's what it felt like. And then, bear in mind I was somehow able to have the fortitude with that pain to use the knowledge I had to fight the demon off. I'm thankful to this day it wasn't an extremely strong one."

"Me too." I could see why she didn't want to use the board. And being as sensitive to the supernatural as she was, it left her more susceptible. "I'll do it by myself."

She blinked. "Do what by yourself?"

"Use the board. That way you don't have to risk going through that again." It was time I grew a set and stopped dragging her into my stuff. She hadn't signed on for this. The least I could do was make it as easy on her as possible.

"No way, Jimmy. No fucking way. Do you have any idea how easy it is for a demon to gain purchase on this realm through one of those boards?"

"It's been done, though, right?" I blocked out what I'd seen happen in the movies. Better to think positively.

She glared at me. "Very rarely, and I wouldn't trust it. No, you and I will be talking to this thing, but it sure as hell won't be at night."

"Fine by me." Hey, if she was going to refuse to let me do it on my own, fine. But if she had nightmares over it, she'd better not blame me.

"And I never want to hear you talk about using the board by yourself again. The last thing I need is for you to be possessed."

While I had to admit that would be bad, I wasn't exactly sure a marker could even be possessed, but if it was possible, that would not be cool. "Okay. No problem. Let's stop talking about that now and do some normal stuff."

"Normal sounds very good."

#

Normal turned out to be taking a walk once we got back into Tombstone. Old Town was lit up with old-style lanterns at night. Tabby seemed a lot more carefree, for which I was thankful. The tension we added at dinner seemed to slip away and I felt almost like we were back before things went sour.

Part of me was willing to ignore what Tabby said and go ahead and use the board without her. Not smart, maybe, but I wanted to avoid causing her pain as much as I could. She was scarred by her past experience. Better to scar myself than let her add any more. I wanted to protect her from all the nastiness. Too bad my current job involved diving into hell and hoping it all worked out. Who knew what started out as a favor could turn into something this complicated? To think, at one time my life had been as simple as get up, perform mass, eat lunch, do counseling, eat dinner, relax, and then go to sleep. It was boring, but I was starting to realize how nice boring could be.

Everything was evolving, including Lucy. Her suddenly being able to pet Isaac had me nervous. I feared her body wasn't faring well. I could call Will to check on her physical form, but things had been strained to say the least after Lucy's exorcism. It probably would be the right thing to do. The kid wanted her family. Maybe, if the conversation went okay, I could let her listen to her dad talk.

"Are you okay?" Tabby asked. "You seem distracted."

"Just thinking." I didn't know if it was a good idea or not. Last thing I needed was for Lucy to shout out to her dad that she loved him and wanted to come home. Yeah. Try explaining that one.

"About what?" She looped her arm around mine.

"Lucy, actually. Her getting more solid has me worried." It did, but I also didn't want to bring the rest of it up to her. She had enough going on without my adding anything to it. But if I didn't start talking, she'd prod me until I spilled the whole bloody thing.

"How so?"

"If she's more solid here, that means she's getting stronger. Wouldn't that mean her body was giving out?" I did not want to think about Lucy dying. I couldn't think of losing her now.

"I don't know. Not necessarily. Why don't you call Will?"

"You know why." I paused. We were in front of a gift shop. In the display rested this little vase. It was exactly like one Mom had when I was growing up. Odd.

"Surely they would appreciate the call?"

"Maybe." But I didn't even know what to say to them. I

mean, "How's Lucy?" seemed kind of contrite.

"What are you looking at?"

I pointed at the vase. "My mom had one just like it."

Tabby let go of my hand and stepped closer to the window for a better look. "Maybe it's a knock-off."

"Or maybe Mom was here once." Which meant that there was a possibility that she'd met Doc.

She walked back over to me. "You should call."

I sighed. She wasn't going to give up; I knew that. I needed to get it over with. I pulled out the phone and clicked on Will's name. After a few rings...

"The number you have reached—"

I disconnected the call. I wasn't surprised. Why would he want to get in touch with me? I'd been the last person to see his daughter before the accident, demon-slaying, whatever you called it. "I got a recording. Will's changed his number."

"Want me to try Tor's?" Tabby asked.

I shook my head. "Nah. I have a feeling that if they wanted to talk to us, they would have called by now."

"Yeah."

"Back to the hotel?" Our evening was ruined now anyway. I guess thinking about a sick kid will do that to ya.

Tabby brushed the hair out of her face. "Might as well."

#

Getting back to the hotel was the easy part. Finding the room trashed, however, was not what I expected.

"What the fuck?" I heard a pop and Doc appeared in from of me.

"What happened?" I asked him.

"A lady came in to steal stuff. She tried to take that thing you always fiddle with."

I almost asked what thing, then I remembered the Order's iPad. "Did she get it?"

"Nope. Lucy scared the bejeezus out of her."

I finally spied it on the floor, face down near my side of the bed.

"And where's Lucy?"

"Too tired. She has to rest before she can show herself again. What she did took a lot out of her."

I hoped it hadn't taken too much. I didn't have a great understanding of Lucy's well-being, but her not even being able to show herself wasn't a good sign. I needed more information and the Order didn't seem to be wanting to give it.

"Isaac?" Tabby searched the room. "Shit."

I dropped the iPad on the bed and ran out of the room. "Isaac!" I dashed around the floor. No cat. So I headed down to the front desk. Maybe they'd seen him. "Anyone see a cat?"

The girl behind the desk had a stony expression on her face. "Animal control has already been called, sir."

Oh, hell no. We weren't going there. "It better fucking be canceled. Your staff broke into my room! Where's the damn cat?"

The girl stared at me like I was lying. I slammed my fist down on the counter. "I want my cat. I want to see the manager, and you'll be lucky if I don't sue your asses."

The girl behind her hopped to it and opened the door to what I guess was the copier room. Isaac snarled and hissed. I pointed at the girl who now wasn't so smug. "Cancel that goddamn call!"

She grabbed the phone and dialed. A man in a suit came out of another back room.

"Are you the manager?" He resembled a sniveling little weasel.

"Yes, sir. If you'll please take it down a notch."

"You can shove your notch up your ass. I suggest you look at the security footage in the hallway near my room." I wanted to drop kick the asshole.

"Hold on." He walked into his office. After a minute, he came back. "Sir, I apologize. It doesn't look like anything is missing."

No help from them. It was a good thing I wasn't able to shoot fire from my eyes, or I'd have burnt the whole building down by now. I guessed that's why the superheroes always were torn people— always weighing the options in any situation. Me, I'd probably make a better supervillain. "No, but my iPad was found on the floor, and if it's broken, I'll expect a replacement."

"You'd have to take that up in court, sir."

I stepped closer to the guy. Didn't he realize my fuse was almost gone? "Any idea how it will look for your hotel if I tell people how pet-friendly you really are? How you almost got my cat euthanized because some worker tried to rob my room?"

"Sir, it's standard procedure to call animal control. Especially when our staff reports being attacked."

Yeah, attacked because she tried to rob me. Fuck him. "I suggest you start paying attention to what's actually happening instead of playing solitaire on your fucking computer all day. And if Isaac is hurt, I'm holding this hotel responsible."

His mouth opened and closed a few times like a fish. "That won't be necessary, sir. Would you like him checked out by a vet?"

"Yes, dammit. That's the least you could do." I swore, if there was something wrong with Isaac, I might just let Tabby kill him.

They let me go behind the desk. As soon as Isaac saw me, he calmed down. "Let's get out of here, bud."

I untangled the rope from around the leg of the copier and off his neck. He jumped into my arms, pressing himself against me so hard. Poor thing. He was shivering.

"How long until the vet gets here?" I asked the girl.

"About half an hour. I'll send him up to your room as soon as he arrives."

I grunted and took Isaac back to Tabby. Isaac was so quiet during the elevator ride that it was starting to look like he was going to need a therapist. That was probably overkill, but whatever.

"Where have you been?" Tabby asked when I opened the door to our hotel room.

"Saving Isaac from idiots. The thief let him out. Though I guess he tore her up pretty good. They called animal control on him." I waited for that little bit of information to hit.

"Shit." She reached forward and Isaac jumped into her arms. "What the fuck was their problem? I swear, if he isn't okay—"

"They're sending over a vet to check him out." I was doing my best not to give her the full brunt of my anger. I wanted to drop-kick the manager. If I amped her up anymore, she would actually do it. But I have to admit, the stress relief of the act would do me good and probably help Tabby too.

"My poor baby," Tabby cooed at him.

I left her to Isaac, went over to the bed, and checked the iPad. The screen seemed okay. After a moment, it opened. I knew better than to count on that, so I went to a few websites and checked my email. Everything loaded fine. I shut it down and put it on the table.

"Are they calling the police?" Tabby asked.

"Who the hell knows?"

"Want to change hotels?" She appeared concerned, but more focused on me than Isaac.

Changing wasn't an option. "This is the only 'pet-friendly' hotel in Tombstone."

"Shit."

"Yeah." Though I had a bad feeling that weasel would

black-ball us at any hotel around Tombstone. We had to come up with another alternative.

"So much for a normal evening," Tabby said. She went over to the little stand in between the beds and picked up the phone. She punched a button and called down to the front desk. "Yes, this is Tabatha Settle in room one-four-oh-eight. Have the police been notified?"

"Uh-huh. Yes, we won't touch anything else...," she paused. "All right. Thank you."

I watched her hang up the phone.

"What did they say?" I asked.

"Cops are coming. Vet's coming. We are supposed to stop poking."

I sat in the chair near the table. "What a night."

"Tell me about it."

#

The cops took our statements. Tabby and I went through everything, including what we'd bought today. Not a thing was missing. I hated to think what Lucy did that scared the thief so badly and left her in such bad shape. Isaac I could imagine. Too bad Doc had once again disappeared or I'd ask him.

The vet had come and gone. Isaac was okay, but stressed. The vet suggested extra treats and plenty of water, anything to make the cat feel loved. I had to force myself not to roll my eyes. Isaac was spoiled enough as it was. This was only going to make it worse, but already Tabby was giving him extra pats.

"Guess we should ward the room again, huh?" I mean, it couldn't hurt. But it was starting to seem like the wards only worked on things connected to the supernatural. Otherwise, how would the robber have been able to come in? Unless Vespa had done something to the ward before. I didn't want to even consider that.

"Probably. I have to wonder if Vespa had anything to do

with this."

Nice to know we were on the same wavelength. "Good question. I just hope Lucy's okay."

"I'm okay," she said. I couldn't see her, but at least she could communicate with us. That made me feel a little bit better.

"Is Doc with you?" Tabby asked.

"No, you are, silly. I'm here."

That was a relief. I didn't want to think she was in between worlds or something. Yet her not being able to show herself scared the crap out of me. It had been bad enough when Lucy was getting more solid. I needed to know what it all meant.

I flipped through the iPad, searching Facebook and a few other social media sites for Will, but it was like he dropped off the face of the earth. I wrote an email asking the Order if they could check on things. I loosely explained what was going on with Lucy's soul. For now, that was the best I could do.

Needless to say, getting to sleep that night wasn't easy. I woke up at any small sound, including whenever the air conditioner kicked on or off. Even though Tabby had warded the room again, I didn't feel safe. What good was a ward when it couldn't keep all the bad people out? I hoped to hell it was just a thief and not something to do with Vespa.

I was tired of the whole thing. I wanted to find out what we needed, deal with Vespa's problem, and go home to sleep in my own bed.

Tabby, somehow, slept like a log. Maybe part of it was knowing that Isaac was okay. Part of my uneasiness could have stemmed from knowing that we were going to use the board. Tabby's experience, now that I'd learned the full story, left me feeling anxious about it. If I knew of some other way to get the information, I'd have used it—even if it did mean trying to hypnotize the demon.

Chapter Nine

Bring Me to Life

"I DON'T WANT to be here when you play with that thing," Lucy said suddenly.

I could barely make her out standing by the bed. Her eyes had this wild look about them and her hands were shaking so badly that her body seemed to quiver.

"I don't know if there's anywhere to go. Do you know any way to contact Doc?" It was the best option, really. If Doc could keep her occupied, then maybe, just maybe, she'd be safe. The last thing I wanted to do was bring in another demon and have it snatch Lucy.

"I can try," she said.

"Okay. Do that. If it doesn't work, we'll come up with something else." What else, I had no idea. Maybe Tabby would have some thoughts.

Soon after, Tabby came out of the bathroom, combing her fingers through her hair.

"Any idea where Lucy can go while we do this?" I figured it was worth it to ask her. I had no more ideas.

She sighed. "No. Not really."

"She's going to try to get ahold of Doc."

Tabby walked over to her side of the bed and sat. "Okay. If she can't get ahold of Doc, then we'll have to use the damn thing somewhere else, but I don't like the idea of leaving Isaac and Lucy by themselves again."

"Me neither. I'd happily get out of this hotel if I could."

Tabby tapped her fingers on her knee. "We should only be in the hotel for a few more days anyway. We'll have to stay where we'll do the exorcism so we can make sure Vespa doesn't have a heart attack or something."

"Good point. But we're back to what to do with Lucy. Vespa's demon did something to her once before. I wouldn't put it past him to do it again."

She paused for a minute. "I could always ward the car. Lucy should be safe enough if I ward it. That way, she doesn't actually come in contact with the demon anymore."

I hugged her. Sometimes, she was so damn smart. "It's stuff like that that makes me want to marry you someday."

She pulled back. "Really?"

"Yes, really."

Suddenly, there was a pop and Doc appeared. "Don't you go getting all mushy on me."

I couldn't help but laugh. For an old-timer, he was funny. "What's up, Doc?"

Lucy giggled.

"What do you need, kid?" he asked Lucy.

"They are going to use that 'thing.'" She pointed toward the bag with the board in it.

Doc crouched down in front of her. She was a little more visible now, almost like colored cellophane.

"What do you want to do?" he asked.

I spoke up. "Lucy and I want to know if there was somewhere you could take her or if you could keep her occupied while we tried to get some information."

Doc stroked his goatee for a minute. "Don't think I can take her away from ya, but Lucy and I can find ourselves something to do."

"Thanks. I appreciate it." And I did. The sooner I could get this out of the way, the sooner we all could go home safe.

Doc nodded and went back to giving Lucy his full attention.

I turned to Tabby. "When do you want to do this?"

"Now, I guess. I want to get it over with."

I got up, grabbed the bag with the board in it, and plopped back on the bed.

Tabby shook her head. "No, let's do it on the floor. I don't want to do it where we sleep in case we end up spending another night in this place."

I got off the bed and plopped on the floor in the hallway next to the bathroom. "How's this?"

Tabby sat opposite from me. "It will have to do."

I pulled the plastic off the box and opened it. "I assume this works like it does in the movies."

"Pretty much, except in the movies they always forget to close the portal."

I didn't bother to pretend I knew what the hell she was talking about. So be it. We needed to get this done. I got the pointer thing out of the box and set it on the floor. Then I put the board down in between our knees.

"Okay, you ready?" I asked her. Would it even work with her being so reluctant?

"No, but do it anyway."

I put the pointer thing on the board. Tabby placed her index finger and middle finger of her right hand on her side of the pointer. I followed suit. "Now what?"

"We ask it things." She stared pointedly at me. "You get to ask."

Great. Thanks. I took a deep breath. "Is anyone there?"

The pointer began moving in a figure-eight pattern. Strange.

"Okay. I need some information about a contract."

The pointer kept moving. I guessed I needed to dumb down my question. "Do you know Vespa?"

The pointer changed direction and moved to the yes on the board. Then, it went back to the figure-eight pattern.

"What now?" I asked Tabby.

She sighed at me. "Keep concentrating on the planchette."

"What's that?"

She rolled her eyes. "The thing that's moving."

"Oh." Now, I felt like a total dumb shit. Using one of these things was supposed to be simple. Evidently, my brain didn't get the message.

"Keep to questions it can answer with a yes or no. But like everything else, they lie. A lot."

I nodded. Got it. Remember that the demons lie. "Okay, spirit. Do you know anything about the contract Vespa made with his visitor?"

The planchette moved to yes. And that's when the lights went out. Holy shit.

I jumped up and tried the light switch on the wall. It didn't work. Rushing over to the window, I pulled the blind away so that I could see. The traffic lights outside the hotel worked.

"Fuck this," Tabby said.

I watched as she flipped the board upside down. "Goodbye," she said.

After a minute, the lights came back on. Too weird.

"See, this is why we don't mess with boards."

So much for a good idea. Not how I expected all of this to go. "Okay. Let's get rid of this thing."

"That requires burning it."

Okay, that couldn't be done in a hotel room. Good thing we were surrounded by desert. "Fine."

#

Tabby stayed at the hotel with Lucy, Doc, and Isaac. I had

the board, a can of lighter fluid, and a lighter. I had to stop by a grocery store to get that stuff, but it wasn't hard.

I drove out of town into the desert. It took me a while to see nothing but sand and sagebrush. I picked a nice spot with lots of sand, pulled over, and got out of the car with all of my accouterments. Making my way down the little hill, I made sure I was away from any vegetation. No sense in starting a huge fire if I could keep from it. At least the wind wasn't blowing. I had the board in its bag along with the receipt. Best to get rid of it all so there would be no connection left.

I doused the bag with lighter fluid, stepped back, set the receipt on fire with the lighter, and then tossed it onto the bag. The whole thing torched immediately. A ball of fire whooshed into the air and then settled back down. The plastic melted first, then there was another whoosh when the cardboard box caught fire. I stood there and watched the fucker burn. Without a doubt, that was going to be my one and only experience with a Ouija board. It wasn't worth the risk, not if it meant losing my soul in the process.

Suddenly, I noticed I wasn't alone. All around me, various desert birds had formed a circle with me at the apex and around the fire. Ravens, crows, several birds I'd never seen before, and one scraggly-looking vulture surrounded me.

Not one of them made a sound. Finally, when all that was left was ash, I grabbed a nearby piece of rotten wood and scattered the ashes.

A crow cawed at me. "Thanks, guys," I said, and they all flew off. One more thing for me to chalk up in my weird file. I couldn't wait for Tabby to hear about this.

#

I got back into the car, turned around, and headed toward Tombstone. A few of the birds followed me for a bit and then, closer to town, they stopped.

"Guess I had my own personal escort."

Once back at the hotel, I parked and went to the room. In my opinion, Tabby should ward the car as soon as possible. The bird thing combined with the board and the damn break-in had me twitchy. I was going to call the Order if I had to. Enough of putting myself and Tabby in danger for an idiot. It was time I took control, and if they didn't like it, they could shove the whole thing up their asses. I was tired of trying to live by their rules. It was time I went back to my own.

Chapter Ten

Forsaken

"TABBY?" I ASKED, closing and locking the door behind me.

"What?" she called from inside the bathroom.

"Never mind. Finish what you're doing." No sense in her stopping when I could wait for a bit.

Lucy and Doc were seated at the table. The curtains were open and the sunlight streamed through both of them. They weren't doing anything, not even talking.

"How's things now?" I asked them.

"Okay," Lucy said. Isaac meowed from the bed.

I walked over and scratched him behind the ears. Then Tabby came out of the bathroom.

"I was thinking. It might be a good idea to ward the car today," I said.

"All right. I can do that."

I was glad when she didn't ask what the rush was. I wasn't sure if I should tell her about the birds or not. She was under enough stress. I grabbed the iPad off the nightstand and loaded it up. Then, I went to my email. I poured over every email I'd gotten from the Order. No contact information. No nothing. "Dammit."

"What?" Tabby asked.

"All they've left me for contact info is email."

"Okay. While I don't like it, it never seemed to bother you before."

"I didn't need to talk to them urgently before." How could I have been so stupid? I remembered a letterhead from the tax forms I signed, but those files were now mysteriously gone from the tablet. Great. Yet another thing to drive me crazy. But tax forms weren't something to worry about now.

Tabby perched next to me on the bed. "We could try to interrogate Vespa. Or maybe help him remember somehow."

"I don't think I want to interrogate a demon yet. But if we could figure out a trigger for Vespa to remember the terms of the contract, I'd be all for it." The less I had to do with the supernatural these days the better.

"You call Vespa. I'll start packing. Tell him we want to begin. And that he'll need to expect houseguests for the conceivable future."

"Works for me." It was an option and better than sleeping out in the desert. Less chance of scorpions, except for the demonic variety. I wasn't all that crazy about going to live with him, especially when we didn't know if he had anything to do with the break-in, but we needed out of a place we couldn't trust at all. I didn't want to visit a repeat of the Isaac affair.

I grabbed my phone and clicked Vespa's number. He answered on the second ring.

"Mr. Holiday. It is good to hear from you," he said.

I rolled my eyes. I wished he would stop all of the faux elegant crap. I knew that part had nothing to do with the demon, just Vespa's perception of what was high-class. "Tabby and I were thinking." I swallowed my revulsion of him. "We've done all the research we can, but now we need your help to finalize things before we begin the exorcism process."

"What did you have in mind?" he asked.

"We were thinking if we could find a trigger, something that would make you remember, it would help."

There was a pause. "I would have no issue with that."

"All right. Sounds good. Also because we plan on beginning the process as soon as we can, Tabby and I figured we could start staying with you." I hoped I didn't sound jakey slipping it in like that.

"That would be fine. I'll meet you at the diner for lunch, and then I'll lead you to my house."

I didn't want him to have to come all the way into town. "You don't have to do that. We have GPS."

"Trust me. It is easier if I help you. The back roads can get confusing. Besides, I have not had lunch."

I thought, yeah, no shit. It was only ten-thirty, but whatever. I knew he was weird, guess this was just one more thing. "All right. What time should we meet you?"

"Oh, eleven-thirty should be fine."

"Sounds good. See you there." I hung up and glanced at Tabby. "He'll meet us at the diner at eleven-thirty for lunch."

"I'm not sure this is a good idea."

"None of this is a good idea. I'm trying to find the least problematic option." And we had to stay with him during the exorcism anyway. Lucy would have to be safe enough in the car. I only hoped we could keep Doc coming and going so we'd have updates.

"Too bad it seems like we've been led this direction from the start," she said.

Tabby had a point. It wasn't like we were getting along better on this trip. We'd had several fights, when back home we'd been fine. It kept happening to us.

"Let's get packing and get the hell out of this place."

Tabby held up a hand. "Wait, speedy. I haven't even warded the car yet."

Oops. I was getting ahead of myself again. "Good point. I'll pack; you go ward the car."

"Now you make sense." She grabbed some witchy stuff and left the room.

I turned to check on Lucy. Poor kid, she'd been through enough, but there wasn't anything else to do. I knew she was going to get tired of the whole thing pretty quick. That meant I had to work harder to get it all done faster. "I hate to do this, but—Lucy, I don't want you leaving that car until Isaac says it's okay."

Now, what made me pick Isaac instead of myself, I don't know. Maybe subconsciously I was sensing that things didn't appear to be what they seemed. Everything with this trip could be described that way. And even though I hadn't heard about it, there wasn't anything that I'd read so far that said a marker couldn't be possessed. I knew a cat could not. He was the safer choice.

"What do you think, Doc?" I asked.

"I think I'll go do some spying."

"Not a bad idea." He disappeared with a pop. "Want to help me pack?" I asked Lucy.

"Nope," she said and giggled. I shook my head.

I got everything we owned into the suitcases. I'm not sure if Tabby would appreciate my packing style, but she could fix things later. I even made the bed. Lucy stayed in front of the TV almost as if she were trying to memorize as much as she could since she wouldn't be watching anything for a while. Part of me hoped this wasn't going to become the cranky young kid in the car thing. But I had my doubts. Lucy knew the ramifications of all this. Vespa scared the shit out of her. And she didn't act like she was six most of the time. I was banking on that.

Finally, Tabby came back.

"We need to get Lucy some books and toys so she'll have

something to do in the car," I said. Better at least get the kid some entertainment. Asking her to do nothing for days would be cruel as hell.

Tabby dumped the little container of sage into her backpack. "I never thought. Is there anywhere in town that sells that type of stuff?"

"What about the hotel gift shop?" We didn't have time to run all the way out to the Walmart and back before we were supposed to meet Vespa.

"Good idea. We'll look while you get us checked out."

"Works for me."

We went downstairs. Tabby helped me get the suitcases to the front desk, and then she sauntered off with Lucy. It was probably better I dealt with the idiots alone anyway. Tabby had a worse temper than me.

There was a different girl at the desk than the sour-pussed one I'd dealt with before. I kind of hoped the bitch got fired, but I doubted it.

"Checking out?" she asked with a smile.

"Yup. Jimmy Holiday."

She pulled up the information and then printed something out. "Just sign here, sir."

I glanced at the paper. It was a letter of sorts stating that I was accepting restitution. Restitution for what?

"What's this?" I asked.

She peered into her computer again. "The owner requested that your bill be on us for all of your trouble."

I could tell she didn't exactly know the story. She seemed a little confused. I wasn't about to go into it. We had to get to the diner.

"All right. That does help things." I signed the paper and handed it back to her.

"Hope you have a nice day, sir," she said.

I nodded, pulled the handles up on both suitcases, and headed out to the car.

Surely, Tabby would realize where I was when she was done finding Lucy toys. If she didn't, she could text.

After I loaded the suitcases in the trunk, I got in the front and turned on the air conditioner. I was not going to miss the Arizona heat.

The car continued to smell like burnt sage. It was a smell I was starting to like. It meant safety after a fashion. And I liked not having to worry about soul-suckers killing me in my sleep, thank you very much.

Tabby came along not much later. Lucy drifted through the door of the car, while Tabby got in the front seat.

"Find anything?" I asked.

"Books and a puzzle," Lucy said.

Tabby held up the bag. "I figured when we pulled into the parking lot of the restaurant, I could unwrap the puzzle for Lucy."

Isaac let out a rowr from his cat carrier.

"You'll have more room to roam around soon, buddy. We just need to get something to eat and find our next place to stay," I said to him. I glanced at Tabby and Lucy. "We ready?"

"As far as I know," Tabby said.

There was silence from Isaac in reply. I drove to the diner, parked the car, and waited while Tabby fixed Lucy's toys in the backseat. She then poured out some water from a bottle into Isaac's travel drink thing. I made sure all the windows were down a good bit and I had parked in the shade. It wasn't quite seventy degrees in the shade, so if we didn't dawdle, Isaac should be comfortable.

When Tabby and I walked into the restaurant, we spied Vespa sitting at the table in the back. I waved off the hostess and Tabby and I headed toward the table.

"You are late," he chided.

I pulled out my cell phone and glanced at the time. We were five minutes late. Shit. "Sorry. It took us a little longer than expected."

He grunted and picked up the menu. I was tired and I didn't feel like kissing anyone's ass today. And he wasn't paying me to be his exorcist, for God's sake.

Tabby, I could tell, was getting annoyed. Her eyes were just starting to take on that blaze I knew so well.

I picked up my menu. Tabby followed suit.

After we gave our order, I turned to Vespa. "One thing I want to talk about."

"All right," he said.

"You need my help. I am not your employee." I was trying to say this as politely as possible.

"Yes."

"This means you need to pay attention to what it is we're doing and what your business relationship is."

He just stared.

"Think of me as your spiritual doctor. I have rules I must follow. You don't have to follow my advice. But you have no claim on me. I can drop you as a 'patient' at any time." And if his pompous ass blew too much more, I would drop it.

"Just as I can fire you."

I shrugged. Like I gave a shit. Go ahead, asshole. Fire me. See if I care. "Difference is, if you fire me, it doesn't affect Tabby and me at all. We'll go home. You, however, will still have a pesky demon."

"Look, I'm sorry," Vespa said. His whole demeanor changed. I wasn't talking to a man anymore; we were back to the scared teenager. His pride had become a deflated balloon.

"Just keep all of this in mind the next time you cop an attitude. I apologized for being late. We were trying to be on time." I forced myself to hold back. There was a hell of a lot more I could say, but they weren't things to be said in public.

Vespa nodded. Little did he know, had I been paying attention to the time, I wouldn't have been happy I was late. I always had this phobia about what would happen if I was late for things. It was bad enough that I was stressed from the hotel mess. Now this? I was really close to saying screw it and going back home. If it hadn't been for Lucy, I probably would have.

"I want to say something," Tabby said.

Vespa's eyes seemed to be captivated by Tabby as she spoke. I wondered if she realized he was crushing on her.

"This isn't an optimum situation. None of us are happy to be here, and we needed to stop pretending. I don't trust you." Tabby narrowed her eyes. "Your deceiving makes me not like you. But this will not stop me from helping you."

Vespa sighed. "Have I hurt you that badly?"

"Hurt, no. Pissed me off, yes." The whites around her irises began to turn red. "I don't care if you're possessed or not, there's no excuse for being a jackass."

Vespa's shoulders slumped. "I didn't mean to be a 'jackass.' I just wanted you guys to believe me."

"That's where you sold us short." I stared at him hard. It was a good thing his eyes were natural green or the elongated pupils might have shown up more prominently. "Our last case was a six-year-old kid. If we believed her, why wouldn't we believe you?"

He shrugged. "I guess I'm so used to being looked at as a suspect by my family that I assumed you'd be the same way."

"The bad part is," I began, "we look at you more closely since you deceived us. To us, you're capable of anything."

"Which we knew the minute we found out that you invited the demon into your body." Tabby crossed her arms over her chest.

I nodded to Tabby. "Yeah. People who do that are kind of divided into two categories: the evil and the stupid. Maybe stupid is too harsh a word. Naive perhaps. But since we can't take your word for what you are, you'll be suspect."

"Just so you know," Tabby added, "it partly has to do with you being possessed. You can never trust a demon; they lie."

Vespa sighed. "Yeah. I found that out... So if you are able to do this, get this thing out of me I mean, will my eyes go back to normal?"

"Probably." I thought that was the least of his worries, but said nothing.

"Just probably?" Vespa asked.

I could see he was starting to shake. He should be scared.

"I don't want to say yes when I don't know for sure. There is nothing absolute about the paranormal." I took a deep breath. "Chances are you'll go back to normal, but there's always that one percent, ya know?"

Vespa's shakes stopped. "Yeah, I know."

Vespa's home reminded me of the *Brady Bunch* house. A split-level thing with the outside partly a slightly muted yellow and the rest red brick. He motioned for us to pull in and park in the driveway to the left side of the house. It was connected to a single-car garage. That meant that him pulling behind me would have me blocked in.

I complied because I didn't want to piss him off, and the ground was flat. If I had to, I'd just drive on the grass and get out of there.

He pulled in behind me, but not right up on the bumper or anything. None of this seemed like Vespa to me. Part of me imagined him hanging around an old Victorian mansion somewhere, not in 1960s contemporary. His car was surprising most of all, I thought. With his age, I expected him to have some old clunker. Instead, he was driving an Infinity SUV. I guessed the demon had helped him some.

Tabby and I got out of the car. Some plant outside was making my nose itch. After sneezing a few times, I closed the car door.

"I'll get Isaac," Tabby said.

She walked around the car, opened the back driver's-side door, and grabbed him. Upon lifting the cage, water spilled everywhere.

"Shit," she said.

"It's okay. Water can't hurt anything." It wasn't like Isaac had taken a dump or something, and it was just a rental.

"Unless you like mold," Nicholas said. I'd started thinking of him as Nicholas again after he stopped acting like a dick-wad. It was like he had two separate personalities, demonic possession notwithstanding.

"I'll go get you a towel," he said and ran off toward the house.

Tabby set Isaac on the driveway. Too bad she didn't have a leash or she could have gotten him out of the now water-logged crate. Poor thing. He was sputtering and glaring at Tabby.

"I can't believe I did that." Tabby sighed.

I crept over and hugged her shoulders. "It's okay. Like I said, it's just water."

"You don't think Vespa was a little eccentric about it, do you?"

I shrugged. "Who knows? This is his part of the country, not ours."

"True."

Vespa ran back out of the house with a few white towels. He handed Tabby one, and then went to dab out the car. That was when the trouble began.

I could see through the window that Lucy was looking at

him wide-eyed. He tried to just get the towel in the car, but the invisible barrier of Tabby's wards kept him out. I wanted to cheer. At least those worked. I had visual proof of it now.

"Let me take that," I said. He handed over the towel, but kept looking back and forth between me and the car.

I leaned inside and was able to wipe up the car without a problem.

Nicholas raised a brow. "You guys are weird."

There was more to it than that. I kind of wanted to chuckle. He was the one who masqueraded as I-don't-know-how-many-great-grandfathers. But he thought we were odd. Okay. I guessed it was all in the way you looked at it.

I handed him back his soggy towel.

"Let's get everyone settled." He plastered this smile on his face that seemed too big. Too clown-like. Poor kid was trying too hard. Or maybe his messed-up family made him think he had to turn into the famous Vespa. That would make all of this not just about an exorcism, but a personality crisis issue. I wasn't a shrink. He'd have to find therapy on his own.

We followed him into his house. The front entry led to a sunken living room. It had kind of an open floor plan with the living room in front and a big dining room table toward the back. Off to the right of the living room was this big staircase. He led us through and upstairs. I swore to God if the place could have looked any more like the *Brady Bunch* house, I'd have pinched myself. All that was missing was the crazy sixties colors. He took us to a bedroom. In the TV house, we would be staying in Mike and Carol's bedroom. Funky.

"You can put your things in here. There is a bathroom across the hall. Will the cat be okay with his litter box in there?" Nicholas asked.

I blinked. "I guess so; at least when we show him where it is."

"All right." He walked out of the room. Just like that. I didn't know if we should follow him or what.

I looked at Tabby. She shrugged.

"I guess we go get the rest of our shit." Boy, the welcome mat had sure been put out for us.

"Yeah, guess so," she said.

#

Later, after we had all our stuff in the house and when Isaac was hiding under the bed in the room we'd been given, Tabby and I sat in the living room with Nicholas. He was trying to seem relaxed, but his posture was too rigid. At least he was just as uncomfortable as we were.

"Okay," Tabby began. "Where were you when you made the pact with the demon?"

Nick raised his hand and pointed at the floor. "In here. Move all the furniture out of the way and pull back the rug. I have a circle etched into the floor."

There were two sofas in the living room: a muted sage-green color and kind of modern in design. They reminded me of baby poop. The rug had these swirly designs in it and some of the things were the same green as the sofas.

"Was there anyone here with you?" I knew enough about the black arts to know that practitioners didn't necessarily have to have a coven, but with what Vespa had done, it probably would have helped. If he'd been smart, that was; I was holding out for some evidence that he had a brain.

"No, just me," he said.

It wasn't easy asking someone questions like this when we didn't even know him. If we knew him, we might have had a clue what would trigger his memory. Right now, it was a crap shoot.

"What did you eat before doing the ritual?" Tabby asked.

"Nothing. You never work with a demon on a full

stomach."

That part, I knew, was probably true. Tabby had said as much before and even the official rite of exorcism recommended fasts and prayer before beginning. After seeing what Lucy's demon did before and during her exorcism, I was glad for my empty stomach.

"Before you did this, how often did you call a demon?" I had to ask. No one in their right mind would wake up one day out of the blue and say, "I think I'll give my soul to a demon today." Yeah, not going to happen.

"It took a while for me to know the process enough to get them to answer."

That made sense, sort of. I bet the demons even wanted to see if he was worth their time and bother.

"If you had to guess," Tabby said, tapping her fingers on the sofa's armrest, "how long?"

"A year. Maybe more."

Yeah. He'd been serious. And stupid. And a pain in the ass, but that was beside the point. I needed to stop dwelling on the stuff I hated about him. If I was going to manage to see this through, I needed to find something about him I liked. I knew that. Otherwise, there was no way I could work for days trying to drive out the demon. It was too hard, and when the final push came, I would need something to keep me going.

"Did you sign the contract in blood?" Hell, that's what they do in movies.

He blinked. "No, I just agreed to it."

"A verbal contract then." I couldn't believe that there wasn't some sort of demonic file reporting in Hell for all the contracts and such, but I wasn't going to go to Hell to ask either.

"In our world, a verbal contract is hard to prove in court," Tabby said.

I leaned back on the sofa. "Why do I have a feeling that Hell has scribes copying down everything a demon needs recorded?"

Nicholas giggled darkly. "You are a funny man."

I was lost on what was funny. Tabby wasn't laughing either. Social grace was not one of Nick's strong points.

"Okay. Mind explaining how this works?" I asked him.

"All I know is that when I agreed to the demon's demands, he entered my body."

That was helpful. About as helpful as saying that to make a hamburger, you need some meat. I wanted to roll my eyes.

"Do you remember how?" Tabby asked.

"Not really. Everything went black and I was out for a few hours."

Great. Things going black told me nothing. If it were me, I'd be trying to figure out anything, as far-fetched as it might sound, that could be helpful. Nick, however, seemed either not too bright, or just simple. There was the possibility that he called us out, but wasn't ready for the help, almost like an addict. If that was the case, I was going to be pissed. Being an exorcist was going to drive me to drink.

"We'll try again later," Tabby said.

Vespa nodded.

He reminded me of a bobble-head. No wonder the demon could take residence so easily.

"Now what?" It wasn't like I had anything else to do. If I could do more research, that would be different, but I couldn't look up shit until I got more information out of him. And since he was information-incompetent, I was screwed.

I missed Doc. Part of me understood why he wasn't showing himself, but it was kind of hard. I'd gotten used to his wit. And Lucy—it just about broke my heart that she was stuck out in the car, but what else could I do? It wasn't like we could trust Vespa's demon. I wasn't looking forward to this exorcism at all.

#

Later that night, after Tabby and I retired to the bedroom for the evening, Tabby set about warding the room. I was glad she was doing it. We needed one safe place to retire. And I needed a place where I could think without having to worry about everything else that could happen while we were asleep.

"When you do the exorcism, where are you going to do it?" Tabby asked.

I paused. That was a damn good question. With Lucy, I'd tried doing it in her bedroom. That didn't work. What worked was doing the exorcism in the area where she'd found the mirror the demon had been trapped in. Worked was one way to put it. More like something was accomplished. I didn't view it as a successful exorcism. If it had been successful, Lucy wouldn't be with me now. No, I just saved her soul. For some priests, that would have been enough. But it wasn't enough for me.

But Vespa hadn't been fooled by a trapped demon in an object. That made everything different. That and the fact that he called the demon to come to him. This house wasn't having quasi-haunted phenomena, so I wasn't sure if there really was a heart in this house. That meant the best option was where Vespa was comfortable. "I guess we'll do it in the living room. That's where Vespa allowed the demon in."

"But a living room?"

I shrugged. I knew it sounded dumb, but I hadn't picked Vespa's demon-working room either. "I'm not sure we have a choice."

"How are you going to secure him in there?"

Good point. The living room was one of the most open rooms in the house. "I'll just have to be creative." I steeled myself. "I doubt he has a big industrial-size freezer."

"Might be a good idea to actually plan it out, ya know? Instead of arranging it on the day you need it."

She had a point. We'd done what we did with Lucy because it was a spur-of-the-moment thing. This time, I pretty much knew where we were going to do the exorcism. I needed to know how I was going to restrain Vespa, how I was going to prepare the room. The last thing I needed was a couch thrown at my head, and what would I do if it didn't work? I needed an escape plan for Tabby and me that was better than driving the car over grass.

Maybe Tabby could make a charm that would automatically ward the front door, maybe all the doors for that matter. Something mostly to keep Vespa in, but that would let me, Tabby, and Isaac out. Now that had possibilities.

"Can a ward be an object that can move?" I asked. I wasn't sure how'd she do this, exactly.

"I never really thought about it before, but I don't see why it couldn't."

"Okay. This is what I want you to do. Make a necklace or something. It doesn't have to be fancy. And ward it to keep me out." Better to test my idea in case I was dead wrong.

She raised an eyebrow at me. "Seriously?"

"Yes! We have to know if this will work." I knew I was getting excitable again, but if she'd bear with me, this might actually work.

She didn't question me anymore. After a bit of rummaging around in her suitcase, she found a piece of ribbon. Then she held it up so I could look at it.

"Will be okay?" she asked.

"It just has to lie on the doorknob." I couldn't see why it wouldn't.

She walked over and snatched a piece of hair from my head. Then she taped it to the ribbon and did her mojo on it.

"Okay, now what?" she asked.

"I'm going to go to the bathroom. While I'm gone, put this over the doorknob." Should be easy enough to see if this was going to work.

"Oookay."

I left. Isaac didn't come out from under the bed. Poor guy, not that I blamed him. He'd been through a lot lately. I wanted to tell him we'd be home soon, but I didn't want to lie. This one had all the hallmarks of taking a hell of a long time.

After I was done in the bathroom, I walked over to the bedroom door, turned the knob and pushed. I stepped back from the door for a minute and looked at it. Then, I tried again. The door wouldn't budge. I tried rattling the knob. It shook a little in my hand but it didn't move. I took my hand off the door. Holy shit, my idea worked.

"Okay, Tabby," I said to the door.

I could hear her chuckling behind it. She opened the door, and I was then able to enter.

"It worked!"

"Yup. And watch yourself, I'm going to remember this."

What the hell had I done? I rubbed my head with my hand. No sense in worrying about it now. I looked at her. "Okay. Now, tomorrow, we need to find out how many doors there are to this place both in and around the house. When we know that, I want you to ward things that will let me, you, and Isaac out. That way, you don't have to try to steal hair from Vespa."

"Good point," she said. "I'd rather not touch him at all."

I didn't want her to have to touch him either, but during the exorcism that was going to be impossible.

#

The next morning, I woke to cat butt in my face. I guess Isaac finally felt it was okay to come out from under the bed. I was glad, don't get me wrong, but I'd rather have had the other end. At least he didn't fart. I think that would have killed me.

I sat up. The room looked like it had when I'd gone to sleep. The walls were painted a baby blue. The bed was big enough and had a white comforter on top. My stuff was stashed in the corner, and Tabby's was on a chair. I looked over at her. She was asleep. I moved around a little, trying to pop my back. All of these strange beds were starting to get to me. I was ready to go home.I heard a soft knock on the door. I threw back the covers on my side and got up.

Nicholas stood on the other side of the door. "Do you all want to go out to breakfast? My treat."

He looked so hopeful. Honestly, I was getting tired of restaurant food, but I didn't want to hurt the kid's feelings. I glanced over to Tabby and then back to him. "Sure. Let me get Tabby up."

"Okay." He grinned and then walked down the hall.

I swear he had a skip in his step. But I knew better. It was only a matter of time before the demon popped in again. The kid was weird as hell, I'd give him that. But he was odd before the demon business. Demons did not skip, unless someone had unleashed a barrage of skipping imps I didn't know about.

Vespa's possession was so different from Lucy's. Her demon, Asmodeus, had taken complete control. Vespa's demon, however, either wasn't that strong or he hadn't gotten his claws fully into Nicholas yet. Which it was, I didn't know, but I couldn't expect this to be easy. He also didn't seem to know a whole lot of things he should. That puzzled me too. I walked back into our room. Isaac peered up at me from the bed.

"You fart on me in my sleep, don't you?" I asked.

No response from the cat. I know he did though. He looked sneaky.

I walked closer to Tabby's side of the bed and knelt down.

"Tabby?"

No response.

"Hey, Tabby," I said a little louder. Again, no response. It was time to break out the big guns.

"Wake up, little rosebud, wake up!" I said in a sing-song voice.

She jerked awake. "You jerk."

I snorted. It worked every time. "Vespa wants to know if we want to eat breakfast out."

She shrugged her shoulders. "It gives us a chance to check on Lucy."

"Yeah and if Lucy heard from Doc, maybe we can get more information on the house."

"Maybe. Let's get dressed."

I looked at Isaac. "I'm watching you."

I could swear he grinned.

#

Vespa met us downstairs with keys in hand. "You guys ready?"

"Sure," I said. With Vespa involved, anything could happen and I wasn't really ready for any of it. I needed to hire a psychic.

Tabby and I headed to the car. We'd left the doors to the bathroom and bedroom we were using open so Isaac could use his litter box. It was going to be interesting to see if he was going to roam to other parts of the house now that he calmed down. I didn't think Nick minded; at least he hadn't said he did. Isaac wasn't known to cause damage to anything except spider plants. He liked to eat those.

As we walked to the car, I couldn't see Lucy, but that didn't necessarily mean anything. My heart hammered in my chest. The closer I got to the car, the further down into it I could see. Finally, I relaxed when I saw that she was lying down on the seat looking at one of the books Tabby bought her. Reading was safe.

I pressed the button on the keys and unlocked the doors. Tabby and I got in.

I kept watching through the rearview mirror as Vespa got in his car and started backing out of the drive.

"Hey, Lucy," I said. "How are you doing?"

"I'm bored," she whined.

No doubt. She had no one to talk to all day. She couldn't go outside and run around. This was hellish for a kid.

"I'll look for more things while we're out this morning," Tabby said.

"Thanks."

I started the car and backed out of the driveway so that I was behind Vespa. There were too many things on my mind and Lucy was only one of them. I watched Vespa in his car, once he was sure I was behind him, he took off. I followed. He led me twisting and turning through various streets until we ended up at a little Mexican restaurant.

"I'll try to convince him to take us to a grocery store." I could come up with an excuse for that. And while we were there, maybe Tabby could sneak and get Lucy a few things in the toy aisle.

"That would be a good idea," she said.

"Tired of eating out?" I knew I was. Maybe if Tabby bought some stuff we could make, Vespa would let us use his kitchen.

"More like, we'll need to eat when we start exorcising him."

"I hadn't thought of that," I said.

She shook her head. "There's a lot you don't think about, Jimmy Holiday."

I laughed. Then I turned my attention to the back seat. "I missed you, Lucy."

"I missed you too. How long do I have to stay in the car?"

Dammit. Cut out my heart with a rusty knife. "I wish I had

a better answer for you, but I don't know. We're trying to find out about the contract."

"It doesn't matter," she said.

I almost pulled over the car. "What?"

"The contract. It doesn't matter."

"How is that possible?" I asked Tabby.

She looked at me blankly.

I stared at Lucy in the rearview mirror. "The exorcism will be normal."

"I didn't say that."

I wanted to bang my head into the steering wheel. I noticed Vespa was standing outside his car waiting on us. Shit. "We'll talk more later, Lucy."

"Okay."

Tabby and I got out of the car. It was not easy to leave that car just when I was getting information, but I couldn't risk Vespa guessing what was keeping us in the car. I'm sure he knew on some level, but the less I made it obvious, the less chance there would be of Lucy getting hurt.

"Sorry about that," I said.

"Nothing to worry about," he said and walked into the restaurant. We followed.

Inside the restaurant, the hostess led us to a table near the front window. The walls were painted to look like fake adobe. The tables used serapes as tablecloths. With the kitchen open enough to the serving area, we could hear the cooks yammering in Spanish. Overall, a nice, homey place. Totally not what I expected from Vespa.

"Ever eat Mexican food for breakfast?" Nicholas asked.

"No, I can't say I have." Back home, Mexican places only opened for lunch; well, unless you counted fast food, and I didn't.

"It's really good," he said.

"Why don't you order for all of us then?" Tabby smiled.

Vespa blushed. I'll admit, it looked weird with his eyes. He was just about doing an evil elf thing with those snake slits.

When the waitress came over, Vespa ordered. After she left, Tabby stared at him.

"What is that migas thing you ordered?" she asked.

"It's my favorite."

God, he was trying to impress her so badly. He was so...high school about it too. I would have felt sorry for him if he wasn't hitting on what was mine.

"It's scrambled eggs with pieces of corn tortillas mixed in," he said.

Tabby grinned. "Can't wait to try them, then."

#

"Hey, before we go to the house, can we go to a grocery store?" I asked as we left the restaurant. I hadn't been this stuffed in a long time. I felt like I'd just been to someone's grandmother's house.

"We can, but why would you need to do that?" he asked.

I raised a brow. Was he afraid of the grocery store or something? "We wanted to get snacks, stuff like that."

Vespa visibly relaxed. "Uh. Okay. Yeah, sure."

He hopped into his car. Tabby and I got in ours. It was such a relief to get out of there, away from him for a bit. He made me feel almost as if I was being suffocated. Everything with him had to be a certain way. I wasn't sure how much longer I could take it.

"Is it just me, or is Nick a little intense?" Tabby asked, reading my mind.

I backed out of the spot. "More like a little control freak."

"What's a control freak?" Lucy asked from the back seat.

"It's someone who has to have everything their way," I said. It was more than that, but it wasn't exactly appropriate to put it in those terms for a kid.

"Like when Daddy says Mommy is…," she paused, thinking, "anal-retentive?"

I laughed. Never mind. I needed to remember Lucy wasn't a normal six-year-old. I kept forgetting. "Something like that."

When we got back to the house with food, Tabby conveniently left a coloring book and some crayons in the car. It was the best we could find at the grocery store. Lucy couldn't play with dolls because she couldn't hold them, so what was the point? Maybe she'd manage the crayons. Luckily, Vespa never asked about any of it. I have no idea what Tabby would have said.

It wasn't until we got to the house that I realized I'd forgotten to ask Lucy to expand on what she knew. We were already inside, putting stuff away in the kitchen, and I didn't want old Nick to know Lucy was in the car. For now, I was thankful he hadn't caught on. Even though I'm sure he guessed something was up when he wasn't able to dab out the water. But I didn't want to give him any ideas, so I couldn't go outside to ask her. I didn't want to raise suspicion any more than I already had. The ward on the car was a huge red flag. Plus, I wasn't sure he couldn't see her. With the demon in him, he probably could.

I wasn't sure if Nick was all that aware when the demon was in control of the body. And I wasn't about to lose Lucy now, not after I'd fought so hard for her. Especially since I had no way of contacting her parents. At least she was almost as opaque as she'd been when we arrived in Arizona. I couldn't imagine what I'd do if I found out that all this had killed off her body.

While Tabby was unpacking the groceries, I ran upstairs. I wanted to see if the Order had sent me anything. Like usual, there was too much I needed to know and no one had bothered to let me in on all of it. If they hadn't, I was jotting off an email about Lucy's parents. I wanted to at least know her body was alive. Surely they could understand that, right?

The iPad booted up. I opened my email. I did have an email from the Order, but not what I was expecting. It was an invitation to meet a fellow Order member in two weeks in New York. Like they expected me to have it all wrapped up in a shiny bow by then? Heh.

I dashed off a quick reply explaining that I was on a case, but I'd touch base as soon as it was over. I wondered what they were thinking. I knew that *they* knew some exorcisms lasted years, so why did they think I'd be done so quickly?

I got the idea that this case might be my test, not that I needed another one, but whatever. God had chosen me; the Order hadn't. So their rules were starting to piss me off. I had more important things to worry about, like saving souls, instead of hoping I passed their stupid test.

I turned off the iPad. Yeah, no job was perfect, but the church and the Order had their own special brand of bureaucracy. It was driving me crazy. I was surprised no rogue priest had gone postal yet. With the way this was being handled, I might be the first.

I wanted to get in touch with Doc, but that would have to wait until tonight. It wasn't like I could stay in the room all day. Isaac seemed content to do so. He was lounging on Tabby's pillow. But I was the one who had to protect everyone. Isaac had it lucky.

"I don't like it here either," I said to him.

He meowed.

"Yeah. I hope it won't be long too." I never thought I would be talking to a cat.

Isaac closed his eyes and went back to sleep. So much for normal conversation.

I put the iPad in my backpack and headed downstairs. I didn't like leaving Tabby alone in this place very long. Especially since Vespa seemed sweet on her. Who knew what secrets this house held? He could have a hidden basement room or something. What did we know about him? In my opinion, he was an idiot. Whether evil or not remained to be seen, but then there were different degrees of evil.

I'm sure that fucking about with conjuring up demons put you in a whole other category than the usual general sins. He was looking at thousands of years in Purgatory, at least. But depending on what he used to do the spells to bring on the demon, it might be worse than that. If he was damned, there was nothing I could do. That was, if inviting the demon in hadn't made him damned already. I could only guess. It wasn't like these things were written down specifically. At least not anywhere that I knew of.

When I made it to the kitchen, I found Vespa trying to make small talk with Tabby. It was kind of sad. He had that tone that made him come on a little too strong.

"Are you sure I can't help?" he asked.

"There's nothing for you to do." Tabby shrugged. "Everything is put away. I just need to find out what Jimmy wants to do."

She must not have noticed me enter. If I had been in a better mood, I might have tried to scare her. Not today.

"What is it I'm supposed to do?" I asked.

Tabby looked up, startled. "Mr. Vespa was wondering what we were going to do the rest of the day."

I focused on Vespa. Maybe I could trick him into some answers. "I would like to speak to Doc."

As soon as I mentioned his name, the demon's eyes began to glow bright green. "Why do you want to speak to the spy?"

I had him. Now, if I could keep him on the string, maybe I

could finish my research. "One, I haven't seen him since we got here. And two, I'm trying to help your host."

He curled his mouth up and snarled. "Once I gain my strength, there won't be any more of these problems."

I was a problem, was I? I wanted to roll my eyes. Yeah, the demon was dangerous, but he was also pedantic. If he was such a big badass, he'd have made something happen by now. I exhaled slowly. "But you haven't gained your strength yet. So where's Doc?"

"If you let me in, priest, I could make you very strong indeed."

I didn't even bother asking why he turned on me. I was the stronger figure. If he was all about power, he'd want a better host. "I don't need your strength. I have my own."

Without warning, Vespa returned to normal. His eyes showed that strange look in them, but the irises were normal green. He lowered his head. Ah-ha. He was aware, somewhat at least. That would be helpful to know during the exorcism.

"I'm sorry," he said.

I sat across from him at the table. "Listen, we've been in this long enough that we know when the demon is speaking and when it's you." Might as well make him feel better. It wouldn't do either of us any good if I flat-out accused him of everything. This way, he thought of me as a friend, thus someone he could trust.

He seemed to relax a little. "I just want this thing out of me so I can go back to normal."

What was normal for him? Dealing with a screwed-up family that stressed him out until he invoked a demon? Jesus Christ.

"What about your family?" Tabby asked.

He jumped up from the table. "You know what? Fuck my family. It's their fault for making me think I had to be something I'm not."

I didn't comment. His being an emotional wreck, sure; let that blame fall to his family. His inviting a demon to possess him? That was all him. They didn't stand over him and force him to learn the rituals, for God's sake. He needed to take responsibility.

"What are you going to do if we get the demon out?" Tabby asked.

Vespa turned and stared at her. "I'm selling this house, leaving this place, and finding a different life."

That was the most intelligent thing I'd heard him say. I swore, if he'd starting talking about using the exorcism as a get-rich scheme or something, I might have crushed his head. Just a little.

"Okay, Tabby. Let's go see if we can get ahold of Doc. I want to see if he has any information for us." That was just what I needed. Let him know just enough that he wouldn't expect what I was doing. Or rather, think he had an idea of what I was doing without him knowing the full story.

Tabby nodded.

"Nick, why don't you go take a nap," I suggested. "You're under a lot of stress and it might do you some good." I meant it. He had dark circles under his eyes and he seemed paler than usual.

"Okay. Yeah. I think I will," he said.

#

I led Tabby back upstairs. I didn't want there to be any more of a connection to Lucy than necessary. If I could have, I would have snuck outside and checked on her, but there was no way. I was probably playing with fire enough by trying to get ahold of Doc. If there had been something wrong with him, Lucy would have told me in the car when we went to breakfast. Now though, she had no way to get ahold of me. I needed to remedy this if there was going to be a next time.

When we got to the bedroom, I closed the door behind Tabby.

"What's up?" she asked.

"I want to know what's going on with that statement Lucy made." I'd been stupid and I was freely admitting it.

"Why not ask Lucy?"

"Because I don't want him near her. If I go outside, you know hed1 be right on my tail, asking what I was doing." I scratched my arm and lounged on the bed.

"He knows she's there. It wouldn't surprise me if he goes outside and watches her." Tabby rubbed her hands over her arms.

I blinked. Shit. "She never said anything about that."

"She didn't have to." Tabby sighed. "I can tell you haven't been around little kids."

"Why?" I was getting so confused.

"Because kids don't always come right out and tell you what's wrong. They want to be saved, but they don't know how to ask for help. And they seem a little nervous when they shouldn't be. Things like that."

Lucy had said something, I'd just been too stupid to pick up on it. She said she wanted to go home. Hell. "He's messing with Lucy?"

"Maybe. I don't know. I just felt weird."

I took a deep breath. I needed to stay on course. "Okay. More reason to ask for Doc."

Tabby stared at me hard. "What are you planning?"

"I don't know yet." I smiled. "Doc? If you can hear me, I need to talk to you." I didn't yell or anything, that would have been stupid. If he could hear me, he'd show up eventually.

Tabby lounged on the bed beside me while I stared at the ceiling.

Yeah, it was dumb, but hell, I always expected him to come from there. Maybe, because in my mind with as much of a badass as he was, he belonged in Heaven, and spirits floated down from Heaven, didn't they? The priest part of me was about to give me a lesson in true theology, but whatever.

After a few minutes, I glanced at Tabby. "Guess he isn't coming."

"Maybe he's busy," she said.

"I hope that's all it is. I don't think I can take much more excitement." And I didn't want to think about him being trapped somewhere because Vespa's demon didn't want to be spied on. If that's what had happened, it would be my fault.

Tabby got up and put her hand on my shoulder. "I know."

#

I figured Doc would get back to me when he could, if he could anyway. There was no sense in me jumping to conclusions when I hadn't heard anything yet. I never heard about him not being able to enter Vespa's house, so I doubt that was it. It left me uneasy. I'd gotten used to him being around.

Tabby and I headed back downstairs. I didn't make any noise. I'd told Vespa to get some rest, and I was going to try to make sure he got it. His room was on the first floor, somewhere in a hallway off the kitchen. I hadn't been invited, so I hadn't bothered looking for it. Tabby and I were in the living room.

"Is it me, or is everything strained here?" Tabby asked.

"Worse than dealing with a failing marriage, you mean?" I remembered how intense it had been at times when Tor and Will's marriage was falling apart in front of our eyes at Blackmoor. I thought that was bad. Somehow, Vespa and his weirdness were worse.

"Yeah. Here, I'm half-afraid to talk," she said.

"It could be the trust thing. This is the first time we've dealt with an active and productive possessed person. The demon wants to live on Earth again. It doesn't just want Vespa's soul." It was a different type of demon. He wasn't any less evil because of it, either.

"How can you tell?" she asked.

"It hasn't taken full possession of Nick. He can be himself. Lucy, however, was always demonic until her soul was separated from the demon." If all the demon had wanted was Vespa's soul, it would have killed him as soon as he'd been invited in.

"Good point. So will the exorcism be easier since Vespa isn't totally possessed?"

"A sort of logic would say yes, but I have a bad feeling that won't be the case." I needed a mentor to explain all of this stuff to me. Or a book. Or something. Flying by the seat of my pants was getting tiring.

"The contract?" she started.

"Yeah. I don't know anymore. Nothing like this is like with Lucy. He hasn't spoken in another language. He doesn't just 'know' things. We should be trying to figure it out, but I'm lost." And then there had been what Lucy said. Maybe she was right and it didn't matter, but I wanted to know why.

Tabby stayed quiet. I didn't want to mention Lucy without being within our warded room. That kid was counting on me to protect her and I was sure as hell trying. Nick probably knew everything anyway, but I felt a lot better being inside the ward before I said or did anything to do with Lucy.

"I always thought that making a pact with Satan required a mark of some sort." I rifled through my brain, looking for some sort of answer. They had all those old movies like *The Mark of Satan* and stuff like that. It had to come from somewhere.

"Like yours?" Tabby asked.

I stared at my wrist. In a way, I almost expected the mark itself to have some sort of special powers or something, but so far, there'd been nothing. It was virtually a tattoo. Only I knew it wasn't normal. You couldn't tell by looking at it. "Yeah, I guess so. Do you think we should ask him if he has a mark?"

Tabby shrugged. "It couldn't hurt. Maybe it would give us something to research. And if we're lucky, it could give us an idea of the contract."

"Have I told you how much I love you lately?" She snickered. She really was amazing.

"Seriously, I don't think I'd make it through all of this if you weren't so smart." In fact, I knew I wouldn't. I wasn't smart enough. I needed her brain.

"You don't give yourself enough credit, you know?"

I shrugged. I didn't care what she said. She was the one who had her head on straight most of the time. I just seemed to do okay when all hell broke loose. Luckily—or unluckily— that happened more often than I liked to think about.

"How are we going to handle this?" Tabby shifted on the couch, likely trying to get comfortable.

I shrugged. "Ask him, I guess." I didn't have any better ideas. If I did, I would have done them by now.

She rubbed her eyes. "Oh, yeah, like that's gonna work. I can just see this. 'Nick, hey man. Do you have any strange markings or birthmarks?'"

"Okay, smarty-pants. How would you take care of it?"

"Simple. We figure out what to do about dinner and I'll ask you how you like my new tattoo."

I chuckled. I couldn't help it. I knew firsthand Tabby didn't have a new tattoo. She had the same one she's always had— a phoenix on her left shoulder blade. Whether Vespa's demon would tell him about the lie was another thing, but hell, it sounded better than what I would have done.

"Works for me," I said.

"Good."

#

Vespa got up about four. Tabby and I had killed time trading the iPad back and forth, reading and playing games. I'd run upstairs and gotten it out of my backpack when it seemed like Nick was going to stay asleep for a while. I never thought I'd need one, but it was coming in handy.

"Were you able to find everything okay?" Nick asked, rubbing his eyes.

"Yeah. No problems," I said.

"What did you want to do for dinner?" Tabby tapped her finger on her chin. "I could cook something."

I liked the sound of that. I'd watched her grab the ingredients she needed to make her chili at the grocery store. It had been too long since I had it.

"No!" Vespa shook himself. "No, I...I think going out is better."

"All right." Okay, I made a point to remember this. Mr. Demon did not like fire. Interesting. I glanced over at Tabby. She seemed a little shell-shocked.

"Oh, sorry." Nick rubbed the back of his neck. "I just...I don't like to cook things in the house."

Tabby nodded. "Okay, then. Guess we'll go out again."

I could hear an almost imperceptible snark in her voice. Honestly, I knew what she meant. I was tired of eating out too. It wasn't like we couldn't talk about the mark just as easily in a restaurant. That part wasn't a big deal. Vespa being a freaked-out idiot? It was becoming a bigger deal as the days wore on.

"Any Italian places around?" I asked. Yeah, we'd been to one earlier in the week, but at least it had a different taste to it. Even if it sucked, the extra garlic couldn't hurt, especially when we didn't know when we were going to start the exorcism.

Vespa nodded and walked back to his bedroom.

Tabby blew out a breath as he left. "That was strange."

"Yeah, tell me about it."

"I mean, even to do his rituals for conjuring the demon, he had to use fire."

I blinked. Okay, she would know. Now his kitchen phobia made no sense. "Really?"

She nodded. "Yeah. You have to call on the keepers, the guardians of the watchtowers: earth, air, fire, and water. Just for what he does, it's backwards."

I took a deep breath. "So the stove or the cooking thing has to be something else."

"Maybe he's afraid of being poisoned?"

"Maybe."

Chapter Eleven

Predictable

VESPA CAME OUT of his room dressed in a suit. I almost fell off the sofa. What the hell was a kid like him doing running around in a suit?

"I'm guessing this is a fancy place?" I asked.

Nick scratched his arm. "No, not really. I just think it's proper to dress for dinner." He smiled at Tabby.

The guy had almost gone cuckoo for cocoa puffs. Damn.

Tabby bit her lip. "Give us a minute, and we'll get cleaned up."

I grabbed the iPad off the sofa and followed Tabby upstairs. This was getting ridiculous. Once we were in the room, I closed the door.

"We're going to have to do something about that," I said.

"About what?"

"The way he looks at you. The way he's acting." No one on Earth could make me dress up for every meal, and even if there were someone, it sure as hell wouldn't be him.

"You think I like it?" she asked.

"No. I know I wouldn't. He needs to lay off."

She sighed. "Right now, it's harmless. Why don't we pick our battles?"

"Good point." Yeah, better not get in yet another argument.

Lucy's demon had fed off that stuff. It would stand to reason Vespa's would too.

After we finished getting dressed, Tabby and I went back downstairs. I had on a dress shirt and some khaki pants—about as dressed up as I got. Tabby had on a flowery summer-type dress. It was black with blue flowers on it. I liked it on her. Made the red in her hair stand out.

Nick leaned calmly against the sofa, waiting for us. "You look nice," he said to Tabby.

"What about me?" I said as straight-faced as possible. It gave me the chance to get under his skin a little.

Nick blinked. "Uh, you look nice too."

I laughed. "Just goofing around. Tabby does look great."

She blushed and gave me a look. I could tell I was going to hear about it later.

"Shall we?" Vespa asked.

We followed him out the door. I was glad to take our rental car. I didn't trust riding with a demon. They were known to cause car accidents if they wanted to kill you. I'd read that in an old book by Malachi Martin.

Some of the stuff in the book sounded fake, but some of it had a ring of truth to it too. The car stuff felt true to me. I didn't care that he'd been eventually kicked out of the church for indiscretions. He had married the girl he'd been...having relations with. Ironically, the same thing I had been accused of that had gotten me defrocked. Conspiracy maybe?

As soon as Tabby and I got the doors closed on the car, Lucy started. "I don't like being in this car."

Uh-oh. Lucy being that blatant meant that things had gotten worse. "I know. It has to be boring." I hoped that was all it was. Please, God. I pulled out of the driveway and followed Vespa down the road.

"I'm not bored. I don't like seeing the faces," she said.

I almost slammed on the brakes. What the hell? This was the first time I heard anything about faces.

"What faces?" I asked.

"When you guys go inside, after a while, these faces look in the windows."

I didn't like hearing that at all. The kid had had enough spooky shit in her life. She didn't need any more. And here I was, forcing her to stay in a car by herself without any way to get ahold of us so we could take her away from the monsters. I was a great guy all right. Maybe it wasn't Vespa fucking with her at all.

"What do the faces look like?" Tabby asked.

"Asmodeus," Lucy said.

I almost lost control of my senses. No fucking way was I going to fight him again for Lucy's soul. I didn't give a shit. He could have Vespa for all I cared, but I knew that wasn't the case. He wasn't the one in charge of Vespa. He would have done a hell of a lot worse in the house if it had been him. No, he'd come because he wanted Lucy.

I did the only thing I knew to do. I started to pray.

Tabby did not join in. I didn't expect her to. Her religion did prayer in terms of rituals, and it wasn't like this was the time or place for that, though I'm sure she could do something small in a car. She just didn't have the stuff with her.

"Could you ward the driveway?" I asked.

"No. Probably not. It isn't a dwelling."

"Damn." It was a thought. Shame there were limitations, but I already knew that.

While we were talking about it, I figured now was the time to ask Lucy about the contract. "Remember earlier when we were talking about the demon contract?"

"Uh-huh."

"What did you mean when you said the contract didn't

matter?" It was the most important thing I needed to know.

"It doesn't."

"How?" Tabby asked.

"The outcome will be the same." She was talking in that weird way that was older than she was again.

"What do you mean, Lucy?" I gripped the steering wheel hard.

She started humming. I gave up. That was all I was getting out of her today. She'd answered my question, but not as much as I'd wanted. At least we had options. The mark idea Tabby came up with. If he had one, and if he let us take a picture of it, maybe we could research the symbols.

My mark had been easy. It was the names of the archangels in their original listed languages. I'd looked up the Aramaic one, Selaphiel. The rest were in Hebrew. I wondered what was so special about old Selly, not that I'd had time to research it ever since we'd come to Arizona.

If we could catch a lucky break, maybe I could take care of this before Asmodeus made his move. Or rather, more of a move than scaring Lucy. I knew with him, there was a hell of a lot more he could do.

The restaurant was nice. White tablecloths, candles, but Vespa had been right. There were plenty of people dressed casually. I let Tabby take the lead. It wasn't like we could come out and ask him if he had any weird symbols or anything and she was a hell of a lot more subtle than me. I would have just tackled him at the house, stripped him, and inspected his body for a mark.

After we ordered, Tabby took a sip of water.

"Mr. Vespa. Are there any tattoo parlors around?" she asked.

Wait. She wasn't doing what she'd talked about with me. I

fought myself not to say anything. It was better if I didn't mess it all up.

He blushed. "Oh, I'm…I'm sure there are, but I've never been to one."

Hmm. Satan boy didn't like tattoos. That wasn't normal. Most of these people who were obsessed with demons covered themselves in them. Not that all people with tattoos were demonics, but the demon-obsessed tended to have head-to-toe tattoos. And here, Vespa seemed squeamish of them. Go figure.

"Maybe we can check. I was thinking about getting another one," Tabby said.

"Added to your phoenix or what?" Maybe she figured it was better not to lie if she didn't have to. Probably smart.

"No. Maybe something to match your mark."

I almost choked. I was going to have to warn her to stick to the script next time. Damn.

"What mark?" Vespa asked.

I guessed it was my time to show off. "When I got involved in all this, I was granted with a mark." I unbuttoned the sleeve of my shirt and showed him my wrist.

His brows rose clear to his hairline. "Wow. That's really cool."

"Thanks," I replied. Tabby and I kept waiting for him to say something, anything, but he remained quiet.

It figured. Every time we thought we'd finally had a leg to stand on, it would be jerked out from under us. Maybe Lucy was right and we should just get on with it.

Yet, before I did something rash, I'd rather talk to Doc first. If he didn't show by bedtime, I was going to figure out how to contact him and find out what the hell was keeping him from coming when I called.

#

I didn't have to worry about it too long. On the drive back

to the house, Lucy suddenly piped up.

"Doc says not to worry. He's working on something."

I blinked. Okay, good to know. "Tell him to keep the big guy away from the car."

She giggled and went back to doing whatever it was she was up to in the backseat. I couldn't exactly stop driving and look around, but she seemed happy enough.

I stole a glance at Tabby. She seemed tired. If I could, I'd let her sleep for a couple of days.

"Are you okay?" I asked.

"Not really. I thought we had it, ya know?"

She wasn't the only one disappointed. It did suck. We needed a break. "Yeah. It sucks, but what can you do?"

"He's really starting to creep me out," she said.

"Does that mean we should say screw it and start the exorcism?" I was tired. She was tired.

"No, that would be stupid."

I sighed. "I was planning on talking to Doc before I made a move."

"That's the smartest thing you've said all day."

I didn't know if I should be insulted or happy about that. I chuckled. "Thanks."

#

When we got back to the house, Tabby and I headed upstairs to change out of our good clothes. Vespa would have to deal with us not dressing every day for dinner. I knew I hadn't packed many dress clothes. It hadn't been necessary. No one wore a suit to an exorcism, except a priest, and I wasn't one anymore.

"You're too quiet," Tabby said.

"Too many places here I can't talk."

Tabby shrugged. "I'm pretty sure he knows what we've been talking about anyway. Lucy always did, even when we were in the library."

"Shit. I'd forgotten about that. It had been Asmodeus' arrogance that kept him from taking our plans seriously."

"I wish we knew what Vespa's demon was capable of."

She wasn't the only one. This thing was such a fiasco. "We know Old Ugly is involved somehow. He wouldn't be screwing with Lucy otherwise."

"I don't like that. I don't like it at all." She pulled a t-shirt over her head.

"It could be worse. At least the demon isn't coming on to you." I could just imagine this scaly thing trying to go all hubba-hubba. It was funny until my head went to what a demon's... thing looked like. I needed brain bleach again.

She rolled her eyes. "I'm not so sure about that."

"Oh, I am." Tabby had only seen a little how Lucy had been manipulated by the demon. It had been ugly. I remembered it trying to seduce me. Uggh.

Isaac mewed from the bed. I glanced at him.

"You tell her," I said.

Tabby chuckled. "You've really taken to talking to my cat."

I smiled and pulled her into a hug. "He's smart. I'm not stupid enough to ignore him."

"No wonder he likes you." She punched me on the arm. "You going to check the iPad?"

"Nah. I'll wait until we go to bed. Let's go back to playing 'let's go entertain you' with ol' Nick. Maybe he'll slip and tell us something."

#

When we got downstairs, Vespa was pouring wine into glasses. What was the special occasion?

"I thought we'd have a drink," he said.

I hoped he hadn't done anything to the glasses. I didn't want to be poisoned or anything. He hadn't yet, but I wouldn't put it past him. Not with the way that demon in him snuck around.

"Do you ever relax?" I asked.

He handed Tabby her glass and motioned for her to sit down on the sofa. Now I understood. This was another ploy to impress Tabby.

"No, not really. My family was all about appearances."

I took my glass when he offered it. At this point, a little drink would do me some good. "Since you're planning on changing your life anyway, why not start now?"

He froze. I couldn't believe he hadn't thought of this before. Kid didn't need out on his own; he needed therapy. In that, I did feel for the kid. His family wanted him to fail.

"Jimmy has a point. Why not just give it all up?" Tabby asked.

Nick sat on the other couch opposite Tabby. "You think so?"

I plopped down beside my girl. Not that she wouldn't normally hit me if I called her that, but I had a feeling that, around Nick, she wouldn't mind. He needed to get the message. Tabby was not up for grabs.

"It would be kind of silly to keep up the charade, right? You aren't eighty for Christ's sake," I said.

He winced. I wasn't sure if it was the curse or if it was my mentioning Christ. He acted like an old church lady who secretly read smut while trying to make people believe she was better than God.

"That will be so freeing," he said.

"I doubt if your 'companion' would care how you carried yourself." I smirked. It was true. I didn't think the demon would even know if a leisure suit was out of style. There was no reason Nick couldn't run around in a t-shirt and jeans.

Tabby snickered.

He needed to learn who he was, not imitate his family member. I had a feeling he'd been doing it so long he'd have trouble telling what was him and what was the persona. But he was a twenty-year-old kid. He needed to start acting like one.

He took a big gulp of his wine. "I don't know what I'd do without you guys."

I did. He'd contact other creepy shit to get revenge on his family who screwed up his life. I guess I should feel good that he thought about contacting me. I just wondered what he'd done to get O'Malley to contact him in a dream. Since it wasn't something that I directly needed to know, I didn't bother asking, but it was a good question.

"It's okay," Tabby said. "Just to try to remember you aren't him."

He swallowed loudly. "Too bad I don't know who I am."

Now that, I knew, he said for Tabby's benefit. A slight change in the tone of his voice gave him away. He was playing the sympathy card.

Tabby didn't bite, though, and said nothing. It was probably better that way. Saying nothing meant she wasn't encouraging him or hurting his feelings.

"Why is Asmodeus here?" I blurted out. Tabby froze. It was too late now. My big mouth had gotten me in trouble again. We could work it to our advantage.

His whole demeanor shifted. I knew I was speaking to the demon now. "You have something that belongs to him."

Says who? Not me. "That is under review."

The demon hissed at me. "I'll see you sleep like the dead, marker."

I fought to roll my eyes. He hadn't done anything to me yet. If he'd been able to, I would have at least been slapped, but there was just old Big Mouth over here. "What is he, your boss?"

The demon chuckled. "He is a prince of Hell. In that respect, yes, he could be my 'boss' as you say."

I nodded. That made more sense. He was some lesser demon trying to gain brownie points. "Tell your 'boss' that he'd better speak to his boss about the legalities of this. Somehow, I don't think he'd like an angel invading Hell to poke around."

It grinned. "Earth is not Heaven."

He thought he was so smart. Too bad; I was smarter. "But my marking of the soul makes the soul marked by God. You could say that your prince is trying to steal a member of Heaven."

"Semantics."

"Just so." I refused to give into him. "The rules are that God and Satan negotiate. If the soul is negotiated to go to Satan, it is up to him to decide where it goes. Not Asmodeus. Somehow, I don't think the devil will take very kindly to his ego."

The demon blinked. "You may be correct. I'll inform the light-bearer and see what he would like to do about my prince."

Yup. This demon was weak. Wouldn't even tell old Assy to get off his lawn. Had to go tattle to the big guys for it. I'd do anything to stop crap from bugging Lucy, even if it meant an interview by the devil himself.

"Sounds good," I said.

Nick slouched over. After a minute, he held his head in his hands. "I'll be glad to get rid of him."

"We'll do what we can." Tabby patted him awkwardly on the shoulder.

He gazed up at her. "Anyone ever tell you that you look like an angel?"

Oh, Jesus. I wanted to puke. Did he ever quit?

#

About nine, Tabby and I went up to bed. The kid didn't

even have a TV. Not that I'd seen, anyway. It made for some interesting conversation. Not really. I was bored out of my mind, but at least I knew that Lucy would be in the same boat in here as out in the car. I didn't feel quite as bad.

I did my evening constitutional, and then went into the bedroom.

"That was fun," Tabby said.

"About as fun as listening to a fanatic try to convert you, I guess." I plopped on the bed and took off my shoes.

"What were you playing with down there, anyway?"

"What do you mean?"

"The thing with Asmodeus." Her hands tangled through her hair. "I mean, Jesus, Jimmy. Like we don't have enough problems?"

"I'm just trying to protect Lucy." Truth was, I didn't know why I'd chosen then to ask. Maybe something else had prodded me. Something supernatural. But I didn't tell that to Tabby. She'd never believe me. Not about something like that.

"And what are you going to do if the big man himself shows up here to interview you?"

"Shit my shorts. Hell, I don't know. It's not my fault the Order expects me to do any of this without guidance." And I did have that thing where I kind of laughed in the face of danger. Maybe that made me a special kind of nuts.

She stood with her hands on her hips. "Now that was a cop-out. Before you had the Order, you lived with what you had to work with. Now it's always, 'If the Order would do this.' I'm tired of it."

I sat there silent for a minute. She had a point. I'd changed the way I saw things, and maybe that was one of my problems. I was confused as to what to do, where to turn, and before, I never worried about it.

"I need to go back to thinking they don't exist."

"Pretty much." She stared at me, and then turned away.

"Okay." I picked up the iPad and put it in my backpack. "For now, they don't exist, and they won't until we're done with all of this."

"Works for me." She left the room to freshen up before bed.

While she was gone, I refilled Isaac's food bowl. He watched me from the bed. When I was finished, he dashed over and started stuffing his face. If I were a cat, life would be so much easier.

"I'm glad somebody appreciates me."

Tabby came in a few minutes later. Her red hair glistened, wet from her shower. I loved her hair. It hung down her back in almost separate locks, it was so thick.

"Forgive me?" I asked.

"Maybe. It depends on how many demons we have to deal with by the end of all this."

"With my luck, we'll have a demon army camped out front." Leave it to me to look at the positive. I wasn't the most fortunate guy in the world. Stuff had a tendency to happen to me.

She plopped on the bed and pushed me. "Don't you even joke about that. One demon, the one in Vespa, is enough."

I agreed with her. I did. I just had a sinking suspicion. Should I have brought up all that about the hierarchy of the demons? Probably not, but it wasn't like I had much else to do. I had to stop Asmodeus from bugging Lucy somehow. I was an exorcist, a marker, not a demon slayer. And if I wanted Lucy to be safe, I had to go with what was at my disposal. Right now that meant my smartass mouth. It was probably already getting me into a lot of trouble.

Suddenly, I heard a pop.

"I hear you been looking for me," Doc said.

I almost jumped out of the bed. Thank God. "Yeah. I have."

"I'm here. Whatcha need?" he asked.

"Hell. Everything." My brain was moving faster than my mouth could. I stopped short of utter madness, got my thoughts in order, and took a deep breath. "Big demon's been terrifying Lucy. Vespa is an idiot, and I know nothing about his contract. Oh, and I might have invited the devil to come up for tea."

Doc glared at me. "What the hell you talking about, boy?"

I closed my eyes for a minute, and then told him about Asmodeus and the conversation I'd had with Vespa's demon.

"I swear. Leave you alone for a while and this is what you make of it?" He muttered to himself and paced across the room.

He glanced over at Tabby. She shrugged and the corners of her mouth were quivering, almost as if she was trying not to smile.

Traitor. I scooted from the end of the bed, making room for Doc to sit.

He took it. It wasn't like he needed to sit or anything, but hell, he was my relative and it was polite. No sense in letting the man wander around all night.

"What is it you need from me?" he asked.

"Help," Tabby answered before I could.

I added, "Some answers."

He laughed. "Maybe I can do that."

"Where were you?" Tabby asked.

"Out and around. Trying to get you people some information." He brushed some invisible dirt off his pant leg.

"And?" I prompted.

"He just doesn't quit, does he?" he asked Tabby.

"No, unfortunately," she replied.

Great. More people to team up on me. What was I, a punching bag?

"What do you want to know first?" he asked.

"The contract stuff. Lucy said something about it not mattering." That was the most important. If I knew that the contract didn't matter for sure, I could get the exorcism done and get the hell out of there.

Doc thought for a minute. "Did she say why?"

"Something about the outcome being the same anyway."

He nodded. "Near as I can tell, it's a case of where there is a contract with a demon like this, the demon can still be expelled. What will happen to the soul, however, is anyone's guess."

"So I have to mark him?" I so did not want to do that.

"Didn't say that," he chided. "The marking is only for those folks that die while you do the exorcism, right?"

"I guess. I mean, I never tried to mark someone who was alive." And there was the little matter of the training I should have had that would tell me all of this. Not that I was bitter or anything.

Doc tapped his fingers on his knee. "That would be something."

"Either way, I don't want to have Vespa with me forever. He gets on my nerves." And if he tried to get with Tabby in her sleep just because he was a spirit, I'd wrangle a soul sucker and let it eat him.

Doc shrugged. "Seems to me that it's up to you if you want to mark him."

"I don't want to."

He snorted. "Condemn the little shit to hell. He isn't exactly a pristine type."

Tabby beamed. "Doc, I like you."

He nodded to her and grinned back. "I like you too, little lady." Then he turned to me. "What else you want to know?"

It took me a minute. I probably should have made a list. "Is there anything I can do to keep Asmodeus away from Lucy?"

He adjusted himself and balanced his foot on the opposite knee. "Near as I can tell, you already did that. I stopped and saw Miss Lucy before I came in here. Kid was right as rain."

"Really?" Finally, something I did right. It would be forgotten when I screwed up again, but at least I'd helped Lucy.

"Yup," Doc said.

So the demon talk worked, but at what cost? It wasn't like any of them could be trusted, and I trusted Vespa's demon least of all. He was a sneaky bastard. And the big guy—who knew what he would do? "What if Satan decides to come investigate?"

"You'd better hope that doesn't happen." Doc wagged a finger at me. "I have no advice for that."

Of course he didn't. He was a ghost, not a paranormal specialist or anything. I was asking a lot of him. It was probably time to stop. Let him do his thing for a change instead of jumping around to my whims.

"Thanks, Doc, for all your help," I said.

"Any time. I think I'll go see what Miss Lucy's up to." He stood and nodded.

"You do that." Tabby waved.

Doc disappeared.

"I guess we gear up for the exorcism, then?" I didn't feel comfortable, but I wasn't sure if anything would make me feel better now. So much felt wrong about all of this, but I was out of ideas.

"That's what it looks like." Her eyes seemed to be assessing whether I was about to fall apart.

"I hate this part," I said.

Tabby patted me on the shoulder.

I wasn't lying. Some people might think that having

permission from God to fight demons would be cool. It wasn't. Especially when everything you did, everything you fought so hard for…and the kid still died because the demon was that evil. I needed a vacation from my problems and anything that was stressful.

Doc had given me a few things to think about though. No, I hadn't tried to mark a live person, and I never would. I remembered how it all went down at Lucy's exorcism. The power that flowed through me trying to fight the demon, and then, when she was felled, instinct took me to her. The magic only worked when Lucy died, and I'd been lucky enough that I marked her in time. It seemed a small thing that her body started breathing again after her mark took. The longer this went on, though, the more it seemed like Lucy never would go back to her real body. That pissed me off. She was a sweet kid, dammit. She didn't deserve to lose her life this young.

"Why don't you try to get some sleep?" Tabby fluffed my pillow and patted it. I lay down beside her. The warmth of her body pressed close to mine felt so good. I'd missed having her next to me.

#

Part of preparing for an exorcism was getting in the mindset to be able to do it. Everything else was secondary. You had to cut off some of the emotion, force everything that could go wrong from your mind, and try to imagine that your faith was your armor.

It wasn't like you could march into the room of the possessed person with a boomstick like the guy in those movies with Bruce Campbell. I wish it were that easy.

A lot of an exorcism wasn't even physical. You had to keep your wits about you. The demon would lie and take everything it could dig up about your life and turn it on its head. Even the good things—they got distorted too. You had to be strong enough to take having your past shoved in your face and made ugly. You had to be bull-headed enough to keep after it until it was finished, no matter what happened. And above all else, you had to somehow keep your faith in God when you were handed a shit sandwich. I guess that's what made me an exorcist.

"Are you okay?" Tabby lay on her side, watching me.

I turned toward her. Trying to sleep was pointless. I wasn't going to make it. I'd been up half the night. "I guess so."

"Moping about everything?"

I snorted. "Yeah."

"Try to get your head out of the low-lying clouds. Nobody said you had to do the exorcism today, you know?"

She was right. I had no specific time frame. That was probably a good thing. But it had to be soon. "Yeah. True."

"Besides. We have to figure out how to outfit the house. Ward that large living room so Mr. Demon can't bring in furniture to hurt us."

"Why not just make a big circle around us and Vespa chained to the floor?"

She blinked. "Or that too."

Maybe my simple brain came in handy after all. "We'll have to get rid of his circle."

I wasn't looking forward to that. With the silver implanted into the floor, it was going to require manual labor.

She leaned back against the pillows. "I forgot about that."

I knew it was going to take more than ripping up the circle. There had to be some anti-magic stuff that had to be done to it too. "How would we do that? I mean, I'm sure it's going to take a hell of a lot more than a belt sander."

She shrugged. "Really, all you need is a chisel and some holy water. We damage the circle and bless it, and it will be just a floor again."

There I went again, making things harder than they needed

to be. "I have a feeling we'll need to figure out how to do that under Vespa's nose. I can't see the demon lying aside while we destroy the circle."

"Okay. So relax. We have a list of stuff to do to prepare," she said.

I could tell I was driving her up the wall. My nervousness was translating into not being able to do anything, and since she shared the bedroom with me, if I wasn't getting any sleep, she wasn't either. The least I could do was be nice to her. I had Vespa to take my frustration out on. "I'm glad."

"I know you are."

#

We got dressed, gave Isaac some water, and went downstairs. There was no sense in putting off the inevitable. Vespa was sitting on the sofa with his head in his hands.

"Are you okay?" Tabby tapped him on the shoulder.

He glanced up with bloodshot eyes. "No. I didn't sleep."

At least I wasn't the only one, but what kept him up? "At all?"

"No. He wouldn't let me." He leaned back on the sofa. His skin had a kind of pasty look to it.

Uh-huh. I wasn't surprised. The whole thing was ramping up. I knew it. I'd known it all along. I'd just been a little too much of a chicken to admit it. If the demon was starting to mess with Vespa's health that meant he wanted another host. Tormenting Vespa would be enough to get under my skin.

"Let me guess. He's telling you to kill us," I said.

He stared at me in shock. "How did you know?"

"It's what they do." Asmodeus had threatened my life multiple times during my stay at Blackmoor. I kind of knew about this stuff.

"Oh, Jesus," he said.

I had a feeling that killing me wasn't what was keeping him

up. I was only on his radar because I could do something for him. Really, he was upset because Mr. Demon was talking about him killing Tabby. His infatuation with her might actually be helpful. If he could keep his backbone, he might even be able to help us fight the demon. But I wasn't holding my breath.

"I don't know how much longer I can do this," he said.

Whine, whine, whine! Shit. I hated to think how he'd react if he suddenly got a serious illness. I walked over and sat beside him. "Listen, you know we are coming up with a game plan. Don't think we're here doing nothing. Everything you tell us, we catalog and use to figure out what direction everything is going to take."

"Really?" His eyes were pleading with me.

"Yup. We aren't here, all this way from home, for nothing, you know?" Though, at times, I felt like that, but I wasn't about to tell him about it.

He nodded.

I had more work to do. Exorcism was going forward. Yeah, I didn't have to do it today, but the timeframe had been sped ahead. I needed to stop thinking about me and get this done. I'd pussyfooted long enough.

"You have that look," Tabby said.

"I know."

She smiled. "I like it."

Truth was, I did too.

Chapter Twelve

How You Remind Me

"WHY DON'T WE do breakfast here today?" Tabby asked. Maybe her charm would make him change his mind about the outside dining issue.

Nick frowned at her. "I don't think that's a good idea."

Oh, good God. This was ridiculous. "Okay. I'll bite. Why don't you want food cooked in the house?"

He took a deep breath. "Because ever since the demon has been in me, any food cooked in this house turns into bugs or rats."

That made sense. Why couldn't he have just come out and said it?

"Have you tried someone else cooking it?" Tabby motioned at the kitchen.

Vespa nodded. "Yeah. My sister was over here before you came. She tried. You don't even want to know what happened to that food."

I had to wonder what it was about food that the demon didn't like. It wasn't keeping Nick from eating, or it wouldn't let him eat out. And because it wanted use of Nick's body, it made sense for it to keep him healthy. At least until I came along, that was.

"Okay, let me get my purse, and we'll go get some

breakfast." Tabby sighed.

I swore, when we got home, I wasn't eating out for a month.

After she left, Nick turned to me. "I don't think I have a chance with her, do I?"

"Probably not. I mean, she and I, we're practically engaged." It was about time he asked.

"You are so lucky," he said.

"To have her, sure. But I wouldn't call myself lucky. Not with the job I have." That, and my penchant for bad luck, but who was counting?

"What's it like?" he asked. "Being an exorcist?"

I closed my eyes for a minute, trying to figure out what I was going to say. "It's hard. It's emotionally draining." I didn't want to get into specifics. Last thing I needed to do was give his demon something to use during the course of the exorcism.

"How do you do it?" Vespa leaned toward me. He was almost a little too interested.

"Perform exorcisms? Or be an exorcist?" They weren't the same thing. You could technically be an exorcist without ever having to perform an exorcism, especially if you were with the church.

"Be an exorcist," he said.

Damn. I hoped I hadn't given him a bright idea what to do with his life after I got him possession-free. He was used to faking people out by being a spiritualist. Taking on the guise of an exorcist wouldn't be far from his comfort zone. "I just do it. I'm kind of stubborn, so that helps."

Tabby came downstairs. "We ready?"

I stood up. "When you are."

#

When we got into the car, Lucy and Doc were playing a game in the back seat. It was kind of sweet, Doc finally having a kid he could call his own. I wasn't sure if he'd had kids while he was alive, but back in those days, he wasn't exactly sticking around home. He'd been out traveling the West, gambling, and participating in gunfights.

"What is the plan, boy?" Doc asked me.

I turned around in the seat a little. "We're grabbing some breakfast. Then, I have to figure out how to prepare the house for exorcism." I turned back and started the car.

Doc was quiet for a minute. "Don't forget to check the basement."

I heard a pop and looked in the rearview mirror. Doc was gone and Lucy was frowning.

"You messed up our game." She sounded so dejected.

"I'm sorry, Lucy. I'm sure he'll be back." I hadn't meant to mess up her morning, but Doc, I'm sure, had needed to do what he went off to do.

She nodded, and then started coloring in a coloring book Tabby had bought her. It was kind of strange to see a crayon move by itself, but I was used to strange by now.

"Now we have to check out a basement." Tabby tapped her fingers on the dashboard.

"Why do I have a feeling Vespa lied again?" If it hadn't been for Doc, I would have been so screwed. Another lie? I wasn't surprised. Lying seemed to be one of the things Nick did best.

"But about what?" Tabby stared out the window.

"The floor." It was all so simple. Slowly, ideas were forming in my brain.

"What floor? You aren't making any sense."

I pulled into the parking spot at the diner in Tombstone. It was weird to be coming back here, but it wasn't like I didn't miss it either. "What if the living room isn't where he does the demon stuff? I mean, wouldn't the whole house feel like the attic room at Blackmoor?"

In fact, I never felt any creepiness at all in Vespa's house. One would think the mere presence of the demon would make the whole house have a different feel, but I didn't feel a thing unless I was standing next to Nick. There had been so many lies at this point, I didn't know which end was up.

"I never thought about it, but yeah."

"Now, I don't know what that circle on the floor in the living room is for, but it sure isn't the heart of the house." I knew our time in the car was growing short. We had to get out there and deal with Nick.

"That's what Doc meant about the basement?"

I opened the car door. "Probably."

#

I'd be lying if I said I didn't want to go down to the basement right away. I needed to know the layout of the place, and get all the crap out of that room before we could start the exorcism, but that meant confronting Nick and I wasn't sure if now was the time to do it. I mean, yeah, I needed to get all of this over and done with, but I'd rather not pick a fight either.

We were on the way back to the house after breakfast, when suddenly, the car froze. Literally. Nothing moved, not the scenery, not the clock. Tabby was stuck in mid-motion of tucking her hair behind her ear. Lucy sat frozen, looking vacantly toward the back of my head. I glanced around. I didn't feel dead.

I stared outside the windshield. Vespa's car was frozen in front of me. The scenery was almost as if it were in a high-quality photograph. Even the leaves on the trees were frozen mid-sway. My stomach felt like it was being pulled in on itself. It wasn't painful, exactly. Just a strange sort of pressure.

"I understand that one of my…wards has been naughty."

I jumped and glanced in the back seat. The car heated all of a sudden. There, sitting next to Lucy, was a man. He looked to be around thirty with black hair long enough to brush his shoulders. His skin had an olive cast to it. He grinned at me. That's when I saw the fangs.

Oh, crap. I'd just landed in a whopping pile of shit. I couldn't not answer him. "If you're talking about Asmodeus, then yes."

He stayed there for a moment, not saying anything to me. Then he opened the car door and motioned for me to follow. I didn't want to, but my body did what he wanted anyway. My arm left the steering wheel and opened the door while my feet brushed the pedals and my body got out of the car on its own. I felt like a puppet.

"I have problems with that one," he said and walked over to a tree in someone's yard. He snapped off a smaller-sized branch. "Thank you for alerting me."

I nodded. This was so many levels of uncool. Getting to meet the devil was never one of my great plans in life. And there was no doubt that this was the real thing. He felt completely wrong, and yet so very polite. No wonder he was considered the great charmer.

"Now, what is it you want in return?" he asked.

I knew better than to make any requests, any agreements. If I hadn't been a stronger man, I'd have asked him to put Lucy to rights, but that was up to God, not me, and certainly, not him. "Nothing. I am just protecting my ward. I know that you and he," I said, pointing to the sky, "have a lot of negotiations to complete concerning her. Asmodeus interfering wasn't supposed to happen."

He grinned at me again. "Not all of us are quite so bad."

Oh, he was a charmer all right. The Father of Lies was a very good name for him. I had to be so careful.

"But Asmodeus is getting a bit ahead of himself. I will deal with him, permanently."

Shivers ran down my spine. Being dealt with by the devil personally was a whole other level of bad I dared not think about. Good thing I didn't have any intentions of doing something that would put me in that type of situation, but I doubt if those who were thought they would end up that way either.

Suddenly, he wrapped his hands around the little branch and fire whisked over it. Instead of a pile of ash, as I'd been expecting, there was what appeared to be a wand. Intricate swirls were charred into the wood. He handed it toward me.

"Give this to your lady friend. She may find it useful."

It was pretty almost. The charring seemed to grapevine around the wand. "No strings attached? This is not a contract of any sort?" I wanted to make sure. No way was I going to take this thing if it meant something else.

He started to laugh. It was deep and as charming as the rest of him. "No. God has his own special plans for you and your lady friend. This is a useful gift. I cannot have an outstanding debt."

Ah, because I hadn't wanted anything, he had to even up the score. Asmodeus must have had his fingers in too many cookie jars. Kind of interesting, getting a tool from the devil.

I took the wand from him. It was a lot heavier than it looked.

"I like you, Jimmy Holiday," he said. "Be careful."

He started walking away. The farther he got from me, the harder it was to see him. I got back in the car and put the wand in Tabby's lap.

Suddenly, time sped up to normal and I found myself having to step on the gas so that the car could continue moving forward.

I was scared now. Terrified, in fact. The devil telling you to be careful wasn't a good sign. It was like an explosives expert telling you that the boom was going to be a little loud.

"What's this?" Tabby asked, looking down into her lap.

"A gift." I almost choked saying it.

"Where did it come from?"

When we stopped at a red light, I closed my eyes for a minute. No way was I getting into it now. "I'll tell you back at the house."

#

Once we arrived, I told Nick I had a headache. It wasn't a lie, not exactly. The whole "meeting the devil" thing took a lot out of me. Tabby followed me upstairs. I was done worrying about what would happen once Vespa knew everything I was thinking. I mean, after all, he wasn't pulling any punches.

Upstairs, I closed and locked the door behind Tabby. The ward would keep him out.

"What is wrong with you?" Tabby asked.

I was pacing back and forth. My whole body shook. I didn't want to sit there. Part of me was afraid time would stop again. It had scared the shit out of me. For something to have that much power just wasn't right. But I knew I had to tell Tabby about it somehow.

"You know your gift?" I asked.

She tossed it on the bed like a pair of socks. "I don't know where you got that thing."

I stopped and stared. She'd just thrown that? We didn't even know what it did yet.

"That thing you just threw, it was made by the devil." I didn't need her accidentally blowing a hole through the wall or something.

She stared down her nose at me. "What?"

"Do you remember me stopping anywhere?"

She paused. "No."

"Remember me going anywhere within the last few days where I could get something like that?" I didn't have time to argue about it, but that's what we were doing.

She blinked. "What the hell, Jimmy?"

I lowered myself onto the bed. I was moving so much I was starting to make myself sick. "On the way back from the restaurant, the devil paid me a visit."

She raised her eyebrow.

"He stopped time, Tabby. You were frozen, putting your hair behind your ear. Lucy was stuck looking at the back of my head."

"If I didn't know you better, I'd say you've lost it."

"And then you'd still have a weird stick that magically appeared." Even she knew magic wands didn't appear out of nowhere.

"Where did the devil get it?"

"He made it right in front of me."

She sat beside me. Isaac meowed underneath the bed.

"See, he's hiding again. Even the cat knows." Isaac was a hell of a lot smarter than she was giving him credit for.

"Dammit, Jimmy." She grabbed a hold of my face. "Calm the fuck down!"

I stared at her. Her eyes were wild and green.

"I need you to relax, Jimmy. I can't understand you like this."

She let go of my face.

I took a few deep breaths. The fact that she was worried instead of pissed woke me up a little. "Okay. I'm all right."

"Now, run all this by me again."

I steadied myself. "The devil came to thank me for letting him know about Asmodeus."

She blinked. "What did he look like?"

"It was horrible. He was a little thinner than I am, and he

wore this expensive grey suit. His hair was black, long, and kind of curly. He was dressed like a normal businessman. That is, until he smiled." Just talking about it started my hands shaking again.

"Why?"

"He had fangs, that's why. Because I wouldn't name something in return for my help, he made you that wand. Said something about how you might be able to use it."

"Do you think you should contact the Order?"

I laughed. "Why bother? They haven't answered one email asking for help. Why would they want to come in if the devil is here?"

Wimps. Oh yeah, let the defrocked one deal with it. He likes it. I rolled my eyes.

"It was just an idea, Jimmy."

I needed to stop taking it out on her. It wasn't her fault that the Order was made up of jackasses. "The sad thing is, the devil isn't what's scaring me."

She stared at me, confused. "Okay, so what has you so freaked out?"

"He told me to be careful." I let that sink in for a bit.

She whistled. "Okay. Asmodeus had soul-suckers and all types of things come after us, right?"

"Yeah." I had no idea where she was going with this.

"We survived that without knowing what we were doing."

I nodded. "Yeah, so?"

"If we made it through that okay, I don't see why this would be any different." She shrugged.

"But the devil said—"

"Did you ever think he meant to watch our backs? Besides, when did you start listening to the other side?"

She was right.

"Okay. Let's go back downstairs." I steadied my hands.

"Old Nick and I are going to have a little talk."

#

I stormed downstairs. Vespa was nowhere to be found. That figured. Tabby ran down the steps after me.

"Don't do anything stupid, Jimmy," she said.

Hah. Stupid was what I did best. "Vespa! Come out here right now!"

"Oh, Jesus. Jimmy, will you just listen to yourself?" Tabby was standing there with her hands on her hips.

"Nick, goddamn it!" I was close to throwing one of those puke sofas. That would get his attention.

The boy scrambled out of his bedroom. "What's wrong?"

"Care to tell me what the fuck this is for?" I threw back the rug that covered the circle.

"I told you, it's where I conjured—"

I grabbed him by the throat and pushed him against the wall. "Listen, you little shit. I don't have time for this. Stop the lies. What the hell is going on?"

His face turned red. No sense in getting charged with murder. I let him go. He backed away from me and rubbed his neck. He actually seemed scared of me for once. Good.

He cleared his throat a few times. "This is my circle. For protection."

Uh-huh. Thanks. A lot. "Now, was that so hard? So where did you do the dirty work?"

"In the basement."

I glanced at Tabby, and then back at Vespa. He hadn't moved. I was seriously thinking about letting Doc shoot him after all of this was through.

"Well?" I motioned with my hand for him to take us to his basement.

He led us down the hallway just off the kitchen. It wasn't even noticeable from the living room. It was narrow with a wooden floor and mulberry-colored walls. We passed by his bedroom as we continued down the hall. The door to it was open and it was a mess, like a normal teenager's room. I even spied a game system. So he had a TV after all.

Tabby held my hand, I think partly because she was tired of Vespa lusting after her and partly because she was uneasy. She might have been trying to distract me enough to keep me calm. The closer we got to the door, the more a steady cold hit me. Strange for Arizona.

At the end of the hallway stood a door with an arch. No other door in the house arched like that. Vespa opened it.

"Be careful of the steps." He motioned forward.

He was right. It was almost like the place had been put together haphazardly. Somehow, the ceiling and the walls were covered in pieces of stone, almost like what you'd see in a castle, but I could spot faint cracks in the mortar. So they were basically tiles then. I had a sinking suspicion that the basement was not originally part of the house, and that Vespa had pieced this whole thing together. We'd be lucky if the ceiling didn't fall on us.

The same tile covered the steps too. I didn't even want to think about how much money he wasted doing all of this. He flipped a switch on the stairway and fake candelabras came to life with fake dancing flames. I could almost imagine the sale at the Halloween store he bought them from.

"Can you believe this shit?" Tabby whispered.

I shook my head. Vespa was showing how very young he was. A Goth would have hired a designer and some professionals, or had someone teach him how to do it properly. They would consider this a disgrace.

Finally, after a curve in the steps, we came to a large octagonal room. More of the candelabras lined the walls. Inset into the floor appeared another circle. This one was made of silver and had different markings from the first one upstairs. A five-pointed star with what was probably the head of Baphomet in the center rested inside the circle. Baphomet's eyes had red jewels. Peachy.

I forced myself not to ponder what the expense was if they were real. I had a sinking suspicion that they were. It made me sick.

"Pretty cool, huh?" Vespa asked.

I raised an eyebrow. "I think you need to reassess your views on things. A room to perform black magic isn't cool. It's dangerous."

The room felt mildly creepy, but nothing compared to the attic room at Blackmoor. Vespa was playing. Mr. Black had been adept.

"It took a lot of work," he said.

"Oh, I don't doubt that." A lot of work for an amateur so-called creepy design.

The edges of the room had a few bookcases. All filled with magic books. Some I could tell he'd bought at the local bookstore. Others were so old they were probably moments from falling apart. Those probably belonged to Nick's great-grandfather.

"How long do you think it will take you to get all of the stuff out of here?"

Vespa stared at me, puzzled. What do you mean?"

I let go of Tabby's hand and started pointing at things. "All of this. How long will it take you to make this a bare room?"

"I don't know." He shrugged. "I just don't understand why."

I stared him, dead in the eyes. "Because this is where we'll do your exorcism."

#

All in all, it took about an hour to haul all of the crap out of there. We put it in a storage room off the garage. I was happy for that extra storage room. I sure as hell would have minded all the crap going into an extra bedroom near the room Tabby and I had been using. Call me crazy, but I didn't want to be near anything a demon had used if I could help it. Stuff like that had an air about it, a sickness.

Half-way through, Vespa froze. His eyes glowed green again. "If you think this will help you, then by all means, carry on."

It was hard to tell if it was a bluff or if the demon was telling the truth. But the subtle tone in his voice led me to believe he was trying to psych me out. Bring it on, Bucky.

"I'm sorry, but I don't feel like being clobbered on the head with a knickknack," I said.

He laughed. "You are a funny one, priest."

I shrugged. "Too bad I'm not funny enough to be a comedian."

Vespa's demon stared at me oddly. "What does a comedian have to do with all of this?"

I blinked. At least my bullshit was distracting him. "You said I was funny."

"Yes."

"So?"

Suddenly, the demon went back to wherever it was when it wasn't in power of Vespa.

"You are so weird," Nick said.

"Says the kid who willingly invited a demon inside his head."

He rolled his eyes. "Now what?"

"Why don't you find out where the hardware store is? We need a chain, a hasp that can be bolted to something. And I don't know where you can get them here, but we need some handcuffs." That was all I had with Lucy. Well, except the mirror. I didn't want to think about the mirror.

He stared at me for a minute. "Do I want to know why?"

I shook my head. "Not yet. We'll hold down the fort while you're gone."

He frowned, and then went upstairs. Tabby and I didn't move until we heard the sound of him starting his car.

"Okay. We need a chisel and a hammer." I motioned toward the floor.

"Garage?" Tabby asked.

"Probably." We ran upstairs and rummaged around for tools. We found the tool chest easily enough. It was a big red case in the garage. Bad part was, it was locked.

"Shit. What do we do now?" I banged on the top.

"Silver's a soft metal, right?"

"Yeah…"

She ogled me like I'd tried to stand on one leg while doing the macarena. "Okay, get a butter knife from the kitchen," I said.

She exhaled and then left the garage. I grabbed a small piece of a two-by-four. If I didn't break my fingers, this was going to work out nicely.

I headed down to the basement. Not long after I got down there, Tabby joined me.

"All right, Mr. Fixit. What's the plan?" she asked.

"All we need to do is break the circle, right?"

"Theoretically."

"Okay." I sat on the floor in the area that seemed the thinnest. It was going to take a bit. The outer edge of the circle was over an inch wide. But since this was all I had to work with, it was going to have to do.

"Put the butter knife here." I pointed to the center of the line of the circle.

Tabby got on the floor and held it.

I raised the piece of wood I was using as a hammer and took a deep breath. "I'm going to try to be careful, but if I hurt you, I'm sorry."

"Just get on with it. We don't know how long he'll be gone." She wiggled a little to get a better balancing point on her knees.

I positioned the two-by-four over the end of the butter knife, aimed, and then I slammed the wood down on the end of the butter knife. The sound was in between a clang and a screech. Enough to give you a headache.

"Did it work?" I asked.

Tabby started laughing. "It's fake! All he did was use glue over the design and hold a piece of paper with a very thin layer of silver over it."

I couldn't believe our luck. Finally, something went our way. I probably should have known better than to think he actually had bought silver and paid to have someone make the bands to fit into the floor.

She began scratching the floor with the knife. Soon, there was a space about an inch wide that no longer had silver. Who knew it would have been that easy?

"That works. I'm glad we didn't have to pound our way through like I thought we would." With a butter knife, that would have taken hours.

She wiped the floor with her hand. The stone was a little scratched, but the circle was clearly broken.

"Put that wood away. I'll put the butter knife in the sink," Tabby said.

We both went upstairs. I went to the garage and put the two-by-four back where I found it. I wasn't stupid enough to think he wouldn't notice, but if he'd been here, we'd have had to fight the demon, it would have been a big mess, and I didn't want the bother. I'd already almost killed him anyway. No need for a repeat performance.

I met Tabby back in the living room. She was sitting on the couch and had a smirk on her face.

"What did you do?" I knew that look.

"Pick up the rug."

I walked over to the edge of the rug and lifted it up. The circle here was scratched out, down to the wood. It smelled foul.

"While I approve of being extra-careful, what's that smell?" I wanted to gag.

"Isaac decided to help."

I snorted. "Where is he now?"

"Went back upstairs. I think he'll be happy when we go back home."

No doubt. I'm sure he was tired of all of this shit too. "He's not the only one."

"One question, though."

I cocked my head to the side. "What?"

"What if he messes with the chain and stuff?"

I flopped down next to her on the sofa. "Have faith. When he brings them back, I planned on storing them in our room until we need them."

"What if he messes with them before that?"

I chuckled. "What do you think we'll be doing before we go to bed tonight?"

"You sure do know how to romance a girl."

I grinned. "You know it."

#

It took Vespa over two hours to get back. No joke. He came in through the front door, his face red and eyes exhausted. He lumbered over and set the bags down next to my feet. "You wouldn't believe how hard it is to find handcuffs if you aren't a cop."

I snorted. "Where did you have to go? Timbuktu?"

He threw himself on the opposite sofa. "Tucson. But man, you wouldn't believe the weird looks I kept getting."

Tabby giggled. "It could be worse. They could have been pink fur-lined."

He froze. "No way."

"Yes, way. So be thankful you were able to find some normal ones." She crossed her legs.

"People are weird."

"I couldn't agree more," Tabby replied.

"Out here, most folks are pretty normal." Vespa rubbed his eyes with his hands.

"Present company excluded, of course," I said. In no universe was he normal, I didn't care what bullshit he was trying to pull.

"I don't know about you, but I'm hungry," Vespa said. I swore, if I didn't know better, I would have thought he was pregnant. That's all he ever wanted to do was eat.

"Want to go get something to eat?" I asked.

"Hell, yes."

We ended up at the Mexican restaurant. I didn't care what we ate at this point. It was all starting to taste the same. Every place used some sort of southwestern rub. At first, it had been kind of nice. Now I just wanted a plain old hamburger with American cheese.

Vespa ordered enough to kill a horse. Enchiladas, burritos, a quesadilla. It was nuts.

"It's almost as if you're eating for two," Tabby said. Yup, she nailed it.

"Nope. I've always eaten like this. Used to drive Mom nuts."

I couldn't imagine being a parent to him. I guess the whole demon business clouded my perception of him, but he wasn't a good kid. I kind of felt sorry for him because his family was partly to blame, but damn. He was a baby in a man's body.

As soon as the food hit the table, he started shoveling it in. It was like watching an anteater go after a nest.

"When are we going to do this?" he asked between bites.

I leaned in closer. "What? The exorcism?"

"Yeah," he wiped his face with a napkin, "I mean, we cleaned out the room."

I relaxed in the chair. "Keep in mind it might take more than one session."

"Yeah. I know."

I took a deep breath. "We could get started as soon as we finish fixing up the room."

"How do you do that?"

"What do you think the chain and handcuffs are for?" It was getting tiresome to having to keep explaining myself. Was he that dense?

"Oh, shit." He sat back in his chair. "Are you going to keep me chained up the whole time?"

"Depends on how the demon reacts. I don't want to die," Tabby said.

Vespa nodded. It figured. To keep Tabby safe he was okay with it.

"Can I at least have a blanket?" he asked.

I almost laughed. "Of course."

"It's not us that's trying to kill you," Tabby reminded him.

What type of people did he think we were? I mean, yeah, being chained to a floor was going to suck, but it wasn't like we were doing it to be mean or anything. In the back of my head, I remembered the warning from the big guy. But that lead to a very important question: why was the devil being nice to me? I wasn't dumb enough to think that he wasn't such a bad guy. Besides, if he wasn't so bad, then why would he have demons like Asmodeus in his employ? He wanted something.

I shook those thoughts out of my head. It was best to deal with the problems I already had.

Chapter Thirteen

Coming Undone

EXORCISM. WITH A willing participant. New ground for me. "Willing" was subjective. It depended on what side I was talking to. But I had to wonder exactly how much he wanted to get rid of the demon. He seemed a little too easygoing with all of it. There had to be something I was missing.

Tabby and I went over every inch of the chain and handcuffs, looking for marks or anything that could have weakened them, but we found nothing. I'd expected something else, but what, I wasn't sure. Things were going too smoothly and I could tell that I was about to get smacked in the face with a giant clod of horse shit. It was coming. I just didn't know when.

I walked downstairs. It was time for another hardware store trip. "Nick!"

"Just a minute!" It sounded like he was in his bedroom.

I stood next to one of the sofas. Tabby was upstairs, making my holy water and trying to help me come up with a new rite of exorcism. We didn't have the one we'd used for Lucy. I'd never thought to pick it up from the attic. I never thought I'd need it again either.

Vespa came out of the kitchen. He was wearing an old t-shirt and a pair of jeans. Honestly, it was good to see him dress his age. I had to do a double-take to realize it was him.

"I forgot a couple of things we need from the hardware store," I said.

"Like what?"

A new brain for you, a piece of chocolate, and my own bed at home. Heh. "Regular bulbs for the lights in the basement. Concentrating will be hard enough without the flicker."

He stood there for a moment, almost frozen. "All right. Let me find my keys."

That was simple enough. Periodically, I could hear water running upstairs. Yep, Tabby had gotten to work. Me, I was waiting on Vespa.

Finally, he came back. "You riding with me?"

I shrugged. It didn't make a difference anymore. Not really. "Sure. Besides, I don't want to leave Tabby without transportation." That was true too.

He led me out the door and into his SUV. The floor had candy wrappers and other trash, but at least it didn't smell.

"Sorry about the mess. I haven't cleaned it out since my last trip."

I didn't ask where he'd gone. It didn't seem important. Being a spiritualist must pay okay. At least if you were one possessed by a demon, not that I was counting. But a fancy SUV covered in candy wrappers? That was a whole other type of brat. One that had been handed everything his entire life. That bothered me. "Do you keep in contact with your family?"

He glared at me from the corner of his eyes as he backed out of the driveway. "For now. I don't like them poking around in my business."

"Ah." There wasn't much else for me to say. It was a good thing we wouldn't have to worry about his family interrupting the exorcism, but something felt off. I couldn't put my finger on what, though.

We got to the hardware store in about five minutes. It was a local place. That was one thing I liked about this part of Arizona—there were plenty of non-megastores. I hadn't even come across a chain restaurant yet. It was a nice change from back home where most local businesses had been run out by big companies. Tombstone would be a good place to live if it weren't for the demon stuff.

Vespa pulled into a spot. "You don't even have to come in if you don't want to."

I knew there wasn't going to be anything to see. "You don't care?"

He shook his head. "Just bulbs for the lights downstairs, right?"

"Yeah."

He closed the car door. The bad feeling intensified and I felt myself starting to sweat. Seemed like, when we got back to the house, it would be time to fix up the basement. But I wanted a night's sleep before I did this. The lack of sleep had been doing its thing all day. Hopefully, Tabby had time to douse both circles with holy water. It was better to be extra sure that none of the bag magic remained when I tried to do this thing.

Soon, Vespa came back to the car with a bag. He opened the door, handed it to me, and got in. I put it on the floor next to my feet.

"Want to grab some pizza?" he asked.

I blinked. We'd eaten a little over an hour ago, but whatever. Gluttony was the least of the sins I needed to worry about. "Okay."

It was almost like the demon inside him amped up his metabolism. The kid was skinny, but he ate so much. It wasn't normal. There was also the possibility that the kid had something medically wrong with him, like a thyroid disorder.

"I think I'd like to begin tomorrow," I told him.

He paused for a minute, and then glanced at me. "Yeah. I think it's about time."

He backed out of the parking place, drove a little ways down the mini-mall and then pulled into a parking spot at the pizza place. "This is my last night of freedom?"

He acted like he was going to be hanged tomorrow. Jesus. "No, don't think of it like that. Just because there have been some exorcisms that have taken years, that doesn't mean yours will."

His cat-like eyes seemed sad to me. The whole effect was kind of spoiled by those vertical slits. He was like an abused animal, wild and broken.

"I'll be back," he said and hopped out of the car.

Shit. I hadn't meant for it all to go that way. Yeah, I'd been a prick, but he'd done stuff to piss me off too. I never said I was perfect. And now, he'd taken it all to an extreme I hadn't meant. I knew this wasn't a happy thing, but hell. This kid had no idea that his possession was nothing like how bad it could be. I still woke up some nights scared to death because of Lucy. He had no idea.

When he came back, he put two pies in the backseat. "Pepperoni okay?"

"Yeah," I said. "Fine by me." I'm sure Tabby wouldn't mind the garlic either. I stayed quiet the rest of the way back to the house. There was nothing else left for me to say.

Unfortunately, the house was not quiet when we got there. A strange car was parked haphazardly in the driveway and a group of people were screaming at the front door. The door was closed. I sat up in the seat.

Before I knew what was happening, Vespa had slammed the car in park and jumped out of the SUV. "What the hell?"

He was stalking toward the crowd at the door. I got out and followed him over to them. Something told me he was going to need backup.

"Oh, thank God. I thought that bitch had stolen your house," the woman in front said.

She was a large lady, about a foot shorter than Vespa. She was at least sixty years old and wore a black caftan with a mosaic border on the edge. She was hideous.

"Don't talk that way about her," Vespa said, his eyes starting to glow faintly.

"Baby, you know how I've always told you that women are bad for you."

Something told me that this was the type of woman that created Ed Gein. Fuck.

"Mom. Look at who is next to me." He pointed at me.

Thanks for putting me on the spot, kid. Nothing like being the target of a behemoth.

"This is my friend, Jimmy," Vespa said. "Tabby is his fiancée."

The lady put her hands on her massive hips. Two other women stood behind her, but they were bowing their heads too. Both had short-cropped grey hair. They were as skinny as Vespa's mom was fat. What the hell were they? Acolytes?

"That *whore* isn't yours?" Vespa's mom asked.

I couldn't keep my mouth shut. I didn't care if she was Vespa's mom or not, Tabby was mine, and she wasn't a whore. I cleared my throat.

She turned her hatred to me. "What are you going to do about it?"

Apparently, no one had ever just smacked the shit out of her. I didn't hit women, and I never would, but she needed someone to take her down a peg or two. I couldn't keep myself from taking up for Tabby. I stepped closer. "Be careful what you say about certain people. Unlike your son, I'm not afraid of you."

"Are you threatening me?" She pumped her head back and forth at me, almost like she was trying to mimic a snake.

I almost laughed. "No. I'm stating facts. Right now, you are out here in the yard for God and everyone to see screaming about whores. One, my fiancée is not a whore, and I think you owe her an apology. Two, you've messed your son up so badly he's going to need years of counseling. Something tells me you should be thinking more about keeping a low profile than screaming in the street."

She slapped me across the face.

I hadn't expected that. I guessed her white trash colors decided to stand out. I stood fixed even though she'd just slapped the piss out of me. If I retaliated that would make me just as bad. And if she knew what was good for her, she'd quit before I let Tabby loose on her. That reminded me—where was Tabby? I took a deep breath and glared at the peons. "I suggest you get your friend and get her the fuck out of here," I told the two women behind Vespa's mom. "Unlike Jesus, I do not turn the other cheek."

I guess I was a scary man when I was pissed off because the two women grabbed her and put her in their car. Score one for the exorcist. Zero for the battle axe.

After they drove off, Vespa turned to me. "That was so awesome."

I snorted. "I can see why you want to get away from here."

He walked over to the SUV and pulled it into the driveway behind my rental car. "Want to help get some of this?"

Tabby came out of the house. "What was that woman's problem?"

"Mom is a pain in the ass," Vespa said.

I snorted. "That's one way to describe her."

Tabby stood on the front porch while I walked back to Vespa's car. I opened the door and grabbed the bag-o-bulbs while Vespa got the pizzas.

"It's a good thing she got out of here," I said as I closed the car door.

"Dude, your hair was standing on end."

"Your face is red," Tabby said. She reached forward and touched it. It burned a little.

"Bitch slapped me." I wasn't trying to get sympathy or anything, but Vespa's mom had a hell of an arm.

We sat at the dining room table. It was this huge oblong thing that seated ten people with no problem. The pizzas were spread out in the middle of the table. We all had plates.

"Remind me to put something on it later," she said.

I nodded.

Vespa came in from the kitchen and handed us all a soda. "I'm really sorry about Mom."

I shrugged. This was the one thing that definitely wasn't his fault. "You can't help who your family is. Don't worry about it."

"What did she say to you?" he asked Tabby.

I had a feeling that if I didn't manage to get the demon out, Mrs. Vespa was going to end up one dead lady.

Tabby opened her soda and took a sip. "I finished getting stuff ready upstairs, so I came down here to wait."

I nodded.

"So," she said. "Suddenly the doorbell rang. I got up, went to the door, made sure the security thing was latched, and opened the door."

"What did Mom do?" Nick tapped his fingers against his soda can creating a tattoo.

"I asked her if I could help her, you know? And she wanted to know where you were. I told her you'd gone to the store, but then she tried to force her way into the house. I managed to get the door shut and the dead bolt on."

"Jesus," I said.

"She screamed for at least ten minutes. I kid you not."

The woman was lucky that Tabby had a long fuse. I'd seen her pissed before, way beyond how mad she'd been with me recently, and it wasn't pretty.

"Just for that, you get the first slice of pizza." Vespa grabbed her plate and loaded her with a hell of a slice. It was almost three slices worth.

"Thanks." She picked it up and took a huge bite out of it.

"Think she'll come back?" I asked. Here I'd been worried about the lighting being a distraction. The battle axe from hell was a whole other dimension.

"If she does, I'll kill her," he said.

Maybe the demon was affecting him more than I realized.

#

After pizza, Nick and I went downstairs. We needed to finish getting the room ready, and I wanted him to get used to the changes we'd made. He froze.

"What did you do?" His eyes began to glow.

"Calm down." I didn't need Mr. Demon right now; I needed Nick. "We had to break the circle. We couldn't risk anything else coming through."

His eyes started glowing full bore. Dammit. Nick was gone again.

The demon cackled. "I don't need the circle to bring more of my kind in. All I need is a little blood."

I stared down the demon. No way was I letting that happen. "It's not time for you yet. Let Nick back. Your show is tomorrow."

The demon laughed again. "I love a good exorcism in the morning."

I rolled my eyes. Either the demon was that cocky or that stupid. I hadn't decided which yet. Nick's eyes went back to normal.

"You aren't going to be doing this anymore anyway, right?" I asked him.

He exhaled slowly for a minute. "I guess not."

"Okay then." His hesitation made me uneasy. What was the point of me exorcising him if he planned to continue messing with demons? Hell if I knew. No sense in worrying about it now. "This will keep us safer. Get a drill and some screws so we can attach the hasp to the floor."

He darted upstairs. I meticulously went around the room changing out light bulbs. There had to be over a hundred. I was starting to think I should have dealt with the flicker. It would have been a lot easier, velvet Elvis setting or not.

"What do you want me to do?" Nick asked when he came back.

"Line up your drill bit with the hold on the installation plate of the hasp. Then pre-drill the holes." He was the one who'd insisted on installing that tile, so let him do the work.

Four zzzt's later and he switched to the drill. He went ahead and screwed the hasp to the floor. It had taken him like five minutes and he was done. I was still changing out light bulbs. It wasn't fair. I had no one to blame but myself; I'd give him the job.

"You guys okay down there?" Tabby yelled from upstairs.

"Yeah. Almost done," I said.

We were waiting until tomorrow for the handcuffs and the chain. I was worried about sabotage. It would be easy enough to check on the hasp in the morning before we began. And I could bless the chain and the handcuffs with holy water if I wanted.

"Want some help?" Nick asked

"Sure." I handed over the bag. The sooner I could get this done, the better off I'd be. I was done with it for the night.

Finally, we made it back upstairs. Isaac was sitting on

Tabby's legs, purring. I guess now that we were going through with the exorcism, he felt it was safe enough to grace us with his presence. She was on one of the sofas. I sat next to her.

"Get it all ready?" she asked.

"As ready as we can." What wasn't ready was my brain, but that was my problem.

Vespa lounged on the opposite sofa. "I don't know if I want to do this."

Why was I not surprised? Just as we got everything ready and busted our asses, he was having second thoughts. I wasn't going to tell him one way or the other, but I was going to speak my mind. I didn't go through this whole experience for nothing. "Listen, I understand you're scared and you have every right to be. But are you going to be able to live like this the rest of your life?"

He stared at the floor. "I don't want to die."

I wanted to tell him he should have thought of that before he dragged us all the way to Arizona, but I didn't. Not wanting to die and not wanting to be possessed were two different things. "I don't think anyone does. Not really. If you decide you don't want to do this, I'll understand. But think about it before you make any decisions."

He got up and went into his room. I turned to Tabby. She shrugged.

"Guess we should go to bed," I said.

"Guess so."

#

"Is it the demon?" Tabby asked once we were safely in the bedroom. Isaac jumped out of her arms and buried himself between the pillows.

I couldn't blame the cat. "I don't know. This demon isn't like Asmodeus at all. He's quiet almost. I don't know if that's good or bad. If it wasn't for the paranormal shit we've seen, I would almost say he isn't possessed at all."

Tabby nodded. "I did get both circles blessed with holy water. And if he isn't possessed, I guess we have nothing to worry about."

I took a deep breath. That didn't sound very simple either. "And the rite?"

"I jotted down what I could from memory. I figured we could work on it."

"Sounds good." There wasn't anything else to do.

Isaac mowed from the bed. I guess he agreed too.

Later, I tried, but a good sleep was something I didn't get. As far as I knew, we had the rite as good as we could get it. We'd gone over it for a couple of hours, but I couldn't see anything that we could add that would make it better. Hell, when we'd written the one I used with Lucy, it hadn't been this much work. Part of it was that we were willing to try anything. And we'd been out of options.

This was different. Something about the whole mess left me with a bad feeling and it wasn't just the devil's warning. It could have been the lies, but I had a feeling it was that I couldn't get a handle on Vespa. One minute, he was this goofy kid, and the next, he was this weird demon. I wasn't used to dealing with a living flip-coin. I'm not sure anyone could get used to that.

I watched the sun rise. Was it smart to start an exorcism on no sleep? Probably not, but Vespa was counting on me. That was if he decided to go through with it. If he changed his mind, I'd go back to bed, get some sleep, and then book my and Tabby's flight home. I'll admit that I was kind of hoping for that option.

"Jimmy?" Tabby asked.

I glanced over at her. "Yeah?"

She picked up her cell phone off the night stand and squinted at the screen. "What are you doing up?"

I shrugged. "I never went to sleep."

She sat up in bed. "Then we'd better hope today goes smoothly."

"I think that's something we better not count on. I swear, if Nick's mother comes back, I might not be able to control myself."

"You?" She uncovered her legs. "I'm going to get my shower."

"You do that." I rubbed my neck.

Almost as soon as she left the room, Doc popped in.

"Stuff startin', huh?" he asked.

I shrugged. You could put it that way. "Vespa didn't want to go through with it last night."

Doc stroked his goatee for a minute. "I'm bettin' that today will be different."

I nodded. "We'll see. How's Lucy?"

His face broke into a smile. "She's okay. Tired of being in that car."

It was so cute. He'd become the doting grandfather. "I bet. Hell, I'm tired of being here, period."

He laughed. "Sooner you get this done, the better."

He didn't have to tell me that. "Yeah, I know. Nick's getting worse."

Doc grunted.

"What?"

He waved me off. "Let me know if you need me. I'm going to go back to Miss Lucy."

And then he disappeared.

One of these days I was going to make him stick around when all hell broke loose. "I need an easier job."

#

After I cleaned up, I got dressed in a nice shirt and some pants, dug out my purple stole, and put the bottle of holy water

Tabby had prepared in my pocket. It was my uniform. Tabby grabbed the bag with the chain, the handcuffs, and a few pieces of ribbon.

"Want to make your confession now?" she asked.

"Probably. If Vespa has decided to go forward with the exorcism, I want to start right away." I took a moment to bring all the things I'd done recently to the front of my mind. Then, I nodded at her.

"Okay. What would you like to confess?" She stood in front of me with one of her hips cocked out to the side.

I sat on the bed. "I don't like Vespa. I hope we can get this over and done with and I don't want to mark him. He's a liar and a cheat, and if it were up to me, I might let the demon have him if it wasn't for the fact that I don't want to be that type of person."

"You'll mark him if you have to?" She sat beside me.

I nodded. I knew I'd been kidding myself. If it was my lot in life to be stuck with his ass, then I'd have to deal with it. But so help me God, if he tried to hurt Lucy in any way, I'd figure out how to un-mark him. Or I could give him to the devil. That might be fun.

"Okay. I think you're ready," she said.

"Thanks for the vote of confidence." Hell, I wasn't even confident in myself. This had the makings of being a very bad day.

We got up and left the room. Isaac stayed behind in the bed, asleep. Lucky shit. Tabby wrapped her ward strings around her wrist. I relaxed a little upon seeing them. At least, Vespa wouldn't be able to go everywhere we could. It was something small, but it was something for me to hold onto.

When we got downstairs, Nick was sitting in the middle of the floor with his legs crossed.

"Everything okay?" I asked. This wasn't exactly how I

expected to find him.

He stared up at me. His eyes were bloodshot and slightly glowing. "I couldn't sleep."

"You aren't the only one," I said. "Have you made a decision?" I needed to know now.

He took a deep breath and then let it out slowly. "If I want to live, I have to get this thing out of me."

"Basement it is, then."

Nick smiled. "Can I get something to eat?"

Him and his stomach. "Exorcism, like magic, is best done on an empty stomach. We do this in shifts almost."

He frowned at me. "I won't be able to eat until it's all over?"

I chuckled. He never listened to me. "No. You won't be able to eat until we're done with the first session."

"Oh. Okay." He got up off the floor and led us down to the basement. I let Tabby go ahead of me. She nonchalantly slipped the ward string over the door knob. I was so damn lucky to have her. If need be, we could run. I hadn't even had that with Lucy.

Vespa sat in the center of the room. I grabbed the hasp and tested it. Then, Tabby handed me the chain and I looped it through the hasp. After I got the handcuffs attached, Vespa allowed me to cuff him.

"You comfortable?" I asked him.

"I guess. This is so bizarre."

I didn't bother mentioning how much weirder it was to conjure a demon, but whatever. I stepped back toward the other side of the room. I nodded to Tabby. She pulled out a piece of chalk. After she'd drawn a circle around us, she set down a small bottle of the holy water, a small packet of sand, a candle, and a feather.

"Hail to the guardians of the watchtowers," she said.

"North, South, East, and West. Hear my call. Bless this circle and keep us safe within it. Bless Nick for the trial he's about to endure. Keep your eyes open and watch out for those that wish us harm." She folded her hands in front of her and touched her nose with her middle fingers. "So mote it be."

Then, she dropped her hands.

Suddenly, I felt a zing pass through my body. I could feel power radiating off the circle. It almost had a rainbow cast coming off it. "Damn, girl."

She blushed.

I checked on Vespa. His eyes were full-on green glow now.

"Most impressive display of power," he said.

I nodded. Yeah, sure, demon. I rely on your impression. He was right, but I wasn't about to let him know that. "Yup. Tabby's special all right."

The lighting dimmed a little. It was time.

"Wretched thing from the dark, state your purpose," I intoned.

It chuckled. "I am here to help. Nicholas Vespa invited me."

Yeah, help what? Kill us all? "Vespa does not like your agreement."

The demon chortled. "So often, they think that they can use us. Make us do their bidding. Instead, we take over the host. Change it. Mold it into something better."

The only thing I'd seen a demon do with a body was destroy it. Either his view of better was different, or there was something else wrong here. "Isn't it limiting to reside in a human body?"

"At first, but once the changes begin, it is perfect."

I blinked. Okay. Time to start with the real stuff. "What is your name?"

"You didn't think it would be that easy, did you?"

I shrugged. "Can't blame me for trying."

The demon nodded. "How much longer are you going to continue this charade?"

"It will take as long as it takes. I am in no hurry." And I wasn't. I was in this for the whole thing, even if it did take years.

Suddenly, I heard what sounded like Lucy crying. I waited. As suddenly as it started, it stopped.

"You'll have to do better than that." This demon was a lightweight compared to Asmodeus. I knew Lucy was safe.

It grinned. "Oh, I plan to."

I steadied myself. Enough chit-chat. "Begone, creature of hate. Begone, creature of lies. Go back to your world."

It laughed again.

Something was wrong. It was like my words had no power. There was none of the magic that coursed through me when I'd exorcised Lucy. Either my powers had been snatched away from me, or Vespa wasn't what he was supposed to be.

I stared down at the rest of what Tabby and I had written. Shit. Vespa, for all of his meanderings, wasn't a child of God. Not really. His inviting the demon in had created a grey area. I had to change him back.

"Vespa, listen to me. Renounce it."

The demon laughed more.

"Renounce your contract. Own up to what you've done. Confess!"

I saw a ripple move through the circle and fade on Vespa. This was not good.

"Clever. Too bad; I have him right where I want him." The demon clucked his tongue.

I pulled myself together. "What is your name?"

The demon shifted and wrapped part of the chain around Vespa's neck. "Why, Nicholas, of course."

"What are you doing?" I asked. I didn't like this. At all.

He cinched the chain together. "What would you do to save his soul?"

Dammit. He had me. The demon wanted a lot more. He wanted me. "I am doing what I was sent here to do for his soul."

"Will you mark him?" it asked.

"If it comes to that, yes." I'd made my peace with the idea. If I did have to keep him, maybe I could teach him to be a better person.

It grinned. "Will you take his place?"

Before I could even say no, the air stilled. A piece of dust floated in front of my face. It did not move from its spot.

Shit. Big bad was here and I didn't know why.

Vespa, in the center of the room, was frozen. Not even a muscle twitched. Tabby and I were normal. I could only guess it was her circle of protection that kept her from being affected.

"Is this what happened before?" she asked.

"Uh-huh." I kept searching around the room, but I didn't see anything. Not yet.

Suddenly, the wall across from us undulated. The mortar around some of the tiles cracked with the ripple. The ceiling shuddered. If this didn't get over with soon, we might well die because of the faulty construction instead of the devil. But then, his being here was causing it all anyway. So that would make him responsible. At least that's where my thoughts went. I had no time for anything else.

Loud footsteps sounded, almost like a great hoofed beast was walking across a cement floor. They echoed, but nothing appeared. A few moments later the devil walked straight through the wall.

My heart started beating in time with his footsteps, as if he held my ability to live within his hands. He did not look up at first, but a smile crept at the corners of his mouth. Oh, yes. He knew exactly what he was doing.

Dressed in a long black robe embroidered with a silver edging along the hem, he was no longer the dapper businessman. While his hair was shoulder-length, red highlights seemed to dance within it like the very flames existed within him. His eyes flashed with crimson light whenever he passed the candelabras. And then there were those fangs. He didn't bother to hide them when he looked up and grinned directly at me.

His gaze snapped to Tabby. I watched, helpless, as he stepped to the edge of the circle.

"What a powerful witch," he said, each word falling sharp as icicles. "Only those who have discovered that pain can be sweet would be able to bear power such as this."

Tabby's eyes went wide and she swallowed hard. "Ah. Thank you."

He shot a grin of fangs and cocked his head to the side. Then, he glared out of the corner of his eyes at Vespa. "It is beginning to look like I need to reassert dominance over my subjects."

"What do you mean?" I asked. I felt stupid for asking. Interrupting him was a sign of disrespect and I had a good feeling that people had been disemboweled for a lot less.

His eyes made their way back to me, slow, deliberate movements that started a deep shiver in my blood. "What makes you think you have the power to ask?"

It wasn't like I thought I was anything. I mean, he was the devil. I was just me. "I'm just trying to understand. No disrespect was meant."

He cackled. My heartbeat started to skip beats in time with each section of his laugh. I sunk to my knees. He could kill me right there. Tabby's protective circle didn't matter. I was toast.

Tabby stared at me. Her body was shaking ever so slightly.

If I could see it, the devil sure as hell could. "They should be punished."

His eyes snapped to her and my heartbeat normalized. *Fuck, Tabby. Don't let him get you too.*

"Everyone has forgotten the things I am truly capable of. Dealing with two souls, that is nothing. Marker or not, none of it matters." His eyes shot upward. "It isn't like *He* can punish me further. I have found that I am very good at my role anyway." His eyes snapped back down to Tabby. "So Tabatha, did you like your gift?"

She blinked and cleared her throat. "It is very beautiful, but I don't know what it does. It isn't like any wand I've ever held."

I don't know how she found the strength to answer him, but I was impressed.

He put his hands together. His nails draped over the tips of his fingers, so long and transparent they could have been made of glass. His face took on more shadows, making him seem more beast than human. "It is a fleshing wand. Most useful."

I frowned at Tabby. I didn't like this. I didn't like this at all.

"I'll let you research it. They are very rare." He stepped farther still, the toe of his shoe touching the edge of Tabby's circle. It sizzled and smoke rose up from it. The pain had to have been great, but he didn't even twitch.

Tabby took a step backward. "Thank you."

He nodded, and then turned his attention again to me. This time, my heart wasn't attacked.

"What do you want to do with this one?" he asked, waving his hand backwards as if to dismiss the man.

I stammered. "My plan is to get him free of his possession and then go on my way."

He shook his head. With each shake, the light in the room dimmed a little more. "Tsk, tsk. Sadly, I can't allow that to happen. You see, things are not what they seem."

I'd had my doubts. I'd never done any of the tests, never saw if he spoke in tongues or could find lost objects. I'd suspected things, sure. But I never did any of the real tests. I'd been distracted. Nicholas never could be trusted. I swiped a hand through my hair, realizing the truth. "He isn't possessed, is he?"

The devil gnashed his teeth. "I knew you were smart enough to figure it out."

I leaned back in the circle. Tabby sat quietly. I felt like I'd been punched in the gut. The demon did want me, but not in the way I assumed. We were doomed. "He can't be exorcised, if he was never possessed."

"Quite correct. I will gladly take a replacement, however."

I gulped, but found a beam of iron somewhere inside me. "I-I think since we both were deceived, he should pay the price. Not us."

The devil stared at me darkly. Images filled my mind. Of me on some torture device. Him licking the blood from my thighs. I shuddered.

"So how is he demonic?" Tabby asked.

The images disappeared. My mind was my own again.

The devil looked at Tabby like a child staring at their new puppy. "A triviality, I assure you. He is my son."

I blinked. Oh, Jesus. We'd been staying with the Antichrist. My bowels would have let loose if there had been anything in them. Once again, I was thankful for that little fasting rule before exorcisms. I was truly starting to understand nuances I never would have guessed.

The devil laughed. "You should see the look on your face. Completely priceless."

He wasn't just evil anymore. The devil was clearly insane.

"He is the Antichrist?" I asked.

He pursed his eyebrows together. "My word, no. I have

many children. The Antichrist you speak of is a myth of sorts. Keep in mind, your book isn't whole."

He was right, actually. Sometime in the fourteenth century, I think it was, the Roman Catholic Church voted on what books were worthy of being in the Bible. Revelation only made it in by one vote. "Either there is no Antichrist, or all of your children are Antichrists?"

He rolled his eyes. "I can assure you that this one is not an Antichrist."

My mind jumped to Vespa's mother. I did not want to think about that woman having sex. Brain bleach on aisle twelve, please.

"You really do need to learn how to protect your mind. Don't make it so easy for me, marker." The devil laughed again. "No, I can assure you, my acolytes are nothing like that woman. Nicholas is a changeling."

Tons of old fantasy stories bounced around in my head. So fairies were of the devil? Maybe? I was starting to realize I didn't know the world as splendidly as I thought I did. Hell, I knew nothing.

"Why did your son bring us here?" That was the question. It had all been a waste of time, mine and Mr. Bad's over there. Surely, he would have something against that. Something that would save my soul.

He shook his head. This time there were no lighting theatrics. "I believe his plan was to try to steal your power. However, Yahweh and I have a very specific agreement regarding markers. You are not to be touched," he said, with an achingly horrific grin spread across his face, "at least not without cause."

I wondered about the intelligence level of his acolytes. I mean, who would want to piss him off? Then I realized: Doc was stuck here, and the original one, there was something there too. "What about Vespa? The real one?"

"There was an old charlatan who was around during the time of your relative. He had a few gifts. But Nicholas is not part of that family."

"He's half-demon?" Tabby asked. I'd almost forgotten she was there, she'd been so quiet. The devil had a way of making you pay attention to only him. I didn't like it.

He smirked. "Correct. His actual name is Arees."

"What will you do with him?" Tabby swallowed.

He shrugged. "Give him time to think about his misdeeds. Show him what happens to those who disobey me."

"Like Asmodeus?" I asked.

"Precisely." He growled and waved his hand toward the being I'd known as Nick. And Nick disappeared. "Tell Yahweh I said hello."

He began walking toward the opening in the wall. Right before stepping through, he glanced over his shoulder at me. A strange gleam lit his eyes. He said two words only with his departure: "Be careful."

Then, the devil was gone. The lighting went back to normal. The hole in the wall was no longer there, but you could see the outline of it in the cracked plaster around the tiles.

Tabby stood up and scuffed the circle with her foot.

Part of me wanted to tell her to leave it, but I'd been too late. I still wasn't quite in control of my mouth.

"Now what?" she asked.

I shoved the exorcism rite in my pocket. "We get our shit and get the hell out. Hotel sounds good."

"It sounds good to me too."

Chapter Fourteen

Always

WE ENDED UP driving all the way back to Tucson. I think
we'd all seen enough of Tombstone by that point. And no way
were we going back to the place that had wanted to kill Isaac.

"Pet-friendly hotel?" Tabby said.

"Pull out Mr. iPad. Try to find that one we stayed in when
we first got out here."

"Jimmy?" Lucy asked from the backseat.

"Yeah?" I peered at her in the rear view mirror.

"Is everything okay again?"

"For now."

Tabby and I grabbed some food from a burger place before
we arrived at the hotel. Fast food was good enough. I just
wanted to sleep. I hadn't been this tired in a long time. After we
got checked in and set ourselves up in the hotel room, I noticed
that Lucy was staring at the corner of the room.

"Whatcha doing?" I asked her.

"Waiting for Doc."

I didn't have the heart to tell her that she'd probably never
see Doc again. He was one of those ghosts that kind of stuck
around a specific place, and Tucson wasn't it.

"Lucy, why don't you come with me for a while," Tabby
motioned toward the door. "Let's let Jimmy get some rest."

"Okay," Lucy said.

My eyes slammed shut the minute I heard the door click closed.

I don't know how long I was asleep, but when I woke up, I felt like I'd been asleep for hours. My back hurt and my eyes felt heavy.

Doc was in the chair next to the table. The layout of the room was almost the same as our original hotel. The furniture was just different. The bed had a brown comforter and the table near the window was square instead of circular.

"What's up, Doc?" I asked, snickering.

"Funny. Very funny." He narrowed his eyes. "You and I need to have a talk."

I sat up on the bed. This didn't sound very good. "Okay. What you do need?"

"I need a favor."

#

Tabby and Lucy came back about a half an hour later. Tabby carried a bag from a toy store. I could tell right now that Lucy was going to be one spoiled little soul.

"Sleep good?" Tabby asked.

"Yeah. But I have something to talk to you about." I patted the bed beside me.

Tabby set the bag on the table and walked back to the bed. "Okay. Tell me you didn't get a call about another exorcism."

I snorted. "No. Just sit here a minute."

"Okay." She sat next to me. "What's this about?"

"How'd you like to add to our family?" I watched her for a minute. Yup, she was starting to freak. Her body grew rigid and her eyes went wide.

"No fucking way."

I started chuckling. "Not like that! Not yet anyway."

She took a deep breath. "You scared me."

"I didn't mean to." Actually I did, but she didn't need to know that.

"Okay," she said. "Back to this family stuff. What are you talking about?"

Doc popped into the chair. "How'd you feel if I stuck around for a while?"

Lucy squealed. "Oh boy!" She turned to us. "Really?"

"As far as I'm concerned, Doc can stay with us as long as he wants." Might as well make him a part of my team. Hell, it had been he who alerted me to half of Vespa's bullshit.

Lucy ran over and hugged Doc. He hugged her back hard.

"Now the house has two spirits?" Tabby asked.

Or we were making a unique family. I was for either one. "Yup."

"If you keep collecting like this, we're going to need a bigger place." She wrapped her arm around my shoulders.

I laughed. "Let's hope we can relax for a bit."

Lucy separated herself from Doc and walked over to where we'd stashed all our stuff.

"What's this?" Lucy asked, reaching for the damn wand sticking out of Tabby's backpack.

"No!" Tabby and I jumped up.

"Don't ever touch that." I snatched the wand out of her reach.

I could see the water pooling at the corners of her eyes. I handed the wand to Tabby.

I reached up and stroked her face. Wow. I could feel it. Something had gone wrong, very wrong. Lucy was no longer transparent at all. As my hand grazed her cheeks, I felt it. I felt flesh.

THE END

Thank you for reading! Find book three in the Marker Chronicles, SORROW'S TURN, in 2017, and catch the included special excerpt next!

Please sign up for the City Owl Press newsletter for chances to win special subscriber-only contests and giveaways as well as receiving information on upcoming releases and special excerpts.

www.danielledevor.com

@sammyig

All reviews are welcome and appreciated. Please consider leaving one on your favorite social media and book buying sites.

For books in the world of romance and speculative fiction that embody Innovation, Creativity, and Affordability, check out City Owl Press at www.cityowlpress.com.

See the next page for a sneak peek at book three in the
Marker Chronicles,

BOOK THREE OF THE MARKER CHRONICLES
SORROW'S TURN

BY: DANIELLE DEVOR

Coming Soon from City Owl Press

Chapter One

Every Little Thing She Does is Magic

IF I EVER thought things couldn't get any weirder in my life, boy was I wrong. Getting out of Arizona was interesting to say the least. No way could we take Lucy on a plane—not without documentation or permission from her parents, which wasn't going to happen. Poor kid had it rough learning how to walk on real feet again. And then, the airplane thing. She'd had enough having been possessed, separated from her body, and then left with me to take care of her. Now this.

How did you call up someone to ask them if you could take their daughter's spirit that had just developed its own body on an airplane while they still had her real body in Virginia? It was enough to make my head hurt.

Also, I didn't have their new phone number, but that was beside the point.

Like I said, things had just gotten a whole lot weirder.

"Are you going to help me or not?" Tabby asked from outside the car.

I was in trouble again. It was starting to be a trend. One of these days, she was going to clobber me. I could see it coming. I got out of the car, took the monstrous suitcase from her, and loaded it in the trunk.

"Car rental place said we can have the car, but there's a fee,"

I said.

Of course there would be. It wasn't like some big organization was going to be nice or anything. Hell, I had trouble with people in general, why would a corporation be any different?

"How much?" Tabby asked.

I shrugged. "I didn't ask."

Thwap. My head rocked forward. "Did you just hit me?" I looked at her. Maybe being psychic was another added bonus to this Marker thing. Nah, if that was the case, I wouldn't have screwed up in Arizona.

Tabby stood with her hands on her hips. Her red hair was framing her face like she was some sort of pissed off goddess. Her eyes darkened, and I was reminded of that guy on TV who kept hitting his workers on the back of the head.

"Yes, I did," she said. "Just because you love that magic black card, it doesn't mean you don't have to worry about it."

I rubbed my head. Damn she hit hard. "If this was my sort of normal, then yes, I'd be worried. But, how else are we getting this menagerie home?"

"Good point."

I was glad she saw it that way because there wasn't another option. It wasn't like I had some amazing powers like flight or anything.

"Was that the last of it?" I asked. The trunk was almost full. I could maybe fit a small stuffed dog in there, but that was questionable.

"Yep," Tabby said.

"Okay. Let's blow this popsicle stand." I jumped behind the driver's seat and looked in the rearview mirror. Lucy was strapped in the car seat Tabby had bought at Wally world after the fleshing rod had done its business. Doc sat beside her, showing her card tricks. I was glad for Doc. Who knew having the sentient ghost of Doc Holiday hanging around would be so useful? That he was my relative was beside the point. No way was I going to complain about his help with Lucy.

I turned to look at Tabby. "Ready?"

"As I'll ever be."

It took roughly three days, fourteen hours, and seventeen minutes to get back home. I knew because I counted every single one. I probably should have let Tabby drive, but I needed something to hold on to and take my frustration out on. Clenching the steering wheel seemed to be serving that purpose. My brain wouldn't stop coming up with various worst case scenarios.

Every so often, Tabby would ask if I wanted her to drive, but I refused. It was a shitty enough trip as it was. There was no sense in making it worse for her. I might as well keep my asshole behavior to myself.

Plus, I had to get used to a child's bladder. Lucy—now that she was whole—had normal bodily functions again. Yet another thing I hadn't counted on. The next time I saw the Devil, I was going to hit him with that rod. Well, not really, but it was nice to think about it.

Still though, it was good to be home. The old house with its white siding and black shutters never looked so good. It might be old, but it was mine. As soon as I stepped foot outside the car, the smell of the Virginia air hit me and I smiled.

"What?" Tabby asked, brushing her long red hair away from her face.

I glanced at her. "Just glad to be home."

She shook her head. "We better get on it."

I blinked. "Get on what?"

"Get the car unpacked?"

Lucy stared at her with wide eyes. Doc was looking at the sky.

"I don't want to start anything, but I'm too tired. Let's unpack tomorrow."

Tabby stared at me for a minute, and then slumped her shoulders. "Okay. We can wait until tomorrow."

I hugged her. Nothing in there that couldn't wait. At least as far as I was concerned.

"Shouldn't you get your holy iPad?" Tabby asked as she was unbuckling Lucy from her car seat.

Even Lucy looked tired. Her long blond hair hung stringy.

"Someone probably wants to talk to you," Lucy said.

I looked at her through the car window. The kid was staring right at me. "Okay. Fine."

I closed the door of the car, handed Tabby the house keys, and started pulling all the crap from the trunk. Guess it wasn't in the cards to wait until tomorrow after all. Fine. But, I wasn't unpacking all the shit right that instant either.

Tabby chuckled and went to open the door to the house.

As soon as I got all the crap inside, I noticed Lucy perched in her usual spot in front of the TV. Doc hovered next to her. It was kind of nice having Lucy solid. She could turn on her own TV whenever she felt like it. Though, eventually, I was going to have to come up with something else to entertain her. And more importantly, some sort of schooling for her.

"If you want a chair, feel free to grab one," I said to Doc. Just because he was a ghost didn't mean he shouldn't make himself comfortable. I mean I knew he was just being polite since this was the first time he'd been in my home, but I didn't want him to feel like a guest.

Doc nodded in his way. "Mighty obliged."

"Hey, might as well feel at home." Since he was going to be staying with us for the unforeseeable future, he should act like family.

Isaac let out loud meow as I put his pet carrier down and let him out of it. He sauntered over to the couch, hopped up, and promptly went to sleep.

"Yes, your highness," I said. "I swear, in my next life, I want to be a cat."

Lucy laughed.

"Jesus, Jimmy. That's just what we need," Tabby said.

I snorted. Part of me thought it would have been great to have her wait on me hand and foot, but the lack of sex part would suck. I didn't even want to think about her threatening to neuter me.

"You hungry? I'm going to throw something together," Tabby said from the kitchen.

"Good luck," I replied.

#

I can't lie and say I wasn't happy to be in my own bed. Lucy stayed downstairs like she had before. Oddly, even though she seemed to have normal metabolic processes, she still didn't appear to be able to sleep. How this worked? I didn't know. It made me uneasy. A kid needed to sleep, and if her body didn't change to adjust, I didn't even want to think about what type of health problems she could get. I needed to figure out a way to spread the worry a bit; otherwise, I was going to give myself high blood pressure.

"What has you so," Tabby turned to me, "odd?"

I rolled over in the bed to look at her. "I'm worried about Lucy. Nothing about this seems right."

She nodded. "Did you check your email?"

"No."

Tabby rolled her eyes at me. "Didn't Lucy say that you should?"

I could have kicked myself. If I didn't get my shit together, things were going to end up completely craptastic. "I'll be back."

I headed downstairs. Lucy was watching some documentary on the effects of uric acid on the brains of chickens. I looked at Doc and raised an eyebrow. He shrugged. At least she was getting an education about something.

"Everything okay down here?" I asked.

Lucy glanced up from the TV. "Uh huh."

I snatched the iPad off the table where someone had put it. I hadn't even unpacked it before I went to bed. Then, I jogged back upstairs. Might as well leave Lucy to her chickens.

"Everything okay?" Tabby asked once I got back into bed.

"So far." I fired up the tablet. Sure enough, there was an email waiting for me. I took a deep breath and tapped it.

Mr. Holiday,

It is my pleasure to inform you that you have been accepted into the next class of Exorcism at the Vatican— Exorcismo E Preghieri Di Liberazione. We will be sending you your requirements shortly.

Fr. Martin

"Fuck me," I said. Granted, I'd been whining about wanting help, but this wasn't exactly what I had expected. Looked like the church did want me in some capacity after all.

"What?" Tabby asked.

"They are sending me to school to become an exorcist."

Tabby guffawed. Literally, guffawed. In fact, she laughed so hard she fell out of bed. No joke.

"What's so funny?" I asked. Granted, I already was an exorcist, but it wasn't like I knew what the hell I was doing.

"Do you even speak Italian?"

"Well, no." Damn. She was right. The school for exorcism was at the Vatican. I was so screwed.

"Oh, God. This is going to be interesting," Tabby said.

I glared at her. "Okay. Yeah. But this does nothing to help with Lucy now does it?"

I didn't mean to be a bastard, but Lucy was a hell of a lot

more important than making fun of me going to exorcism school. We needed information the help the kid. The sooner the better.

Tabby got quiet. "No, it doesn't. Question is—do you want to let them know about her?"

I thought about it for a minute. I'd been Lucy's protector for so long now, it would feel wrong to hand her over to someone else. And well, not to be mean, but she was likely to end up as some Vatican experiment. I wouldn't put anything past any of them. The Order of Markers was connected to the Vatican, but not run by them. I had to be damn careful. Periodically, I found myself looking in corners of the rooms for micro-cameras or something, but I never found any. Still, since the Order had broken into my house before (when they set up the holy iPad), I knew they were watching. The question always was: how much?

"No, we aren't telling them about her," I said. It was better that way. Maybe, if they just had footage of her entering the house, they would think Lucy was a relative.

"All right then, what are we going to do?" Tabby asked.

I sighed. Sometimes, I wished she wouldn't expect me to have all the answers. I needed more of a give and take. "Get some sleep."

#

The next morning, I got up to nothing. There was no sound. No weird events. It almost had me worried. Kind of sad that I was getting so used to the unusual that when something normal happened, I felt suspect.

I got up out of bed, went downstairs, and found Tabby, Doc, and Lucy sitting on the sofa. They all looked like their pet rock had died.

"What's up?" I asked.

"Something's wrong," Lucy said. She stared at the floor.

The TV wasn't even on. That was a bad sign where Lucy was concerned.

Nothing like those two words to scare the shit out of me.

"Wrong how?" I asked. It could be anything: a new demon, bad luck about to befall me. I started to sweat.

"I don't feel very good," she said.

Her skin had a sort of waxy appearance to it. Okay. I could work with sick. Lots of over-the-counter remedies to try. I waved at Tabby.

"Is she running a fever?" I asked.

Tabby shook her head. Doc's lips pursed together. If she was normal sick, Doc wouldn't be acting so strangely.

"Make it stop," Lucy said suddenly. She held her head with both hands.

I patted her arm. "If I can, honey. I will."

"Any ideas, Doc?" Tabby asked.

He huffed. "All I know is that this ain't natural. And when something ain't natural, lots of bad can happen."

I ground my teeth together. It wasn't like we could take Lucy to a doctor. It was just not what any of us needed right now. Not to mention the the that the kid was in pain and I didn't know how to fix it. "We better look into what a fleshing rod actually does."

"Guess so," Tabby replied.

ACKNOWLEDGEMENTS

First of all, I have to thank Tina Moss at City Owl Press--she's not only an amazing editor, but an even more amazing friend. I'd also like to thank my family, friends, and everyone else for putting up with my incessant desire to watch more goofy horror films. And, finally, I have to thank my mom for her sense of humor. Without my folks, Jimmy Holiday wouldn't be alive.

ABOUT THE AUTHOR

Named one of the Examiner's Women in Horror: 93 Horror Authors You Need to Read Right Now, Danielle DeVor has been spinning the spider webs, or rather, the keyboard for more frights and oddities. She spent her early years fantasizing about vampires and watching "Salem's Lot" far too many times. When not writing and reading about weird things, you will find her hanging out at the nearest coffee shop, enjoying a mocha frappuccino.

www.danielledevor.com

ABOUT THE PUBLISHER

City Owl Press is a cutting edge indie publishing company, bringing the world of romance and speculative fiction to discerning readers.

www.cityowlpress.com

Made in the USA
Charleston, SC
03 November 2016